Just as the boys were about to leave, they heard a loud explosion upstream...

"What's that?" Beau exclaimed.

In an instant a fireball shot to the sky.

The boys rushed to the edge of Blue Boulder.

"Wow! Look at that!" The fireball lit up the night.

"What could have exploded?"

"Firecrackers?" asked Beau.

They heard a police whistle.

"What's going on?"

"That's a police whistle."

"From upstream."

Who-cooks-for-you, who-cooks-for-you-all. The call came from the ridge.

"A barred owl!" Jaime exclaimed.

"Or Eric," Jorge said.

"Eric, is that you?" Beau called out.

"Someone's on the creek," Jaime whispered. "Tayanita Creek. Look."

Over the rhythmic splash of oars they heard a man say, "Oh, shit."

Suddenly they were blinded by a spotlight. Jaime held the trowel over his eyes. Jorge and Beau stared at the source of the light. The three stood stock still. Finally the canoe disappeared around the bend and left them in darkness. Upstream they could see a fire.

The mayor of the small north Georgia town of Witherston and one of its prominent attorneys are being blackmailed by a mysterious Donna Dam, who threatens to expose the two men's shameful activities of forty years ago if they do not take a paternity test and pay a hefty sum of money—and if Mayor Rather does not withdraw his proposal to build a dam, creating a lake on top of a sacred Cherokee burial ground. Blackmail leads to murder, and when Detective Mev Arroyo and her two teenage twins investigate, they discover some dark secrets, putting all their lives in danger...

KUDOS for *Dam Witherston*

In *Dam Witherston* by Betty Jean Craige, we are reunited with all the delightful and zany characters in Witherston, Georgia. This time, Mayor Rather is trying to dam the stream and flood a sacred Cherokee burial ground in order to build a lake for recreation. But then someone blackmails the mayor, threatening to reveal what he did forty years ago if he doesn't pay a hefty fee and back off the dam project. When the shack where the blackmail money is to be dropped off explodes, killing someone, Mayor Rather is the prime suspect. Now Detective Mev Arroyo and her two teenage sleuth sons, Jaime and Jorge, have to prove his innocence—or guilt. Like the first two books in the series, Craige has combined mystery, humor, and suspense in a clever tale of murder and mayhem as you can only find in Witherston. ~ *Taylor Jones, Reviewer*

Dam Witherston by Betty Jean Craige is the story of greed, revenge, and what happens when the past comes back to bite you in the butt. Someone is blackmailing the mayor of Witherston, as well as one of its successful attorneys, threatening to reveal what they did on a night in November forty long years ago, if the two men don't pay a large sum of money, take a paternity test, and if the mayor doesn't put the brakes on a project to dam the town stream and create an artificial lake, flooding an ancient Cherokee burial ground. When the local law enforcement investigates the blackmail scheme, they discover a murder, and that's when the trouble really starts. Craige has a unique voice, and her character development is superb. I love that I can never figure out who the villain is until the protagonist does. *Dam Witherston* is a worthy sequel to the first two books in the series. Another keeper to put on the shelf and read over and over. Bravo, Craige. ~ *Regan Murphy Reviewer*

ACKNOWLEDGEMENTS

Mystery writers need mystery readers, both before and after the mystery has been published. I am fortunate to have some wonderfully sharp-eyed friends who read *Dam Witherston* critically for me before I sent the manuscript off to Black Opal Books. They each found different mistakes and offered different suggestions for change. Together, they helped immeasurably to make my story better. *Dam Witherston* is the third novel in the *Witherston Murder Mystery* series that they have read for me.

I thank Susan Tate and Margaret and Wyatt Anderson for spending their valuable time reading my manuscript critically. Susan, whose knowledge of Georgia's history and geography is vast, acquainted me with beautiful north Georgia and inspired me to set my mystery series there. Susan also helped me understand the legal issues I encountered in writing the stories. Margaret Anderson, a member of my Mystery Lunch Club and an impressive critic of mysteries of all kinds, read the manuscript with an eye to the logic of the plot. I am also grateful to Margaret and Wyatt for teaching me about evolution and genetic ancestry over the three decades of our friendship.

Sue Moore Manning, who was already skilled in drawing when we became friends at the age of six, did the cartoon of the mayor as Humpty Dumpty. Holly Marie Stasco, a graduate of the University of Georgia Lamar Dodd School of Art, did the maps.

I am fortunate to have such talented friends.

I have learned about Georgia's Cherokee culture, past and present, from many articles on the web and in print. But I would like to single out one which awakened me to a fundamental difference between the traditional Cherokee culture and the culture of the whites of European ancestry who settled this region in the eighteenth century. It is the difference between the Native American and the European attitudes toward women. "The Power of Cherokee Women," on the website of the *Indian Country Today Media Network*, summarizes the research of Carolyn Johnston, Theda Perdue, Faye Yarbrough, and Wilma Dunaway into the lives of Cherokee women before the Cherokees adopted the Christian and patriarchal values of their conquerors. I recommend it.

Finally, I have to thank my many other friends who read my earlier mysteries *Downstream* and *Fairfield's Auction* and encouraged me to keep writing. So that's what I do. I keep writing.

DAM
WITHERSTON

A Witherston Murder Mystery

Betty Jean Craige

A Black Opal Books Publication

GENRE: THRILLER/SUSPENSE/WOMEN'S FICTION

DAM WITHERSTON ~ A Witherston Murder Mystery
Copyright © 2017 by Betty Jean Craige
Cover Design by Jackson Cover Designs
All cover art copyright © 2017
All Rights Reserved
Print ISBN: 978-1-626945-98-2

First Publication: JANUARY 2017

Published by Black Opal Books **http://www.blackopalbooks.com**

DAM

WITHERSTON

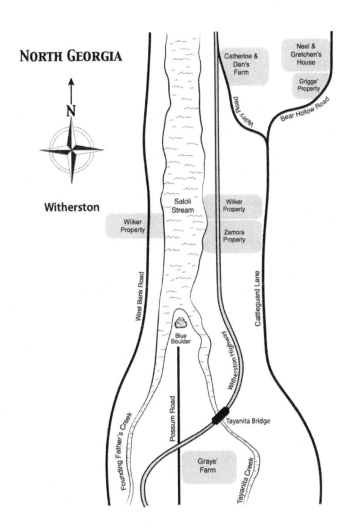

NORTH GEORGIA

N

Witherston

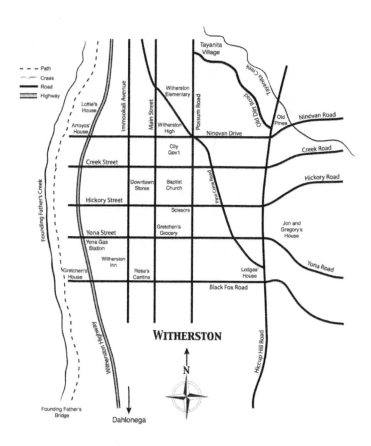

WITHERSTON

PROLOGUE

Mayor Rich Rather grabbed his cell phone when a beep signaled the arrival of an email.

"Excuse me," he said to Trevor Bennington, Jr., President of Bennington Financial Services and member of the Witherston Town Council. "I'm expecting an estimate from Appalachian Landscape Contractors."

He opened his email.

From: Donna Dam (donotreply@xxx.com)
To: Rich Rather

PAYBACK TIME
Fri 03/10/2017 9:31 a.m.

Dear Mayor Rather:

Do you remember what you were doing on the night of November 5-6, 1977? I bet you do. You will pay for it.

There is a wooden shed 1/4 mile upstream from Withers Fork on east bank of Saloli Stream. It's on the Zamora property. Bring $9,900 in cash at 5:00 pm tomorrow. Leave the money in an enve-

*lope inside on the table. If you do not show up
on time, I will go public with your secret.*

*Donna Dam
Sent from my iPhone*

"Anything wrong, Rich?"

"No, nothing, nothing at all. Thanks, Trevor." Rich
stood up. "But I'm afraid I've got other business to attend
to. I'm sorry to be cutting our meeting short. So sorry."

The mayor showed him out of his office and deleted
the email.

❧❧❧

Grant Griggs sat down for Friday morning coffee
with Patrick Davis, President of Witherston Savings and
Loan. As was their custom at the Witherston Inn Café,
they'd taken a back table.

"Looks like Rich will give the contract to Appalachian Lakescape Contractors, Grant," Patrick said. "I lob-
bied him hard."

"Thanks, Patrick. I promise that will work out for
both of us."

Grant's cell phone beeped. "Do you mind if I check
my email, Patrick? I'm expecting a message from Phyllis
Graph."

*From: Donna Dam (donotreply@xxx.com)
To: Grant Griggs*

*PAYBACK TIME
Fri 03/10/2017 9:31 a.m.*

Dear Mr. Griggs:

Do you remember what you were doing on the night of November 5-6, 1977? I bet you do. You will pay for it.

There is a wooden shed 1/4 mile upstream from Withers Fork on east bank of Saloli Stream. It's on the Zamora property. Bring $9,900 in cash at 5:00 pm tomorrow. Leave the money in an envelope inside on the table. If you do not show up on time, I will go public with your secret.

Donna Dam

Sent from my iPhone

"Shit," Grant muttered. "Patrick, I'm sorry to have to leave you, but I've got to see a client. I must go now." He deleted the email and walked out of the restaurant.

 споро

Red Wilker was vacuuming the stuffed black bear the taxidermist had just delivered to Wilker's Gun Shop when he got the email.

From: Donna Dam (donotreply@xxx.com)
To: Red Wilker

PAYBACK TIME
Fri 03/10/2017 9:31 a.m.

Dear Mr. Wilker:

Would you like for the people of Witherston to know that you are buying up property in Saloli

Valley with inside information about the pro-
posed lake? I bet you wouldn't.

There is a wooden shed 1/4 mile upstream from
Withers Fork on east bank of Saloli Stream. It's
on the Zamora property. Bring $5,000 in cash at
5:00 pm tomorrow. Leave the money in an enve-
lope inside on the table. If you do not show up
on time, I will go public with your secret. And
you could get jail time.

Donna Dam

Sent from my iPhone

"'What the duck is this? Look, Grace. Who in crea-tion is Donna Dam?" He handed his cell phone to his wife.

Grace read the email. "Is she referring to your land buy-outs in Saloli Valley?"

"How could she find that out? How could anybody?"

"Rich knows. Grant knows. Phyllis knows. Patrick knows."

"They all have a stake in the lake. They won't be talking."

"What are you going to do?"

"Don't ask. You don't need to know."

Red deleted the email.

WITHERSTON ON THE WEB
Saturday, March 11, 2017
NEWS

Mayor Rather Wants a Lake

On Friday, March 17, Mayor Rich Rather will present a plan to the Witherston Town Council to make a 45-acre fishing and boating lake in Saloli Valley above Withers Fork. Information regarding the actual site of the dam, the site of the proposed lake, and the diversion of Witherston Highway has been kept secret.

Last January, Mayor Rather solicited proposals from North Georgia Landscape Designers, Georgia Brothers Environmental Engineers, and Appalachian Lakescape Contractors.

Mayor Rather issued a public statement yesterday: "The $1 billion that Francis Hearty Withers bequeathed to Witherston two years ago has hardly been touched. In fiscal year 2016 we used $5 million of interest to create Founding Father's Wildlife Preserve. To make the lake we would have to use some of the principal. But we could afford to spend $400 million to create a recreational lake that would make Witherston the most attractive town in Georgia, maybe in the whole United States of America. And we would still have $600 million in the bank."

In answer to a question from this reporter, the mayor said, "Amadahy, $600 million can produce $24 million in yearly interest."

Much of the $400 million that the mayor an-

*ticipates spending would be used to buy proper-
ty owned by farmers in Saloli Valley, some of
whom are living on land their families have occupied for two hundred years.*

Amadahy Henderson, Reporter

Mayor's Wife Opposes
Mayor Rather's Dam Proposal

*Rhonda Rather, wife of Mayor Rich Rather,
has invited all Witherstonians opposed to Witherston's construction of a recreational lake to
join her in a demonstration tomorrow afternoon.
The group will assemble at the entrance to Tayanita Village at 1:00 p.m. and parade up Possum Road to Emmett Gray's farm a quarter-mile
this side of Withers Fork. Mrs. Rather urges op-
ponents of Mayor Rather's dam to bring their
tractors, trucks, and vans to carry everyone to
Mr. Gray's anti-lake barbecue. Tayanita Village's mule Franny will pull a wagon. Gregory
Bozeman's donkey Sassyass will pull a cart.*

*At 2:00 Mrs. Rather, Chief Atohi Pace,
Gretchen Green, and Molly Schlaughter will
speak.*

*Mayor Rich Rather will not attend the
event. He said that he had always given his wife
Rhonda freedom to express her views. He said
that he loved her for her independence but that
he intended to present his proposal to the Town
Council despite her opposition. He asked Witherstonians to contact their Council representative—Trevor Bennington, Jr., Smitty Green,*

Ruth Griggs, or Atsadi Moon—if they wished to express support for a Lake Witherston.

The mayor had no comment when told by this reporter that his secretary Molly Schlaughter would participate in the demonstration.

Amadahy Henderson, Reporter

Detective Mev Arroyo Is Honored

Yesterday the Witherston Roundtable awarded its annual Witherston Citizen Award to Detective Mev Arroyo at a luncheon at the Witherston Inn Cafe. Frederick Zurich, president, cited Detective Arroyo's leadership in solving Witherston's two recent murder cases as the reason members of the Roundtable named her the 2017 recipient. Detective Arroyo thanked first the members of the Roundtable and then her family. "My husband Paco, my 16-year-old twins Jaime and Jorge, their friends Beau Lodge and Annie Jerden, and my aunt Charlotte Byrd are my personal in-house deputies. So are Gretchen Hall Green and Neel Kingfisher," she said. "We solved those crimes together—with, of course, Chief Jake McCoy, police officers Ricky Hefner, Pete Koslowsky Senior, Pete Koslowsky Junior, and our new IT security officer John Hicks."

Catherine Perry-Soto, Editor

ANNOUNCEMENTS

Keep Nature Natural (KNN) will meet today at 10:30 a.m. to plan our opposition to Mayor Rather's proposal for a dam. Usual place: Picnic shelter at west end of Hickory Street on Founding Father's Creek.

> *Beau Lodge*
> *President of KNN*
> *Witherston*

The Witherston Roundtable will hold its annual Witherston-to-Dahlonega Slow Pedal on Wednesday afternoon, March 15. Mayor Rather will lead bicyclists of all ages down Witherston Highway to Dahlonega. He will depart from the Witherston police station in his black Chrysler at 3:00 p.m. If you would like to return to Witherston on the chartered bus, please be at the Gold Museum (the old Dahlonega courthouse) with your bicycle at 6:00 p.m. A chartered U-Haul will bring the bikes back to Witherston. THIS IS NOT A RACE. We ask only that you wear a helmet and goggles for your safety.

> *Frederick Zurich*
> *President of Witherston Roundtable*

LETTERS TO THE EDITOR

To the Editor:

The residents of Tayanita Village beg the

*residents of Witherston to think about the Cher-
okee history you will obliterate if you dam up
Saloli Stream. Our ancestors' bodies are buried
on the land you want to flood.*

*Witherstonians: How would you react if
people with different ancestry from yours—say
the Cherokees—flooded your church graveyard?*

*John Hicks
Tayanita Village*

To the Editor:

*Our mayor wants to create a lake to bring
hunters and fishermen and people with money to
our town. He's threatened by environmentalist
idiots like his wife. It's time for right-minded
Witherstonians to stop Mayor Rather's oppo-
nents.*

*Red Wilker
Witherston*

To the Editor:

*Mayor Richard Rather wants to build a dam
and make a lake. He should know better.*

*Does he not remember where he was at
1:30 a.m. on November 6, 1977? He was in Toccoa engaged in shameful activity. I can prove it.*

Mr. Attorney Grant Griggs was also in Toc-

coa engaged in shameful activity on the night of
November 5-6, 1977.

And Mr. Red Wilker is engaged in shameful
activity here in Witherston now.

Other folks: More could come out about
you.

If the mayor does not reverse his position
on the dam, I will reveal what I know.

Donna Dam
Former Toccoa resident

EDITORIAL

As editor of Witherston on the Web since
Smitty Green retired last October, I have published every single letter-to-the-editor I have received without any editing.

However, the last letter in today's edition
will provoke some questioning of this policy. The
letter was emailed to me at 6:30 p.m. yesterday.
The writer signed her (or his?) name "Donna
Dam." I could not find any record of a Donna
Dam in Georgia.

However, I did learn what happened at 1:30
a.m. on Sunday, November 6, 1977, in Toccoa,
Georgia, only 50 miles east of Witherston in
Stephens County. After days of torrential rains,
the Kelly Barnes Dam broke. The 40-acre
Barnes Lake, used solely for recreation by 1977,
flooded the valley, leaving 39 people dead.

So-called "Donna Dam" threatens the
mayor if he continues to support the lake.

Does this letter constitute extortion? Probably. Do I want to censor letters-to-the-editor? No.

Catherine Perry-Soto, Editor

WEATHER

Today's temperature will rise to the high 60s by noon and will drop into the high 40s by midnight. The skies will be sunny today and tomorrow. Sunshine on my shoulders makes me happy. Spring break starts today.

Tony Lima, Weather Dude

WHAT'S NATURAL
By Jorge Arroyo

Are chickens "natural"?

Did you ever stop to think that if there weren't humans on Earth, there wouldn't be any chickens, at least not the broiler kind that most of us in Witherston have. (We thank Dan Soto for the 4,000 broilers he brought to Witherston in last year's blizzard.) There wouldn't be any dogs either. Both chickens and dogs are domesticated. They're not wild animals we tamed. They're animals we created from wild animals, who were their ancestors. Chickens are bred through artificial selection, which is selection by humans, not by nature. Humans decide what traits they would like to have in their fowl—like good meat or lots of eggs—and they mate birds to each other who have those traits. That's how we get different breeds, such as broilers, orpingtons, and bantams.

My brother Jaime and I got a flock of broilers for Christmas in 2015. They are named Moonshine, Sunshine, Henny Penny, Mother Hen, Feather Jean, and Feather Jo. During the day we let them run free behind our house, but at night before we go to bed, we lock them in their chicken coop to protect them from coyotes.

To most people our chickens look identical (like my twin Jaime and me). But Jaime and I can tell them apart. They each have a distinct personality. Moonshine is the dominant hen. Sunshine and Henny Penny like to be petted. Feather Jean and Mother Hen come when called. Feather Jo is the littlest and cutest. They all know their names. Jaime and I love them, just like we love our dog Mighty.

NORTH GEORGIA IN HISTORY: THE WITHERS
By Charlotte Byrd

Soon Witherston will celebrate the 157th anniversary of its founding. And soon we will celebrate the birthday of Witherston's benefactor Francis Hearty Withers, who was born on May 22, 1915. So I will devote my next few columns to the history of the Withers family.

At noon on Tuesday, June 5, 1860, on the front steps of Saloli Creek Methodist Church,

Harold Francis ("Harry") Withers honored his father, Hearty Withers, by giving the name "Witherstown" to the old Cherokee settlement downstream from his 40-acre homestead. The Cherokees had called their village Galunadi, or "Shoals." Witherstown soon became Witherston, and brick buildings replaced the Cherokees' clay huts. The town's population, which was recorded as 205 on the date of its founding, grew to 400 by 1870.

Harry Withers, as Harold Francis Withers was called, will be remembered in north Georgia history for changing the Cherokee names of geographical landmarks to English names. For him, naming was a form of conquest, and he, heir to his father's fortune, was conqueror.

Three years prior to the naming of Witherston, Harry Withers gave the name Harry Withers Fork to the fork where Saloli Stream split into two branches. It's now called Withers Fork. He gave the name Founding Father's Creek to the branch of Saloli Stream that ran along the west side of his property. He wished to honor Abraham Baldwin, Georgia's representative to the Constitutional Congress and first president of the University of Georgia, which he had attended.

The Cherokees, who occupied the southern Appalachian Mountains for a thousand years, had called it Saloli Creek. Saloli is the Cherokee word for squirrel.

Harry Withers did not rename the branch of Saloli Stream that flowed east of Witherston, perhaps because it did not cross his property. He allowed it to remain Tayanita Creek. Taya-

nita is the Cherokee word for beaver.

The land and the wealth stayed in the Withers family for five generations, until the billionaire centenarian Francis Hearty Withers was murdered in May of 2015.

As you all know, Francis Hearty Withers bequeathed $1 billion to the municipality of Witherston and $1 billion to the 4,000 residents of Witherston. In the summer of 2015 everybody in this town who had been a resident on May 24 inherited approximately $250,000.

We owe much of our inheritance to the Cherokees whose land and gold Francis Hearty Withers's ancestors took.

The naming of Witherston symbolizes for me the burial of one civilization by another. As an historian, I always wonder what lies hidden, what is lost forever, and what we may yet discover beneath our words and our buildings.

LOST AND FOUND

7:30 a.m. Pastor Paul Clement reported that Esmerelda, his ten-year-old nanny goat, has disappeared. Esmerelda answers to her name. If you find Esmerelda, please email pastorpaulclement@aol.com.

CHAPTER 1

Saturday Morning March 11, 2017

Good morning, Red," Mayor Rather said as he approached the counter at nine o'clock in the morning. "Nice bear you got in your window. I assume that's Bearwithus."

"Hello, your highness." Red Wilker was the owner of Wilker's Gun Shop, which his father Bullet Wilker had passed down to him. Bullet had been Witherston's mayor in the 1980s. "Yes, Bearwithus will bother us no more."

"Can you sell me a gun this morning? Quietly? I may need it for protection. But I don't have time for a security check."

"A handgun, Mr. Mayor? One befitting your elevated status in our fine town?"

"Whatever you have, Red. I need it now. Now."

"How about a pretty pink Beretta Nano nine millimeter? I got it from Marjorie Parker last summer. She said she couldn't use it in assisted living." Red laughed. "Want a powerful pink pistol?"

"Whatever."

"Let's go in the back."

"Confidential, okay? We need to keep this confidential," the mayor said.

"Understood."

"And I need bullets too."

"Have you ever fired a handgun, Rich?"

"No, why would I have fired a handgun?"

"For fun, Rich, for fun. That's why I shoot. That's why I sell guns. For fun."

 entranceentranceentrance

"What if Donna Dam is lying? What if Mayor Rather wasn't even in Toccoa that night?" Detective Mev Arroyo asked her family. "What if Donna Dam wrote the letter to make people think the mayor had committed a crime when he hadn't?"

Jorge had his iPad open to *Witherston on the Web*, which locals called *Webby Witherston.* He had just read aloud the letter from Donna Dam.

"Wow," Jaime said. "I could write a letter to the editor and ask 'What were you doing with your guns on March 11, 2011, Mr. Wilker?' Since he sells guns, Mr. Wilker wouldn't remember. So everyone would think he's guilty of something."

"I could write a letter and ask, 'What did you throw off the Tallahatchie Bridge, Mrs. Wilker?'" Jorge said.

"Boys, this is serious. The mayor is being blackmailed," Mev said. "Publicly."

"So what are you going to do about it, dear?" Lottie asked her.

Detective Mev Arroyo of the Witherston Police Department sat at the dining room table with her husband Paco, their identical sixteen-year-old twins Jaime and Jorge, her aunt Lottie, known to the Witherston community as Dr. Charlotte Byrd, and Doolittle, Lottie's talkative African Grey parrot. Doolittle had hopped onto Jaime's left hand.

The boys' dog Mighty lay under the table.

As was their custom, Lottie joined them on Saturday mornings for Paco's breakfast of scrambled eggs, bacon, grits, and biscuits. Lottie and Doolittle, that is. In the year since acquiring him at Hempton Fairfield's auction, Lottie seldom went visiting without her bird, to everyone's delight.

When Lottie lost her only son in Iraq and retired from Hickory Mountain College, Mev invited her to move next door to them in Witherston. In the last several years she'd watched Lottie regain her spirit and her energy. Lottie devoted her time to writing a daily column in *Witherston on the Web*, studying north Georgia's past, and advocating for human rights, animal rights, and environmental rights. She'd just published *Invisible Persons*, a book about the Cherokee civilization that once flourished in north Georgia.

Now she was working on a history of Witherston. Mev found Lottie's research skills to be applicable forensically.

Mev's family loved Lottie for her wit and wisdom, her knowledge of fine wine, and her culinary talents. They joined her every Sunday night, when she gathered her family and friends together for dinner. Lottie was merry, full of laughter and love despite the tragedies she'd suffered. She came of age in the sixties, and she'd taught Jorge and Jaime to love the music of that decade. Her collection of records and CDs was huge. Her Smart Car bore the bumper sticker *THE EARTH DOES NOT BELONG TO US. WE BELONG TO THE EARTH.*

"I'm going to find out what Rich Rather did in Toccoa the night the dam broke," Mev said.

"He heard the Earth roar," Lottie said.

"Wikipedia says the flood didn't just kill thirty-nine people," Jorge said. "It also destroyed nine houses, eighteen trailers, many vehicles, and two buildings on the campus of Toccoa Falls College."

"I bet Mayor Rather was making love to a girl named Donna," Paco said.

"What was Mr. Griggs doing?" Jaime asked.

"Making love to a girl named Dam," Jorge said.

"Who would be old by now," Jaime said.

"As old as the mayor. Maybe sixty years old," Jorge said.

"Not as old as I am," Lottie said.

"And not as pretty, Aunt Lottie," Paco said. "*Hijos*, what are you all doing today?"

"This morning we're going to the KNN meeting Beau's called. This afternoon we're walking with Beau and Eric up to Withers Fork," Jaime said.

"Take some food," Mev said, opening the refrigerator door.

"Thanks, Mom."

"I want to get a picture of Saloli Valley before the mayor floods it," Jorge said.

"Use a wide angle lens," Lottie said.

"Be home by dinner," Paco said.

"Dinner," Doolittle repeated. "Doolittle wanna dinner." The parrot poked his beak into Jaime's grits.

cʌɔcʌɔ

"Mom, Pop, did you all read Jorge's column in *Webby Witherston*?" Beau asked. "It's about breeds of chickens. Are different races of humans like different breeds of chickens or dogs?"

Sixteen-year-old Beau Lodge was sitting at the breakfast table with his iPad open in front of him and his dog Sequoyah at his feet. The only child of an interracial couple—Dr. Jim Lodge, a very dark African American, and Judge Lauren Lodge, a very blonde European American—Beau had lately asked lots of questions about race.

"No, Beau," Jim said. "In the first place, breeds are *bred*, by humans. That's what breed means. Breeds of animals emerge by artificial selection. Races emerge by natural selection, such as by geographical separation of populations over thousands of years."

"Also by social separation," Lauren added. "By social prejudices that turned into laws that forbade marriage between races. Anti-miscegenation laws prohibited marriages like ours until the U.S. Supreme Court ruled the laws unconstitutional in 1967."

"The laws helped keep the blacks black and the whites white," Jim said.

"A girl at school told me I was a different breed from her."

"Oh, Beau! How awful! How mean!"

"How ignorant," Jim said. "There's far greater genetic diversity among dogs than among humans. And there's greater genetic diversity within so-called human races than between them."

"How should Beau respond to this girl, Jim?"

"Don't worry, Mom. It's no big deal."

"Do you know why your father and I named you 'Beau'?"

"Why?"

"Because you were a beautiful baby, cocoa-colored, with huge inquisitive eyes and the sweetest face we ever saw. Beau means beautiful in French."

"In a hundred years, Beau, most Americans will be cocoa-colored just like you," Jim said. "Then race won't be on anyone's mind."

Thanks, folks. I love you all." Beau got up and closed his iPad.

His mother kissed him.

"I have a Keep Nature Natural meeting this morning. We're going to fight Mayor Rather's lake proposal."

"We hope KNN succeeds, son."

"When will you get back, Beau?"

"Late afternoon. After the meeting, I want to go with Jorge and Jaime and Eric to Withers Fork. With Sequoyah and Mighty. We'll walk. Okay?"

"I'll pack you a lunch," Lauren said. "Take your cell phone."

"You know John Hicks? He wears a sweatshirt that says 'Happy Half-Breed.' I think I'll get one like it."

ⱯⱯⱯ

"You're gorgeous, Rhonda," Scissors's owner Jon Finley said to the mayor's wife after blow-drying her short, wavy, platinum-blonde hair. "Now would you like me to clip Coco Chanel's whiskers?"

Coco Chanel was Rhonda's platinum-blonde Pomeranian who usually could be found in her arms.

"Thanks, Jon, please do."

Jon carefully snipped Coco Chanel's whiskers.

"As I was saying, Rich will meet with the Town Council on Friday," Rhonda went on. "He thinks the Council will approve his proposal to make a lake with some of the money old Francis Hearty Withers left Witherston. Rich says a lake will attract tourists and bring growth. He thinks it will make him and Witherston famous."

"I'm an anti-growth man. I like being unfamous in an unfamous mountain town with a population of four thousand unfamous people and no tourists whatsoever."

"Me too. Who needs more than one bank, one gas station, one hotel, one drug store, one fire truck, and one liquor store?"

"Three cafes, two patrol cars, and one fabulous beauty shop, owned by a handsome man with no hair." Jon had developed alopecia in high school. He was completely hairless.

"Jon, did you see *Webby Witherston* this morning? The letters to the editor?"

"I saw the letter from Donna Dam."

"Have you heard what that's about? Rich won't tell me. After he read the story he left the house. He said he had to work all day. On a Saturday for heaven's sake."

"No, sweet baby. I've heard nothing about Rich's doings in 1977."

"That was before I went out with him."

"Did he know Grant back then?"

"They were fraternity brothers."

Jon held the mirror up for Rhonda to view the back of her head.

"Anyway, do you and Gregory want to join our protest march tomorrow?"

"Sure. And we'll bring Renoir." Jon and his life partner Gregory Bozeman, a retired EPA ecologist, took their white standard poodle with them wherever they could.

"Be at Tayanita Village at one o'clock. We'll go in a convoy up Possum Road to Emmett Gray's farm, just before you get to Blue Boulder. Rich wants to build the dam there at Withers Fork where Saloli Stream splits into Founding Father's Creek and Tayanita Creek."

"At Withers Fork?"

"Yes, but don't tell anyone. The exact location is not yet public knowledge."

"What does he want to call the lake?"

"Witherston Lake or Lake Witherston. I don't know which. But Rich said the Council is calling it Mayor Rather's Lake."

"Call it a flood, and then nobody will support it."

"Good idea. Mayor Rather's Flood."

Rhonda picked up Coco Chanel and headed toward her red Chevy Volt convertible.

"See you all tomorrow," she called over her shoulder. "You and Gregory and Renoir."

∾∾∾

Grant Griggs ran into the mayor at ten forty-five as he passed Rich on his way out of Witherston Savings and Loan. Grant had extracted from his safety deposit box ten thousand dollars in cash and a small handgun, both of which he'd put into his briefcase.

"Hello, Rich," Grant said. "We've got to talk. Who in hell is Donna Dam?"

"How do I know, Grant? I never heard of her."

"What's she got on us?"

"Nothing. She just wants to stop the lake and ruin my career. So she's saying we know about dam breaks because we were in Toccoa that night."

"We were, but we weren't doing anything illegal."

"We were drinking."

"How old were you then?"

"In November of 1977? Twenty."

"I was nineteen. But the legal drinking age in Georgia in 1977 was eighteen."

"So she's just trying to scare us?"

"Yeah. What are you doing today?"

"Usual business, Grant, just usual business. I'm headed down to Dahlonega. What are you doing?"

"I'm going fishing."

"Do you think we should sync our stories about what we were doing in Toccoa? Our trusty *Webby Witherston* reporter will be sniffing around."

"I don't remember a thing, Grant. Maybe we fished in Barnes Lake that day."

"And played pool that night."

"Right."

"We didn't want to go to the Georgia-Florida game."

"Right."

"I hope you don't change your mind on the dam, Rich. There's a lot of push-back, you know."

"Yeah. From my wife. But I will not change my mind. No, I will not. Anyway, it's too late to back out."

ণ্ড

"Blanca, *ven acá.* Come here." Ernesto Zamora held a letter in his hand. "Do you understand this letter?"

Blanca read it. "Hernando, *por favor.*" She showed her son the letter.

Their son Hernando was accustomed to translating documents for his parents. He read the letter.

"A real estate lady named Phyllis Graph says that someone wants to buy our land for four hundred thousand dollars."

"But our land is worth more than that," Ernesto said. "*Mucho más.* And it's not just our land. It's our home. It's our way to make a living. We can't sell it."

In the spring of 2000 Ernesto and Blanca had come to Lumpkin County from Seville with their newborn son, bought forty-five fertile acres on Saloli Stream, planted grapes, built a small winery, and founded Zamora Wines. They'd recently remodeled the ninety-year-old farmhouse and turned the interior into the Spanish home of their dreams, as they thought appropriate for prosperous winemakers.

"We won't, Ernesto. We won't sell it, ever."

"What if the mayor builds his dam? The lake would flood us."

"The mayor won't succeed. I am sure of it. God will protect us."

"We need to protect ourselves," Hernando said. "God may be protecting the mayor."

"I wish Witherston had elected me to the Town Council instead of Mrs. Grant. She will vote for the lake because her husband wants it."

"I'm going on Mrs. Rather's march," Blanca said.

"I'm biking over to a KNN meeting this morning to figure out how to stop the mayor," Hernando said. "I'll be back by noon. This afternoon I want to go fishing."

"I'll plan on trout for dinner." Blanca gave her son a kiss.

მ~ა~ა

"Will the meeting of Keep Nature Natural please come to order."

Beau, president of Witherston High School's environmental group, stood at the end of a long pine picnic table and pounded his gavel.

On the benches sat KNN members Annie Jerden, Jaime Arroyo, Jorge Arroyo, Mona Pattison, Christopher Zurich, Eric Schlaughter, Sally Sorensen, and Hernando Zamora. Under them lay Mighty and Sequoyah.

"We have one order of business today," Beau said. "To figure out a campaign to block Mayor Rather's dam proposal. The floor is open for discussion."

"I think Jorge should do a cartoon of our Humpty Dumpty mayor watching a bulldozer make a dam," Mona Pattison said. She squeezed Jorge's hand.

"It could be a comic strip. In the second frame Jorge could draw the bulldozer pushing Mayor Rather into the lake," Jaime said.

"And in the third frame he could draw Mayor Rather floating belly up with his itty bitty arms waving in the air," Beau said.

"And a speed boat headed his way," Mona said.

"Okay, Jorge?"

"Onkey donkey. I'll draw something."

"A cartoon won't stop anything," Christopher said. "Let's actually do something."

"I agree," Sally said. "What can we do?"

"Is there anything that would make building the dam immoral?" Beau asked. "Let's concentrate on that."

"It's already immoral," Hernando said. "Think of the people who would be displaced by the lake, like my family."

"Think of the people who would be killed if the mayor built his dam and the dam broke," Eric said.

"And think of the people who would lose their water supply if Tayanita Creek dried up," Jaime said. "Our Cherokee friends in Tayanita Village depend on Tayanita Creek."

"Immorality doesn't bother our esteemed mayor," Eric said.

"Then what would make building a dam illegal?" Beau asked.

"Indian ruins," Christopher said. "I've been working on this. If we find Indian ruins alongside Saloli Stream, the state of Georgia will forbid flooding the valley."

"Beau has dug up arrowheads in Saloli Valley," Sally said.

"Saloli Valley is where Cherokees and whites killed each other. I'll bet there are a lot of bullets in the ground there too," Jorge said.

"So how are we going to find Indian ruins before Friday, Christopher?" Beau asked.

"I've planted them," Christopher said. "I planted

some bones and made an Indian burial site. Do you want to know where it is?"

"I want to know where you got human bones, Christopher. Did you kill someone?"

"Who said the bones were human? A few goat bones could look like a grave," Christopher said.

"Geez, Christopher, you've already been arrested for your idiotic pranks. If you get caught, you'll never get into college," Jaime said.

"So you don't want to know where my burial site is?"

"No."

"Don't tell us, Christopher," Beau said.

"Do you have a better plan, Jaime?" Christopher asked.

"Way better. I say KNN sends a letter to *Webby Witherston* explaining what happens to wildlife when a dam gets built. We give the Town Council information they don't have. Then the supporters of the dam will change their mind."

"Good idea, Jaime," Beau said.

"You write the letter, Jaime, and see how successful you are," Christopher said.

"Okay, I will," Jaime said.

"And I will draw a comic strip," Jorge said. "Or at least a cartoon."

After more discussion, Beau adjourned the meeting.

"KNN will meet here on Friday morning at ten o'clock," he said. "Friday afternoon the mayor will present his proposal to the Council."

"Don't forget Slow Pedal on Wednesday afternoon," Sally said. "Who's going?"

"I'm going," Beau said.

"Let's all go and wear our KNN sweatshirts," Jorge said, "so we can recognize each other."

"This will be my first time riding," Eric said. "I'll borrow my stepfather's dirt bike."

CHAPTER 2

Saturday Afternoon, March 11, 2017

T he mayor is going to dam up Saloli Stream probably right here at Withers Fork," Jaime said.

Jaime, Jorge, Beau, and Eric stood on the granite
outcropping locals called Blue Boulder, which split Saloli
Stream into Tayanita Creek and Founding Father's Creek.
Jorge took a picture of Saloli Valley north of Blue Boulder.

"Wow," Beau said. "All those farms up the valley
will be flooded."

"The cows will need life vests," Jorge said.

"No, they won't," Jaime said. "Cows can swim."

"Because they're full of methane gas," Jorge said.

"Beep beep, beep beep, the cows went beep beep
beep," Eric sang to the tune of the Playmates' 1958 song
"Little Nash Rambler."

Almost every Saturday afternoon for as long as they
could remember Jaime, Jorge, and Beau had explored the
woods. The three boys had grown up wading in the
creeks, hiking, climbing, fishing, and recently bow hunting. They'd captured salamanders, caught trout, shot wild
turkeys, and glimpsed boars, bears, foxes, cougars, and
coyotes. They'd camped out all night by themselves.

They believed they knew the area as well as any Indian scout.

Often they hiked along Founding Father's Creek downstream to the bridge where they would fish and gather shells. Sometimes they hiked upstream to Saloli Falls, where in warm weather they would skinny-dip in the pool under the falls. Occasionally, they hunted for arrowheads in Saloli Valley to add to Beau's collection.

Today Jaime, Jorge, Beau, and Eric, with Mighty and Sequoyah, had trekked up Possum Road all the way to Withers Fork. Beau had named his dog Sequoyah after the Cherokee man who put the Cherokee language into writing. While Mighty and Sequoyah, forty-pound lab-terrier mixes, chased each other into and out of Tayanita Creek, the teenagers unpacked the breakfast bars, peanuts, apples, and gouda cheese they'd carried in their backpacks.

"Look! A coyote!" Beau pointed to the woods west of Founding Father's Creek. "Look!"

"Where?"

"There, over there!"

Eric cupped his hands over his mouth. "Aaah oooh aaah oooh."

"Wow, Eric. You'd make a good coyote," Jaime said.

"I wish I had my bow," Beau said. Beau had saved his allowance and bought a sixty-five-inch Cherokee longbow—that is, a reproduction of the nineteenth-century weapon—for three hundred and sixty dollars.

"Let's come back while we're still on spring break, with our bows," Jaime said.

"I could come Wednesday morning," Eric said. "I'm taking the whole day off so I can do Slow Pedal with you all."

Jorge and Jaime had less expensive recurve bows,

but they also had good aim. They'd each shot a turkey in April.

Jaime, Jorge, and Beau attended Witherston High, where they were good students, although not above mischief. Beau had been president of the ninth grade and was now president of KNN. He wanted to be an historian. Jorge, who could draw as well as he could write, wanted to be a journalist and a cartoonist. Jorge had been president of the tenth grade. Jaime, who was first in their class academically, wanted to be an ecologist.

The trio had befriended Eric in August when Eric entered Witherston High as a new student hailing from Rome, Georgia. Eric's mother Molly Schlaughter had become Mayor Rather's secretary, and his new stepfather, Sam Staples, had joined the Witherston Police Department. Jaime, Jorge, and Beau found Eric, who was a year older, different from students their own age, more sophisticated, more mature, more independent from his parents, or rather, from his mother and stepfather. Eric worked at the Yona Gas Station on weekend mornings and holidays. He hoped to get a scholarship to the University of Georgia to study wildlife, especially birds of prey. He had straight black hair which he pulled back in a ponytail. He owned a Harley. And he sang in Tony Lima's Mountain Band.

Jaime and Jorge resembled their Spanish father. They had dark brown eyes and unruly brown hair, which Jaime parted on the right and Jorge parted on the left. And like their father they sported neat moustaches. At five feet, ten inches, they were already taller than their father and a good bit thinner. To most people they were indistinguishable from each other.

Beau did not have a moustache. As the only dark-skinned boy in his class, he sought the well-groomed look. He shaved, wore a buzz cut, and dressed in khakis.

He was short for his age, only five feet, six inches tall. He hoped to find a girlfriend, as Jaime and Jorge had, but he knew no black girls. He liked Sally Sorensen, but she was white and he was reluctant to ask a white girl for a date.

The three boys' parents were best friends. The twins' father Paco was Witherston High's biology teacher, and their mother Mev was the Witherston Police Department's detective. Beau's father Jim was Witherston's gynecologist, and his mother Lauren was Lumpkin County's probate judge. Lauren commuted to Dahlonega, thirty minutes down the mountain.

"May I bring one of my stepfather's guns?" Eric asked. "He's got some Confederate rifles."

"Real Confederate rifles?" Beau asked.

"He's a Civil War reenactor," Eric said.

"No firearms," Jaime said.

"You can use my bow and see if you feel like a Cherokee," Beau said.

"I look like a Cherokee," Eric said.

"You do."

"Because I've got Cherokee blood in me," Eric added.

"You can use my bow too," Jorge said.

"We can share," Jaime said.

"Do you all want to have an adventure out here?" Eric asked them when they finished eating their apples.

"What kind of adventure?" Beau asked.

"A trip."

"Like a trip down Tayanita Creek? We've done that," said Jaime. "On a raft."

"I mean a mental trip," Eric said, pulling out of his backpack a green plastic case the size of a cigar box. "We're going to smoke some of Georgia's best cannabis, and we're going to do it in style," he said.

"Marijuana? Marijuana is illegal. We could go to jail."

"Wait, Jaime. Let's see what Eric wants to show us."

Eric opened the case and took out a royal blue glass pipe.

"Wow. That looks expensive," Beau said.

"I bought it on the web for sixty-five dollars. It's called a Sherlock pipe because Sherlock Holmes smoked one like it. It's blown glass."

"Wow," Jorge said.

"Smoking cannabis in a glass pipe is pure bliss," Eric said. "No chemicals pollute the smoke."

"Where's the marijuana?"

"Here." Eric removed the false bottom from the case and extracted a small plastic baggy filled with the weed.

"Did you get that on the web too?" Beau asked.

"No. I got it from a grower I know. I've been saving it for a special occasion, like today."

"We should try smoking it, Jaime," Jorge said. "We're sixteen years old. We need to find out what marijuana does to us."

"I don't know," Jaime said. "It's illegal."

"Just this once," Jorge said to his brother. "Aunt Lottie would approve."

"For sure," Jaime said.

Eric put a generous bit of marijuana into the pipe, tapped it down with his forefinger, lit it with a match, and took a drag.

The four boys sat cross-legged facing each other on Blue Boulder. Eric passed around the pipe. Again and again. The sweet scent filled their nostrils. The smoke filled their lungs. When the pipe was empty, he refilled it.

Beau told a long, long story about the black workers in the Georgia gold mines of the 1830s who were his father's ancestors. Jaime whistled the witchdoctor song,

"Ooo eee ooo ah ah ting tang walla walla, bing bang, Ooo eee ooo ah ah ting tang walla walla bing bang." Jorge regaled his companions with tales of Henny Penny and Mother Hen, Feather Jo and Feather Jean, and Moonshine and Sunshine.

And Eric led the boys in singing "She'll Be Coming Round the Mountain When She Comes," including the verse "She'll be wearing pink pajamas when she comes."

When he got to the verse "She'll be carrying three white puppies when she comes," Jorge said, "Okay, Eric. Okay, okay, okay!"

"Where did that song come from, Eric?" Jaime asked.

"Appalachia. In the nineteenth century. Could be from right around here," Eric said.

"It has the same tune as 'When the Chariot Comes,'" Beau said, "which is an African American spiritual. Starts like this. 'O, who will drive the chariot when she comes?'"

"You're right, Beau," Eric said. "But in the nineteenth century somebody from these mountains put new lyrics to the tune. Tony Lima likes the 'Coming Round the Mountain' version, so we may sing it tomorrow."

The boys lay down on the warm granite.

"Have you ever thought about how many people have sat on this boulder and listened to these rapids like we're doing?" Beau said, looking at the blue sky. "Humans have lived here for twelve thousand years, probably more. Just imagine, twelve thousand years ago, four guys like us may have been lying here in the sun, talking about their tribe, smelling the pines, listening to the birds. Maybe cleaning the fish they'd caught."

"Do you think those guys saw the same birds that we see?" Jaime asked, pointing to a hawk soaring overhead.

"That red-shouldered hawk? Listen. *Kee-rah, kee-*

rah, kee-rah," Eric said, mimicking the hawk's call.

"Wow, Eric."

"Want to hear a barred owl?" Eric mimicked the *Who-cooks-for-you, who-cooks-for-you-all* call of the barred owl. "If you hear that at night, you know it's a barred owl."

"Or else it's you, Eric," Beau said.

"Right. I'd be sending you all a signal of danger."

"How would we know the difference between you and an owl?"

"If I'm good, you wouldn't. By the way, do you all know that birds see the world differently from us humans?"

"They see it more clearly," Jaime said.

"Lots of birds see into the ultraviolet ranges of light," Eric said. They can see colors of feathers that we humans can't see, because feathers reflect ultraviolet light. Hawks and eagles can see urine on the ground because urine reflects ultraviolet light. That's one way they spot their prey."

"I'd better pee in the bushes," Jorge said. "I don't want to attract a hawk when I'm doing my business."

"Twelve thousand years ago those guys probably saw birds we won't ever see, birds that are now extinct," Beau said. "Extinct like the ivory-billed woodpecker."

"But these creeks were here. They must have been here for twelve thousand years," Jaime said, "making the same sound of water splashing over rocks."

"I like to think the creeks will be here for another twelve thousand years," Jorge said.

"They won't if Mayor Rather builds his dam," Eric said.

"I don't think humans will be here for another twelve thousand years," Beau said.

"I know one thing those guys didn't see twelve thousand years ago," Jaime said. "That jet trail. The first Americans didn't mark up the sky."

After a minute of silence Beau asked, "What do you think those guys looked like?"

"No way to know. They didn't take pictures," Eric said.

The boys grew quiet. In the warmth of the sunshine all four fell asleep.

When the daylight waned and the air cooled, Mighty and Sequoyah bounded into their midst, shook themselves dry, and barked.

"Oh, no! It's past six," Jaime said, looking at his phone. "Get up, everybody. We've got to get out of here before it gets dark."

The boys stood up and stretched.

"I hear a car," Jaime said. "Up there." He pointed to the ridge behind them.

"I just hear white water," Beau said.

"You're hallucinating, Jaime," Jorge said. "You're hearing a car while we're hearing rapids." He giggled.

"Seriously, bro, I heard a car up there. It stopped."

"Why would someone come to Withers Fork at sundown?" Jorge asked.

"I'll climb up on the ridge to see who's there," Beau said. "Come on, Sequoyah, Mighty. Let's go." They disappeared into the thicket.

"Okay, guys. Let's bury the pipe," Eric said.

"Why?"

"If we bury it nobody can prove we've smoked anything," Eric said. "I'll be in big trouble if I get arrested again."

"You've gotten arrested?"

"Yes. Once. For drinking. It was in Rome. A year ago."

"We'll all be in trouble," Jaime said.

"Where should we bury it?" Eric asked, looking around.

"I have an idea," Jorge said. He climbed twenty feet up the rock face to where the granite jutted out of the ground. "Under the granite. Behind these bushes."

Jorge crawled, with some difficulty, through the rhododendron.

"Great! This is like a little cave."

Eric pulled a trowel out of his backpack. "Use this."

"It is a cave," Jorge said as he leaned into it. "It's a dry cave. Big enough for a bear to hibernate in."

"I'll dig," Jaime said and took the trowel. "I'm a good digger."

Jaime followed his brother through the bushes.

"Some animal has already been digging here," Jorge said. "He got halfway to China." He backed out to make room for Jaime.

"I'll take us the rest of the way," Jaime said. He crawled into the cave with the trowel. "There are a lot of rocks here, like an underground wall."

Jaime passed several rocks out to Jorge.

"Why do you have a trowel in your backpack?" Jorge asked Eric.

"I always carry one."

"What else do you have in there?"

"A Swiss knife, a flashlight, plastic baggies, a wallet with a fake driver's license, a bottle of water, a bag of peanuts." Eric showed them the backpack's contents. "And a condom. You never know what you'll need."

"A condom?" Beau asked.

"Like I said, you never know."

"You have a girlfriend, Eric?"

"Yes. Back in Rome. But please keep that confidential."

"Cool," Jorge said.

"What do you have in your backpack, Jorge," Eric asked.

"My iPhone, my iPad, a bottle of water, a KNN sweatshirt, and a granola bar. Maybe I should carry a condom, too."

"We need some light in here," Jaime said.

Eric handed the LED flashlight to Jorge. Jorge leaned in behind his brother and aimed the beam down the hole.

"The hole has to be deep enough that the pipe won't be discovered," Jorge said to Jaime. "Deep enough that the rain won't wash the pipe away."

"It's very dry in here," Jaime said. He piled the dirt and rocks at the cave entrance.

"Here's the pipe case," Eric said. He had put the case into a plastic zip-lock bag.

Eric handed the case to Jorge, who handed it to Jaime, who dropped it into the hole.

"Hurry, guys," Eric said. "Fill in the hole, and let's go."

"Whoa, Jaime," said Jorge, who was lying almost on top of his brother watching him work. "You're hitting something white, a tree root or something."

Jaime put down the trowel and reached into the hole.

"Yikes," he said. "It's a bone!" In a minute he'd uncovered a six-inch-long curved bone. He pulled it out and handed it to Jorge. Jorge laid it on the ground.

"Looks like a rib."

"Maybe it's a wolf rib."

"Maybe it's a human rib."

"That wolves licked clean."

"Yuk."

"Dig deeper, Jaime," said Jorge. "We've got to find out what else is down here."

"Give me more light."

Jorge handed him the flashlight.

"What are you finding?" Eric asked from outside.

"This," Jaime said. He backed out of the cave holding a checked ceramic pot eight inches in diameter. He set the pot on the ground beside the rib.

"Jaime!" Jorge exclaimed. "That's an old Cherokee pot. We saw one like it at Oconaluftee Indian Village."

Jaime turned the flashlight on it and caught something gold and shiny in its beam. He handed Jorge a small rock.

"Look, Jorge. What kind of rock is this?"

"That's a gold nugget! Real gold."

"Let's see," Eric said.

"Guess what, guys," Jorge said. "We've found a burial site. A Cherokee burial site."

"Hold the flashlight, bro."

Jorge turned the flashlight into the hole.

"Look, there are more bones."

"What should we do?" Eric asked.

"Put everything back in the hole and cover it up," Jorge said. "This spot is sacred."

Jaime carefully returned the rib to its resting place in the ground.

"I'm going to get a picture of the pot." Jorge took a picture with his iPhone. He then handed his brother the pot with the nugget.

Jaime put the pot back where he'd uncovered it.

"Let's get out of here," Eric said. "It's getting dark."

"Jorge, there are lots of bones down here," Jaime said. "I can see them."

"Someone's coming!" Jorge whispered.

Beau crashed through the brush, followed by the dogs.

"Who's on the ridge?" Eric asked.

"Officer Hefner. He asked what we were doing. I said we were talking."

"Cripes. Was my stepfather with him? They're partners. Or they're supposed to be."

"I didn't see him, but he might have been in their patrol car."

"Or he might have gotten out to have a smoke."

"I didn't see him," Beau repeated.

"I'm gone. Keep the trowel," Eric said. "I'll hoot if there's trouble." He disappeared into the woods.

"We've got to fill up this hole before we leave." Jaime said. He started pushing sand back into the hole. "Help me, bro."

"What's going on?" Beau asked.

By now Jorge and Jaime had filled the hole with sand. They shoved a few dead branches into the cave entrance and then backed out of the rhododendron bush.

"We're done," Jaime said.

Jaime and Jorge and Beau climbed up on top of Blue Boulder.

"Nobody will ever find that cave, Jaime. Good work, *hermano*!"

Just as they were about to leave, they heard a loud explosion upstream.

"What's that?" Beau exclaimed.

In an instant a fireball shot to the sky.

The boys rushed to the edge of Blue Boulder.

"Wow! Look at that!" The fireball lit up the night.

"What could have exploded?"

"Firecrackers?" asked Beau.

They heard a police whistle.

"What's going on?"

"That's a police whistle."

"From upstream."

Who-cooks-for-you, who-cooks-for-you-all. The call
came from the ridge.

"A barred owl!" Jaime exclaimed.

"Or Eric," Jorge said.

"Eric, is that you?" Beau called out.

"Someone's on the creek," Jaime whispered. "Tayanita Creek. Look."

Over the rhythmic splash of oars they heard a man
say, "Oh, shit."

Suddenly they were blinded by a spotlight. Jaime
held the trowel over his eyes. Jorge and Beau stared at the
source of the light. The three stood stock still. Finally the
canoe disappeared around the bend and left them in darkness. Upstream they could see a fire.

"I'm calling Mom," Jaime said. "The police need to
know about the explosion."

"But don't tell her what we've been doing," Jorge
said.

Jaime called.

"We're okay, Mom…We're sorry…We're still on
Blue Boulder…We'll explain…Mom, something exploded up here. We saw a fireball…Something's on fire…On
Saloli Stream north of Withers Fork…The east
bank…We're on our way home…Okay, bye."

ↄ☙ↄ

"*Dios mío!* Oh, my God! Ernesto, what's that?"

The explosion shook the house.

Blanca and Ernesto Zamora rushed onto the back
porch in time to see the fireball ascend into the night sky.

"It's the shed," Blanca said, "where Hernando goes
to read."

"Where's Hernando?"

"He went fishing."

"Hernando!" Ernesto shouted.

Blanca blew her silver police whistle to call her son home, as she'd done since he was a little boy. She wore it as a pendant.

"Hernando! Come home!"

"I'm coming!" Hernando shouted from the other side of Witherston Highway near the stream.

"Where were you?" Blanca asked her son minutes later, when he walked into the house. He was covered with soot.

"I was fishing on the property the Armours used to own, maybe a quarter mile above our shed. I heard a shot in the direction of the shed and walked down to look. I was only a hundred yards from the shed when it blew up."

"*Jesús!* You could have been killed!"

"Good thing I wasn't inside."

"*Qué pasó?*"

"*No sé, Papá.* I don't know. I think somebody set the fire."

"*Dios mío!*"

Hernando pulled three trout out of his backpack fish cooler. "Here's dinner."

ಀಀ

Mev heard the siren of Witherston's fire truck as she climbed into Chief Jake McCoy's Chevy Tahoe. Tracker, Jake's hundred-pound bloodhound, was in the back seat. Jake turned on his siren. Deputies Pete Senior and Pete Junior followed them in their patrol car and turned on their siren. By the time they arrived at the scene of the explosion Fire Chief Mike Moss and his two volunteers Atsadi Moon and Shorty O'Rork were pumping water from the creek.

Jake grabbed Tracker's leash as he and Mev jumped out of the vehicle.

"Hey," Mike greeted them.

"Hey, Mike," Pete Senior said. "What's cooking?"

"Very funny."

"Did anyone live here?" Jake asked.

"No. Might have been an old fishing shack. It was no bigger than a storage shed. Made of pine. Pine burns fast and hot. This was a hot, hot fire."

Mike stood with the police officers while Atsadi and Shorty put out the fire.

"Maybe it was a storage shed," Jake said.

"Out here?"

"Maybe it was a meth lab," Mev said.

"Could have been a meth lab," Jake said, aiming his flashlight into the water-soaked rubble.

"Something went nuclear." Mike said.

"Do you see any bodies?"

"No. Hard to see in the dark."

Tracker started barking. He strained at his leash.

"Wait. Give me some light over here," Jake said. "Looks like Tracker's found a body."

"Good God! It is a body. Was a body. It's just bones now."

"I smell gasoline," Mike said. "This fire was set."

"Take pictures, Pete Junior," Jake said.

"Will do, chief."

"Pete Senior, bag the remains."

"Will do, chief."

Jake's cell phone rang. It was reporter Amadahy Henderson.

"Hello, Amadahy," Jake said. "I figured you'd call. I'll tell you what's happening…"

⇜⇝

Following their dogs, Jaime, Jorge, and Beau made their way up the steep brushy slope to the ridge.

With the light of the full moon, the boys started walking down Possum Road. Jaime told Beau about the bones he found in the cave.

"Do you think those are the bones Christopher planted?" Beau asked.

"Oh! What if they are?"

"They can't be, Jaime. They looked really old," Jorge said. "And where would Christopher have gotten a gold nugget?"

"Right. And if Christopher had gotten a gold nugget he would have kept it for himself."

"Like a dog with a bone."

"I'll call my father and get him to pick us up at Mr. Gray's farm," Beau said.

Beau called his father.

"Pop's coming now," he said.

"I bet the man in the canoe set off the explosion," Jorge said.

"To hide something?"

"Maybe he was doing something illegal there and had to get rid of the evidence."

"Maybe he was making meth. Meth is explosive, you know," Jaime said.

"And now he's going to kill us. He must know who we are."

"He held the spotlight on us for a long time."

"That was so we couldn't see him."

"What was Officer Hefner doing on the ridge?"

"I don't know. Maybe just looking around."

When the boys arrived at the farmhouse, Lidia Gray greeted them with a wide smile. She was a short, plump, pretty, silver-haired woman in her early seventies.

Jorge and Jaime knew her because she'd been the

Witherston Police Department's secretary.

"Twins, your father just called," she said. "He and Dr. Lodge are on their way. You all come in. Emmett's out."

Ten minutes later Jim Lodge and Paco Arroyo pulled up in Jim's new green Outlander.

"Where were you?" Paco asked the boys, opening the car door. "You were supposed to be home by dark."

"We went exploring," Jorge said.

"And then we fell asleep on Blue Boulder," Beau added.

"The sun made us drowsy," Jaime said.

"Where's your friend Eric?" Jim asked.

"He went home before us."

"Okay, boys," Jim said. "Call your dogs and get in the car."

"Mighty, Sequoyah, get your tails here!" Jorge yelled.

"*Vámonos*," Paco said.

CHAPTER 3

Saturday night, March 11, 2017

C ome and get it or I'll throw it out," Gretchen
called from the kitchen. That was her usual sum-
mons to dinner.

"Do I smell buffalo on the grill?" Neel called back,
as he did every night, each time mentioning a different
mammal. All-organic Gretchen had turned him into a
pescatarian, that is, a person who eats fish and seafood
but no meat.

Neel Kingfisher, Jr., MD, sat at his computer in the
living room of the old farmhouse he and Gretchen had
renovated. He was writing a book he called a biography
of Green Acres which would start with the arrival there of
the first humans some twelve thousand years before.
Green Acres was the name he and Gretchen had given to
their thirty-acre plot of wooded land in Saloli Valley
where he imagined his Cherokee ancestors once lived.

Neel sat down at the chestnut dining table, and
Gretchen brought out baked trout, leeks, and peas, with a
salad of olives, tomatoes, and cubes of Georgia white
cheddar cheese over raw spinach. Plus home-baked
whole wheat bread. Gretchen poured the wine, a chardonnay from a local vineyard.

"Lovely, dear Gretchen."

"Thanks, dear Neel."

"I got our genetic reports today. Do you want to know what I am?"

"I know who you are. You're a handsome Cherokee, with straight gray hair, brown eyes, brownish skin, impressive muscles, and a good brain. You're fifty-seven years old. You're six feet tall. You weigh 185 pounds."

Neel identified himself as Cherokee, although he was only three-fourths Cherokee. His grandparents were Mohe Kingfisher and Penelope Louise Withers, who moved from Georgia to Oklahoma in 1930 when Penelope's father, Witty Withers, disinherited her for marrying an Indian. They had one son, Neel, before dying together in a bus accident. Twenty-nine years later, in 1960, Neel Kingfisher and Ayita Nance begat Neel Kingfisher, Jr., who eventually studied medicine at the University of Oklahoma College of Medicine and became Neel Kingfisher, Jr., MD.

In 2013 Neel had come to Witherston from Tahlequah, Oklahoma, to search for his north Georgia roots, and had taken the job of director of Withers Retirement Village. Here he grew to know and despise his first cousin once removed, the billionaire on the hill, Mr. Francis Hearty Withers, who never acknowledged their kinship.

He retired from his position when he fell in love with Gretchen Green and realized he didn't want to spend the rest of his days dispensing drugs to old men. He and Gretchen bought Green Acres, plowed and planted a vegetable garden, sent the vegetables to Gretchen's grocery store, and, in their late fifties, found happiness. They lived with Gandhi the Great Dane, Swift the white German Shepherd, Ama the sibling of Mighty and Sequoyah, and Barack the black cat.

"Do you want to know who I am genetically, Gretchen?"

"Hang on, Neel. You're a physician who prefers philosophy, art, and Cherokee history to medicine. You collect Cherokee bone knives. And you're in love with me. Right?"

"Right. I'm also sixty-nine percent Native American, twenty-two percent British and Irish, five percent northern European, two percent French and German, two percent undetermined. One percent of my DNA can be traced back to Neanderthals."

"So you're not seventy-five percent Native American."

"I'm not. That surprises me. At least one of my Native American forebears made love to a white person. Do you want to know what you are?"

"I am fifty-seven years old, five foot six inches tall, with two long gray braids and a dove tattooed on my right arm. I am a liberal environmentalist feminist foodie in love with you."

"Genetically, you are seventy-seven percent British and Irish, ten percent northern European, five percent Native American, three percent Ashkenazi Jew, and five percent undetermined. Two point six percent of your DNA can be traced back to Neanderthals."

"So at least one of my white forebears made love to a Native American. I hope it was in the bottom of a canoe. Maybe we're cousins, Neel!"

"Maybe, maybe not, dear Gretchen."

"Here's to my favorite Indian," Gretchen said as she and Neel clinked their wine glasses. "That is, my favorite mostly-Indian person."

"Here's to my favorite mostly-white person."

"Neel, Rhonda asked me to speak at her demonstration tomorrow."

Gretchen had participated in demonstrations since the age of eight. Upon learning that her father had been fatally shot in the battle of Khe Sanh in 1968, she and her mother had joined the anti-Vietnam movement. At the age of eight she had carried a MAKE LOVE NOT WAR sign while her mother carried a NOT ONE MORE DEAD sign in a peace march in Columbus, Georgia, where they lived. In later years she'd celebrated Earth Day, crusaded for the Equal Rights Amendment, crusaded against nuclear power, and become a vegan, then a vegetarian, and finally a pescatarian. After she married her friend Smithfield Green, whom she met at the University of Georgia, and moved with him to Witherston, she opened her all-organic, meatless grocery store. Their marriage hadn't lasted because Smitty craved meat, but their friendship had.

"Do you want to come with me?" Gretchen asked Neel.

"Not really. You know I think words influence more people than feet."

"The lake may flood our farm."

"What?"

"Did you read *Webby Witherston* today? According to Amadahy Henderson, the proposal calls for a lake of sixty acres. The lake could extend a half mile up the valley from Withers Fork. I did the arithmetic. We could drown."

"You've convinced me."

"I'll email Rhonda that we'll both be there."

coco

"I've fed the animals and cooped up the chickens for the night, Catherine," Dan said as he entered the kitchen. "Now I'm hoping you'll feed me and coop me up for the night."

"Oh, Dan! I've gotten another letter from Donna Dam. I just checked my email."

A year ago Catherine Perry and Dan Soto had married and moved into a hundred-year-old farmhouse on a thirty-acre apple orchard they leased from Rhonda Rather for a dollar a month. Dan had just quit hauling chickens for Love Me Tender Poultry and fallen in love with Catherine. The deal with Rhonda was that they would provide sanctuary for needy barnyard animals in exchange for the low rent. Currently they were caring for a tired old donkey named Lewis, a one-eyed horse named Honeybunch, and a three-legged nanny goat named Cabbie, as well as a flock of seventeen healthy Broiler chickens and a rooster named Luciano Pavarotti. Plus their basset hound Muddy and their cat Calico.

"Let's see it," Dan said.

Catherine held up her smartphone.

From: Donna Dam (donotreply@ddam.com)
To: Catherine Perry <catherineperrysoto@webwitherston.com>

PUBLISH THIS
Sat 03/11/2017 5:29 p.m.

To the Editor:

Would Mayor Rather and Attorney Griggs be willing to take a paternity test?
If not, why not?

Donna Dam
Former Toccoa resident

*PS. IF YOU DO NOT PUBLISH THIS TO-
MORROW (SUNDAY), YOU PUT MAYOR RA-
THER AND ATTORNEY GRIGGS IN DANGER.*

Sent from my iPhone

"This letter will turn Witherston catawampus."

"It would turn me catawampus if I got such a letter."

"If you got such a letter, love, I would not be happy either."

"There's something weird here," Dan said. "Donna Dam sent the email to you at five twenty-nine this afternoon. So she's not waiting to see whether the mayor retracts his proposal."

"She's not just trying to stop the dam, Dan. She's trying to punish them for something."

"Are you going to publish her letter?"

"If I don't, I endanger the lives of two people. But if I do, I get them into another kind of trouble. What would you do?"

"I'd publish it. However, I'd give the mayor a heads-up."

"I'll phone him now," Catherine said.

e⁄ɔe⁄ɔ

"Where have you been today, Rich? It's Saturday."

"Working, Rhonda. In Dahlonega. Trying to make a living while you were blocking my plans."

"If your plans were any good, Rich, I wouldn't block them."

"Rhonda, please call off the march tomorrow. You're undermining my authority. You're humiliating me." Rich Rather poured himself two fingers of bourbon. "And I'm in a mess."

Rhonda looked at her husband. He was overweight, overly talkative, overly insensitive, and overly concerned with other people's opinions of him. Also, overly fond of Wild Turkey. Your average politician. Why had she married him? she wondered. Oh, yes. She'd wanted children. And in 1984, as a senior at the University of Georgia desperate to get married, she'd found him suitable. So they got married. He inherited his father's used car business in Dahlonega—Rather Pre-Owned Vehicles, which everybody called Rather Used Cars—and they moved to Witherston. She gave birth to dear Sandra, who made her marriage worth the pain. Now her stout husband had been elected mayor for a second term. For the life of her she couldn't figure out how he'd gotten enough votes. She had cast her vote for his opponent, Gretchen Green.

"A big mess. Rich. If you create your damn lake, you're in a big mess. You'll flood farms of families who have lived here for generations. Farms that grow our vegetables. Those folks will hate you for the rest of your life."

"They'll get paid for their land, Rhonda. Well paid."

"And everybody else in Witherston will hate you too. We'll have to truck in our vegetables from other places. They'll be more expensive."

"They can eat chicken."

"On top of that you're going to stock your lake with foreign fish. Lord have mercy, Rich! You're already mayor. Do you want to be God?"

"Rhonda, could you please hush up for a minute. Something terrible is happening."

"Right. Your proposal of a lake."

"I just got a phone call from Catherine Perry-Soto. She's publishing another letter from Donna Dam in tomorrow's *Webby Witherston.*"

"Why won't you tell me what you did on November 6, 1977?"

"It's irrelevant."

"Who is this Donna Dam?"

"I told you this morning. I don't know. I never heard of a Donna Dam."

"She's blackmailing you, Rich."

"I know. About something I did forty years ago."

"What did you do?"

"I witnessed the dam break."

"That can't be all."

"I'll tell you about it tomorrow," he said.

"I'll look forward to tomorrow," she said. "Did you read the letter that arrived from that new realtor in town, Phyllis Graph?"

"No, Rhonda. I don't read your mail."

"She says she has a buyer for the Gunter farm. She says he'll pay five hundred thousand dollars."

"Excellent. A year ago you bought it for four hundred seventy-five. Now you can turn it over for a twenty-five thousand dollar profit. Good work."

"The buyer must not know the farm will be twenty feet under if you get your way."

"So sell it, Rhonda."

"No. I won't sell it, Rich. I'm leasing it to Catherine and Dan for an animal sanctuary."

"For a dollar a year."

"Right."

"And the animal sanctuary is more important to you than twenty-five thousand dollars."

"Yes, obviously. But a used car dealer won't understand."

"I don't."

"What do you think Red Wilker has done? He's being blackmailed by Donna Dam too."

"No idea, Rhonda. I have no idea."

The phone rang. Rhonda saw Ruth Griggs's caller ID.

"Hello, Ruth."

"Turn on Toccoa Radio, Rhonda. Now. Bye."

Rhonda and Rich listened to the last part of a news report from the Toccoa radio station:

"...twice-elected mayor of Witherston. Donna Dam, whoever she may be, suggests wrongdoing on the part of the mayor and his attorney friend Grant Griggs on the night of Toccoa's flood. You may ask, what were they doing here? What is their secret? I ask, will Donna Dam's letter to the editor derail Mayor Rather's ambitions to run for the state legislature? Our lines are open. Call in now.

"And we have a caller. Hello, this is Trip Hill on your favorite Toccoa radio station. What do you have to say this evening?"

"Hello, Trip. This is Harmon from Fair Play, Georgia. I like your show. I knew Rich Rather in college. I'll bet he was smoking marijuana that night. Or drinking Jim Beam."

"Thank you, Harmon from Fair Play. And now we have a second caller, Abbie from Toccoa..."

Rich turned off the radio.

"Who is Harmon, Rich?"

"He was president of my fraternity."

"Do you know who Abbie is?"

"No, I don't. I don't know her."

🙖🙖🙖

"Where's Mom?" Eric asked when his stepfather walked in the door at nine o'clock. "I thought she'd be here to fix dinner."

"I have no idea," Sam said. "She got up this morning

after you went to work. Said she needed to spend time with a friend and would be back tomorrow. I said okay and kissed her goodbye. She's been a little temperamental lately."

"You think so?"

"Where are you going, Eric?"

"Out. Don't wait up." Eric put on his helmet and drove off on his Harley.

At the age of fifteen Eric had lost his father, Nat Schlaughter, who fled the law, and at the age of sixteen he'd gained his stepfather who enforced the law.

"I went from the frying pan into the fire," Eric had told Beau when he moved to Witherston. "Now when I go home there's a patrol car in the driveway and a cop in my living room. How can I ever make friends?"

☙❧

"Are you going to tell Annie about the marijuana?"

"I don't know. Are you going to tell Mona?"

"No. If we tell our girlfriends, they'll tell their parents."

"Who will tell our parents."

Since the age of two, the twins had shared their thoughts and feelings with each other before falling asleep. They were each other's best friend.

"Let's not tell anybody right now. We can tell our parents when we're older," Jorge said, "when we come home from college and we're all grown up."

"Good idea, bro. But we should tell them about finding the skeleton and the gold nugget. And the ceramic pot."

"We can't do that without explaining why we dug the hole."

"Why I dug the hole."

"Right. You dug the hole to bury Eric's glass pipe."

"Which we used for smoking marijuana," Jaime said.

"Let's not tell them about the skeleton, not yet."

"Maybe we could talk to Neel. He knows a lot of Cherokee history. And he'll understand."

"Let's take him with us up there."

"Could the skeleton belong to somebody killed recently?"

"Who was buried nekkid?"

"With a few of his favorite things?"

The boys giggled.

"Jorge, are you positive that the skeleton belonged to a human and not a goat?"

"A goat is much smaller. Anyway, Neel will know."

"Tomorrow let's tell Mom and Dad we want to search for arrowheads with Beau and we've asked Neel to go with us," Jorge said.

"We'll say we might find a Cherokee grave!"

"They'll laugh."

"Write Neel."

Jaime Arroyo
iMessage
Saturday, March 11, 11:04 p.m.

Hi neel
Will you meet us at blue boulder
tomorrow morning
We found a skeletonthats maybe cherokee

Yes.
I'd be happy to join you boys.
Thanks for inviting me.

You can tell gretchen but nobody else

I promise. What time?
Where do I meet you?

Ridge above blue boulder at ten

Confirmed.

"Done. Neel will meet us."
"Now write Beau."
"Okay."

Jaime Arroyo
iMessage
Saturday, March 11, 11:10 p.m.

We are going to blue boulder tomorrow
in our car
Want to come

Ok
What time

9:45 our house

See u tomorrow

"Beau just texted me back. He'll come.
"*Buenas noches, hermano.*"
"*Buenas noches.*"
Jaime moved Mighty from his pillow to the foot of the bed and promptly fell asleep.
ZONGZINGZING.
"I've got it," Jorge said. He looked at his phone. "Oh, no!"
"What?"

Jorge showed the message to Jaime.

XXX
iMessage
Saturday, March 11, 11:29 p.m.

*If you twins or Beau tell your mother or anybody
else what you saw or heard on the creek tonight
one of you will be die. Possibly your mother.*

"Oh my god!" Jaime exclaimed. "This must be from
the man in the canoe. He knows who we are."
"What if Beau talks?"
"We've got to tell Beau. Now."
"I'll write him."

Jorge Arroyo
iMessage
Saturday, March 11, 11:33 p.m.

Have you told your folks about man in canoe

No
*I just got horrible message from someone called
xxx*

So did we

Said someone would die if we talked

We got same message
We r not talking

Omg
Whats happening

Lets figure it out tomorrow in car

See u tomorrow 9:45

Ok

"What do we do? Mom's investigating the fire, and we know something that could help her solve the mystery."

"If we tell her, someone dies, Jaime."

"If we don't, and Canoe Man gets away, someone else could die. How would Canoe Man know if we told Mom?"

"The police would investigate, and someone would leak the story to Catherine or Amadahy."

"So what do we do, bro?"

"We investigate the case ourselves."

"With Beau."

"Buenas noches."

"Buenas noches, hermano."

୧⠒୨

Neel opened his journal as he had done every night since leukemia had taken the life of his only child. That was six years ago. Not long after ten-year-old John's death, Neel's marriage broke up, and in 2013 he came to Witherston. He took a sip of his ginger root tea, which Gretchen had prepared with lemon and honey, and began writing.

> *Today I learned from a genetic ancestry test that I am not three-fourths Native American. What a surprise. I must have more than one white ancestor whose passion overcame preju-*

dice. Think of all the suffering humans have in-flicted on other humans to preserve so-called racial purity.

Here's an idea. What if every birth an-nouncement reported the infant's genetic ances-try? Imagine the consequences. Though such a practice might wreak havoc on some families (!) it would undermine racial arrogance.

Why should a person's genetic history be considered private? Genes tell the truth.

I would like to dig up the remains of Fran-cis Hearty Withers and find out whether he car-ried the blood of a Cherokee.

WITHERSTON ON THE WEB
Sunday, March 12, 2017

NEWS

Human Dies in Fire

8:00 a.m. The remains of an adult human were found in the ashes of a small shack that caught fire yesterday evening. The person has not yet been identified.

The shack was located on the east bank of Saloli Stream a quarter mile upstream from Withers Fork on the property of Ernesto and Blanca Zamora. Jaime Arroyo called his mother, Detective Mev Arroyo of the Witherston Police Department, at approximately 7:00 p.m. to report seeing an explosion and a fireball. 16-year-old twins Jaime and Jorge Arroyo and their friend Beau Lodge were picnicking on Blue Boulder when they witnessed the event.

Fire Chief Mike Moss arrived on the scene at 7:25 p.m. with volunteers Atsadi Moon and Shorty O'Rork. They put the fire out quickly.

Detective Arroyo, Police Chief Jake McCoy, Tracker, and Deputies Pete Koslowsky Senior and Pete Koslowsky Junior arrived shortly thereafter. Chief McCoy will report their findings at noon today. When questioned later last night Fire Chief Moss said that he noticed a small marijuana patch, about 4 ft by 6 ft, in the woods behind the shack.

Amadahy Henderson, Reporter

Witherston Is Split on Dam Proposal

A Witherston on the Web telephone poll taken yesterday shows our community to be almost equally divided on Mayor Rather's proposal to create a Lake Witherston. Here are the numbers:

46 %In favor
44%Opposed
10%Undecided

And 30-40 people are expected to join the anti-dam rally organized by Rhonda Rather at 1:00 p.m. this afternoon at Tayanita Village. Demonstrators will go to Emmett and Lidia Gray's farm for speeches, music, and a picnic.

Catherine Perry-Soto, Editor

ANNOUNCEMENTS

Rhonda Rather invites all Witherstonians concerned with the damming of Saloli Stream to express their opposition by joining a convoy of cars, trucks, tractors, and mule-drawn wagons departing from Tayanita Village at 1:00 and parading up Possum Road to Emmett Gray's farm. After speeches Emmett will grill hamburgers, Gretchen Green will roast organic vegetables, and Ernesto Zamora will supply wine. Tony Li-

ma's Mountain Band, composed of singers An-
nie Jerden and Eric Schlaughter, Tony Lima on
the banjo, Jaime Arroyo on the guitar, Dan Soto
on the harmonica, and Sally Sorensen on the vi-
olin, will provide music.

LETTERS TO THE EDITOR

To the Editor:

Rhonda Rather, who only a year ago was
arrested for releasing chickens from Dan Soto's
chicken truck, is embarrassing her husband
once again.

Mayor Rather recognizes the importance of
a lake to the future happiness of Witherston's
residents. He was reelected in November on a
platform of making Witherston the most attrac-
tive town in north Georgia.

Now the mayor's flakey wife has opposed
him publicly. In fact, she's leading the opposi-
tion. Who does she think she is, Eleanor Roose-
velt? God save us from another Eleanor Roose-
velt.

Alvin Autry
Witherston

To the Editor:

Who cares what anybody did in the 1970s?

If Donna Dam is allowed to ask Rich Rather and Grant Griggs publicly what they were doing, then we should be allowed to ask Gretchen Green publicly what she was doing.

I say, don't dig up the past. It could embarrass you big time—any of you.

Red Wilker
Witherston

To the Editor:

Saturday night someone killed Buffy Saint-Cherokí, Tayanita Village's oldest cat. We think it was a coyote.

Galilahi Sellers
Tayanita Village

To the Editor:

Keep Nature Natural is opposed to damming up Saloli Stream. We will march with Mrs. Rather today. Our ecosystem is like our body. Rivers and streams circulate through an ecosystem like blood flows through a body.

If we build a dam to block the natural flow of water, we'll give our ecosystem a heart attack, killing birds and squirrels and frogs and other living things.

Beau Lodge, President,
Keep Nature Natural

To the Editor:

Would Mayor Rather and Attorney Griggs be willing to take a paternity test? If not, why not?

Donna Dam
Former Toccoa resident

POLICE BLOTTER

On Saturday, March eleventh, at 10:30 p.m. Deputy Pete Koslowski Junior arrested Eric Schlaughter, age 17, for showing a fake ID in Rosa's Cantina. When Mr. Schlaughter asked for a beer and produced the driver's license of a man 31 years old, bartender Ignacio Iglesias became suspicious and called the police.

Mr. Schlaughter was fined $50 for the first-time offense and released into the custody of his stepfather, Deputy Sam Staples of the Witherston Police Department. His mother, Molly Schlaughter, who works for the mayor, was out of town.

NORTH GEORGIA IN HISTORY:
THE WITHERS
By Charlotte Byrd

Today, my fellow Witherstonians, I write about the origins of our inheritance. I have pieced together the story from diaries, court records, and newspaper clippings from the Cherokee Phoenix.

In April of 1829, not long after gold was discovered in the Cherokee Nation, Hearty Withers and his wife Penance moved from Savannah to north Georgia in search of their fortune. They were part of "the Great Intrusion," as the Cherokees called the influx of gold seekers in the area. Hearty had been a mule breeder in Savannah, owner of a jack and three jennies. Hearty believed that gold miners would pay good money for his mules, and they did.

Hearty and Penance built a one-room log cabin on Yahoola Creek in the part of the mountains the Cherokees called Talonega and the white settlers renamed Dahlonega. His son Harold Francis Withers, or "Harry," was born there in 1830.

Talonega, meaning yellow, probably referred to the gold dust in the streams and soil. Hearty panned for gold in Yahoola Creek and found a ton of it. Hearty Withers became rich.

And then Hearty Withers became richer still. In the 1832 Georgia Land Lottery, he won 40 acres on Saloli Creek. The Land Lottery was the means whereby the state transferred to white settlers the land the Cherokee and Creek Indians had occupied for a thousand years.

In possession of gold and land, Hearty sold his mule business and moved his wife, his four-year-old son James Edward, and his two-year-old son Harry, who was baptized Harold Francis, some 20 miles north of Talonega to the spot where the Withers lodge stands today. James Edward died in 1835.

Hearty Withers contracted syphilis shortly before his death, according to Penance's diary. But he did not die of the disease. He died while tending his garden on May 30, 1838, at the hands of a young Cherokee who slit his throat.

In her diary entry of June 6, Penance wrote, "Fortunately, little Harry and I have our property. The Indian took my husband's life, but he didn't take our land or our gold."

Because the Cherokees had begun to exact retribution for the theft of their land and gold, Georgia authorities sent 16,000 of them to "Indian Territory" west of the Mississippi in the winter of 1838. A fourth of them did not survive the journey.

WEATHER

Morning has broken, like the first morning.

Today will be sunny with a high of 65 and a low of 55.

But heavy rain will fall tomorrow. Find an ark.

The moon will be full tonight.

Antonio Lima, Hombre del Tiempo

CHAPTER 4

Sunday Morning, March 12, 2017

At half past eight Sunday morning, daylight savings time, Mev knocked on the front door of the Zamora house. Blanca answered in her bathrobe and invited her in.

"*Buenos días, señora Arroyo. Pase, pase. Le gustaría café?* Would you like a cup of coffee?"

"*Gracias, Señora Zamora.*"

Blanca offered Mev a seat by the fireplace, called Ernesto and Hernando into the living room, and brought out from the kitchen a silver tray with a silver coffee pitcher, a silver cream pitcher, and a small silver bowl with silver tongs for the cubes of sugar.

"How lovely. Thank you," Mev said, looking around. "Your home is beautiful. I like your blue tiles."

"Thank you," Blanca said. "We wanted a reminder of our lives in Spain."

"First, property records show that the fire last night was on your property. Is that correct?"

"Yes, *señora*, it was. Our old shed burned."

"I am so sorry. Did you keep anything valuable there?"

"No. We once kept farm equipment there, but we have a new bigger shed now."

"I'd like to know more about the shed. How old was it? What was it used for recently? Did you keep anything flammable in it?"

"Hernando, you speak," Blanca said.

"I'll tell you about it, Detective Arroyo," Hernando said. "The shack, as everybody is calling it, was already run down when my parents bought this property in the year 2000. It might have been a woodshed once. My parents used the shed for farm tools, and I used it for my bike, my baseball bat, all my kid stuff. When my parents built their new tool shed near the winery, I fixed up the shed for me with a table, chairs, and a lamp. I kept my fishing gear and my canoe there."

"You kept a canoe in the shed?"

"Oh, no! I guess my canoe is burned. It was my prize. It was a dugout."

"Blanca and I never go back to the old shed," Ernesto said. "We decided not to plant the five acres between the stream and the highway. Our vineyard is on the thirty acres between the highway and Cattleguard Lane."

"Did you hear anybody in the shed Saturday afternoon?"

"No," Blanca said. "But somebody could have driven up Witherston Highway and gone to the shed without our hearing it."

"I didn't hear anybody in the early afternoon," Hernando said. "I picked up my fishing gear at two-thirty on my way to my fishing spot. And I wouldn't have heard anybody later because of the rapids where I fish."

"Did you go to the shed often, Hernando?"

"I'd go there whenever I went fishing to pick up my gear, and to get my canoe whenever I wanted to go out on the stream."

"You kept your fly collection there, Hernando," Blanca said. "Your beautiful flies."

"I tie flies. That's my hobby, Detective Arroyo," Hernando said.

"Tell Detective Arroyo about the shot you heard, *hijo*," Ernesto said.

"Okay. I thought heard a gunshot downstream in the late afternoon about a half hour before the explosion. At first I just thought it was a hunter, and I kept fishing. But after a while I realized that it's not hunting season now for anything except coyotes. So I packed up my fishing rod, picked up my bucket, and headed back to the shed. I saw the explosion."

"Did you see anybody nearby?"

"I saw a man paddle away in a canoe. It was getting dark, so I didn't recognize him. I didn't realize he might have been in my canoe."

"Did you keep firecrackers in the shed, Hernando?"

"No, I didn't keep anything that would explode. I'm not a hunter, so I don't keep bullets there either. Nobody in my family owns a gun."

"What about meth?"

"Meth? No way. No way would I get involved in meth, sir."

"Do you ever use drugs?"

"No. Well, I do smoke marijuana occasionally, Detective."

"*Marijuana? Por Dios, hijo!*" Blanca exclaimed.

"*Mamá*, it's no big deal. And I don't smoke it much."

"Hernando," Ernesto said. "Marijuana can ruin your taste for wine. Wine is better. When you appreciate good wine, you won't want to smoke marijuana ever again."

❧

"Good God! Grant, come here. Did you see today's letter?"

Ruth Griggs had her tablet open to *Witherston on the Web*. She and her husband were having their usual breakfast of coffee and Danish.

"Who is Donna Dam, Grant? And what does she know about you?"

Grant looked over her shoulder.

"I don't know, Ruth." He sighed. "Please stop asking."

"Why does she want you to take a paternity test?"

"I don't know."

"Well, if you don't tell me, I might change my mind about the lake."

"Please don't change your mind, Ruth. We'll make a lot of money if Rich's proposal passes the Council."

"Have you had an affair?"

"No, Ruth. No. Of course not."

"Okay. I believe you. So on the night the dam broke did you have some sort of amorous encounter?"

"I don't remember any amorous encounter, Ruth."

"Well, if I'd had an amorous encounter on the night the dam broke I'd remember. I remember all my amorous encounters. Or most of them."

"Ruth! How many have you had?"

"Enough to know that all men are not created equal." Ruth went back to the online newspaper.

On the evening that they had celebrated the thirty-first anniversary of Grant's passing the Georgia bar, the thirtieth anniversary of their marriage, and the twenty-sixth birthday of their daughter Sarah Sue, Ruth decided she needed a life for herself. So she ran for Town Council in November and won, defeating Ernesto Zamora, who had a Spanish accent.

"Do you think Rhonda's demonstration will change anybody's mind on the Council?" Grant asked her.

"Who knows? If we're split down the middle, Mayor

Rather will break the tie. We're probably split down the middle. Trevor will vote for the lake because he's pro-business, like me. Smitty could go either way. Atsadi Moon will vote against it because he's an Indian."

"Tayanita Village will be against it, you're saying."

"Atsadi and Amadahy live in town now. But those young half-Cherokees in Tayanita Village will all be against it. They act like their ancestors still own our land."

"You've got to keep Rich from changing his mind."

"No problem, Grant. I've got something on Rich."

✌♋✌

"So you're being asked to take a paternity test, Rich. For God's sake, will you tell me why?"

"I don't know why, Rhonda. I tell you, I don't know why. Believe me. This Donna Dam is out to get me because I'm proposing a lake."

"Are you having an affair with some young thing?"

"No, Rhonda. No way."

"So what did you do forty years ago that you still want to keep secret?"

"I confess. I may possibly have had a one-night fling with a girl in Toccoa the night the dam broke."

"Was she your age?"

"About. Or a little younger. I was twenty then."

"So do you recognize anyone around town who is fifty-nine or sixty who looks vaguely like the girl you bedded the night the dam broke?"

"No, and I don't remember what she looks like. I never saw her again."

"Would Grant remember? He was with you, right?"

"I doubt that Grant remembers that night either. We were both tanked up."

♥ↄ♥ↄ

"Paco, did you read Donna Dam's letter? There's more to this than environmental extortion."

It was nine fifteen, and Paco was putting the breakfast dishes into the dishwasher. Mev sat at the kitchen table reading the news online on her laptop. Jorge sat on the living room floor with his back against the sofa drawing a cartoon. Jaime lay on the sofa watching him with Mighty on his stomach.

Paco poured Mev her second cup of coffee.

"I think Rich Rather and Grant Green were making babies when the dam broke," he said. "I think Donna Dam is one of those babies."

"Mom, I'm drawing a cartoon of Mayor Rather drowning in his own lake."

"Be kind, Jorge. The mayor has a good heart."

"He has a better heart than head," Jorge said.

"You didn't make him fat enough," Jaime said.

"Okay, is this better?"

Mev went back to *Webby Witherston*.

"Oh, no," she said. "Eric Schlaughter got arrested last night for showing a fake ID. It's in Police Blotter."

"What?" Jorge put down his sketchbook.

"Boys, do you all know anything about Eric getting arrested?"

"No."

"What time was it?"

"Ten-thirty."

"We were here."

Jaime and Jorge read over their mother's shoulder.

"What a dumbass! He must think he looks thirty-one years old!"

"*Hijos,* did Eric offer you alcohol when you were out hiking yesterday?"

"No."

"No, Dad."

"We don't drink."

"You'd better not. Everybody watches a police officer's sons. You all could get in big trouble if you were caught with alcohol," Paco said.

"In our family all four of us have to be model citizens, boys," Mev said.

"We're trying, Mom."

"May we go back to Blue Boulder this morning? Beau wants to look for arrowheads," Jorge said.

"How long will you be?"

"Two or three hours. We'll drive up."

"Okay."

"Beau's coming here at a quarter to ten."

"Don't forget Mrs. Rather's protest rally this afternoon. I'm on duty for it."

⌒⌒⌒

At a quarter to ten, Jorge, Jaime, and Beau piled into the twins' 2010 gray Jetta. It was Jaime's turn to drive, Beau's turn to ride shotgun, Jorge's turn to ride in the back seat. Before they set off Jorge stuck another bumper sticker on the trunk. This one said *SUPPORT YOUR RIGHT TO ARM BEARS.*

Witherstonians wore their hearts on their bumpers.

Jorge and Beau opened their iPhones and compared their threats from XXX.

"If we told Mom she'd tell Chief McCoy, who'd tell the deputies. Then they'd look for Canoe Man in connection with the fire," Jorge said.

"And Canoe Man would kill one of us."

"Or our parents."

"That's why we have to find Canoe Man ourselves."

"But if we showed her Canoe Man's instant message,

your mother could be careful to hide the source of her information," Beau said. "And she could ask John Hicks to trace the message."

"Then John Hicks would know. And he might tell Chief Pace," Jaime said.

"Who'd tell all of Tayanita Village," Jorge said.

"And Amadahy Henderson would put the story on *Webby Witherston*," Jaime said.

"And then the whole wide world would know," Jorge said.

"We can't tell our folks about Canoe Man, Beau," Jaime said. "At least not until we figure out who he is."

"So we won't tell Neel about Canoe Man. Or about XXX, who must be Canoe Man. We just tell him about the skeleton because he knows a lot about Cherokee history, right?"

"So do you, Beau. You know lots about Cherokees."

"Thanks. You know, I've been thinking," Beau said. "If that skeleton is really Cherokee, it may be from between 1828 and 1838. Guess why."

"What happened here in 1828?" Jorge asked.

"The Georgia Gold Rush," Jaime said.

"Right," Beau said. "And the skeleton was buried with a gold nugget."

"The skeleton was a human at the time," Jorge said. "He became a skeleton after the worms ate his flesh."

"Or her flesh," Beau said. "Anyway, as soon as the Cherokees started carrying around gold nuggets the white settlers noticed, took the Cherokees' land and gold, and sent the Cherokees packing to Oklahoma."

"In 1838," Jaime said.

"After 1838 the Cherokees wouldn't have been carrying around gold nuggets," Beau continued. "And neither would the whites. By 1840 there wasn't much gold left in the ground."

Jaime drove carefully up the unpaved part of Possum Road past Emmett Gray's farm to the top of the hill above Blue Boulder. He parked beside Neel's Jeep Wrangler.

Neel greeted them. "What's this about a skeleton?"

The boys sat down beside Neel on the ground. Jorge told Neel the whole story of Saturday's events, including the smoking of marijuana and excluding the sighting of Canoe Man and his late-night threats.

"Boys, let's look at the skeleton."

"We think the skeleton is Cherokee because we found a Cherokee pot with it," Jorge concluded. "It had a design like a nineteenth-century one we saw at Oconaluftee Indian Village."

"And there was a gold nugget in the pot," Beau added.

"Let's go look at the skeleton," Neel said, after asking a few questions. "I brought along some of my old medical equipment." He opened his backpack. "Surgical gloves so we don't contaminate the bones with our DNA. Dental tools. A flashlight. Also a trowel."

"Wow, Neel. You're cool," Jaime said.

"Way cool," Jorge said.

"Let's go." Neel zipped up his backpack.

Jorge led the way down the steep slope to the cave entrance.

"Boys, you said the cave was dry?"

"Yes, dry and sandy."

"And the bones were dry."

"Good. Because if the bones are still hard, they could have some DNA that will help us identify them."

"They are definitely hard," Jaime said.

"Here we are," Jorge said. "Behind this bush. May I borrow your trowel, Neel?"

"Here's the trowel. Please put on these latex gloves."

Jorge slithered through the rhododendron, pushed aside the dead branches, leaned into the cave, and scooped out the sand and rocks. Then he backed out.

"You look, Neel. I'll hold the flashlight."

Neel put on a pair of latex gloves, crawled through the bushes, and reached into the hole. After several minutes, he backed out with the ceramic bowl and Eric's pipe case. He handed the pipe case to Jaime.

"Boys, you all may have made an historic discovery. This is a grave. The rocks were probably arranged around the body. The bones are human, and they're hard. Except for the rib and the humerus you all moved, the skeleton is largely intact. I think we've got an adult female here. And she was pregnant."

"Cherokee Woman, Cherokee Baby."

"Wow, Neel," Beau said. "My father will want to see it."

"But not now. We need a professional archaeologist to excavate this site. We shouldn't disturb it."

"Now let's look at this beautiful pot," Neel said.

"Someone's coming!"

Jaime stuffed the pipe case into his backpack.

Atsadi Moon, followed by Amadahy Henderson, emerged from the woods.

"Hi, guys, what are you all doing?" Atsadi greeted them.

"Did you follow us?" Jorge asked him.

"We came to take pictures for *Webby Witherston*," Amadahy said. "Of Blue Boulder and Withers Fork and the burned fishing shack. Why are you digging here?"

"Jaime, Jorge, and Beau have made a discovery. If we tell you about it will you please not disclose the location?"

"Dr. Kingfisher, a journalist has to tell the truth but doesn't have to tell all," Amadahy said. "I'll write a story about the discovery and say that the bones were found in Saloli Valley north of town."

"That's fine," Neel said. "I believe that the boys have found a Cherokee grave. They discovered the bones of a woman and a fetus buried with this Cherokee ceramic pot and a gold nugget. I'd guess that the ceramic pot was made in the 1830s, so the grave may be almost two hundred years old. I'll report the discovery to Georgia's Historic Preservation Office in Atlanta today. I know an archaeologist who works there, and maybe I can get him here out right away."

"I'll do the article now," Amadahy said. "This is the biggest story of my career! I'm texting my boss."

She texted Catherine.

Amadahy Henderson
iMessage
Sunday, March 12, 11:15 a.m.

Hi catherine
I have big story about a cherokee grave
in saloli valley which mayor wants to flood

Hi, Amadahy.
Write your story now, right now.

Ok

"Thanks, you all. I'll get your story on the web this afternoon," Amadahy said. "And please keep me posted. We're in this together now."

"Will do," Jorge said.

Amadahy and Atsadi disappeared into the brush.

"I'm putting the pot back in the grave," Neel said.

"I think we'd better tell Mom and Dad today, Jorge."

Neel called Dr. Carter Ellis in the Office of the State Archaeologist.

"Dr. Carter will be here at ten tomorrow morning, boys. Would you all like to come back here and watch him dig up the bones?"

"Sure, Neel!"

"Sure!"

"Sure!"

They climbed up the steep wooded slope to their cars. After Neel had driven away Beau's cell phone rang.

"Hello," Beau said. "Oh, hi, Eric...Okay. We'll come get you after lunch...Bye."

"Does Eric need a ride?" Jorge asked.

"Eric wants a ride."

"He's got his motorcycle."

"He wants a car, so that he can go places with other people."

"If Eric had come to Witherston two years ago, before Mr. Withers died, Eric would have a car. He would have money like us," Beau said. "A quarter of a million dollars."

"And his mother would have a quarter of a million dollars."

"And his mother wouldn't have had to marry Deputy Staples," Beau said.

"Life's a lot of luck," Jorge said. "We were lucky to live in Witherston before the geezer fed the worms, so we're rich. Eric wasn't lucky. Eric must think about that a lot."

"He does," Beau said.

ာာ

"Mayor Rather, do you have a comment on this morning's letter from Donna Dam?"

Catherine caught Rich and Rhonda as they entered Reception Hall after church.

"I have no comment," said the mayor. "I have no idea what the woman is talking about. No idea. No idea at all."

Catherine jotted down his comment in her pocket notebook. "Did you and Mr. Griggs know each other in 1977?"

"We were fraternity brothers. So yes, we did."

"What were you all doing in Toccoa the night of November 5? That was a Saturday night, right?" she asked

"We'd gone bass fishing on Barnes Lake. Okay? But why are you grilling me? Shouldn't you be trying to find out who Donna Dam is? Maybe if I knew the identity of Donna Dam, I'd remember that night."

"The dam broke that night. Do you remember?"

"Yes, yes. Great tragedy. Great tragedy."

"Are you willing to take a paternity test?"

"Miss Catherine, what good's a paternity test if no one's claiming to be your offspring?"

"You have a point, Mr. Mayor."

"Right."

"Are you going to withdraw your proposal to build a dam?" Catherine asked.

"Of course not. No. Now I have to move on. I have to greet these folks." The mayor turned his back on Catherine and shook hands with Red and Grace Wilker.

Catherine approached Ruth Griggs.

"How are you, Mrs. Griggs?"

"Fine, thank you. How are you?"

"Have you any reason to change your mind regarding Mayor Rather's proposal?"

"No. I will vote in favor of it. A lake for recreation will be good for business. And what's good for business is good for all Witherstonians."

"Witherstonians are already rich, Mrs. Griggs. Almost all of us are," Catherine said. "Well, a lake will make Witherston one of the most attractive communities in Georgia."

Rhonda walked up, handed Catherine a glass of lemonade, and said to Ruth, "Only to people who like to fish in a stocked pond or water-ski behind a noisy boat."

"You've made your views very clear, Rhonda," Ruth said.

Catherine left Reception Hall with her husband Dan. "I have the makings of an interesting story," she said.

*ဘဲ*ဘဲ*

At noon Mev stood with Jake and Rich on the front steps of the Municipal Building and faced a small crowd of Witherstonians, most of whom had come directly from church. Jake had Tracker on a leash.

"Good afternoon," Jake said. "I am Chief McCoy of the Witherston Police. Let me thank Detective Mev Arroyo and Mayor Rich Rather for joining me on this occasion. Unfortunately I have little to report. As you already know, yesterday evening there was an explosion in a wooden shack on Saloli Stream just north of Withers Fork. The fire was very hot.

"The shack burned down quickly. My team—Detective Arroyo, Officers Pete Koslowsky Senior, Pete Koslowsky Junior, and my dog Tracker—examined the site after Chief Moss, Atsadi Moon, and Shorty O'Rork had put out the fire. We found the remains of a body, but only the bones. We will try to identify the bones by DNA analysis.

"No missing person report has been filed, so we have no leads. Now we'll take questions."

"Chief McCoy, could the fire have been deliberately set?" Amadahy Henderson asked.

"It could have been, Amadahy. We smelled gasoline at the site. We do suspect arson. Officers Pete Senior and Pete Junior are headed out there this afternoon to look for clues."

"How long will the DNA analysis take?" Officer Sam Staples asked.

"Officer Ricky Hefner carried the bones to Atlanta this morning. We may get a report by five o'clock on Monday."

"What will the report tell us?" Grant Griggs asked.

"If we have nobody else's DNA with which to compare it, then we'll get only an ethnic profile. That will help us narrow our circle of possibilities. As of now we don't know whether the victim was male or female, black, white, Asian, or Native American, young or old."

"Detective Arroyo, did your boys see anything that could help you solve the mystery?" Red Wilker asked.

"No, Mr. Wilker, They would have told me if they'd seen anything suspicious."

"Mayor Rather, as you know, the shack that burned was on property owned by Ernesto and Blanca Zamora. That would be property Witherston would have to buy if you built your dam, wouldn't it."

"Probably, Catherine, yes, probably."

"Chief McCoy, Fire Chief Moss said he noticed a patch of marijuana plants near the shack. Are you going to arrest anybody for growing marijuana?"

"I didn't notice any patch, Amadahy, so the answer is no," Jake responded. "Thanks for coming, everybody."

໐ຽ໐ຽ

Catherine opened her laptop on their kitchen table.

She and Dan had just finished their lunch of grilled cheese sandwiches, and Dan was putting the dishes into the dishwasher. Muddy and Calico dozed by the wood stove.

"Dan, before we go up to the Grays' farm I want to find out more about the Zamora property." She peered at the screen. "According to the Witherston Tax website, the Zamora farm is worth three hundred and eighty thousand dollars. That must be because it's a vineyard."

"You're talking about Zamora Wines?"

"Yes. I've been to their house on Cattleguard Lane. I did a story about Ernesto and Blanca and their son Hernando when Ernesto ran for Town Council. They name their wines after Spanish poets."

"We're having one of their wines for our anniversary, Catherine. A 2012 García Lorca. I bought it for you the other day. It cost thirty-seven dollars."

"Thank you, Dan."

"You're worth it, Catherine."

"If Ernesto Zamora had beaten Ruth Griggs for the Town Council, Mayor Rather wouldn't have the votes to dam Saloli Stream."

"The mayor's lake will destroy the Zamoras' vineyard."

"That reminds me. Let me check out the weather in Toccoa on November fifth, 1977. I want to know whether the mayor actually went fishing that Saturday."

"Don't you trust the mayor?"

"I'm verifying, Dan. Look. According to a U.S. Geological Survey report, the rainfall began on the morning of Wednesday, November second, and ended at midnight on November fifth.

"So it was raining heavily on the day the mayor says he and Mr. Griggs went fishing."

"It was. Here's something from Wikipedia. On November sixth, 1977, at one-thirty a.m., the Kelly Barnes Dam failed after a period of heavy rain. Seven inches had fallen from November second through November fifth. In particular, on November fifth, three and a half inches fell between six p.m. and midnight."

"Mayor Rather lied."

"Or he and Mr. Griggs have mud for brains. So what were they doing that the mayor doesn't want to reveal?"

"Partying," Dan said. "That's what I did when I was twenty years old. Actually, that's about all I did, party and play my harmonica."

"It's got to be more than partying."

"If so-called Donna Dam knows what Rather and Griggs were doing forty years ago, she was at least a teenager then."

"Could Donna Dam be an old girlfriend?" Catherine asked.

"Whom he spurned?"

"Why does she surface now?"

"The dam. It's almost the fortieth anniversary of the break."

"I'm going to share what I've learned with Detective Arroyo."

"Before you publish it?"

"Before I publish it. We're friends. We share information."

☙❧☙

"Thank you, Chief Pace, for allowing us to assemble here. We're delighted that you too oppose my husband's proposal to flood Saloli Valley."

Surrounded by clucking chickens Rhonda addressed Chief Atohi Pace on behalf of the thirty Witherstonians gathered at the entrance to Tayanita Village. Rhonda was dressed in a hot pink corduroy big shirt, a black down vest, black jeans, and black riding boots. She had Coco Chanel on a leash. She carried a hand-lettered sign that said *STOP MAYOR RATHER'S FLOOD*.

Rhonda was flanked on her left by Gretchen who held high a sign that said *LET RATHER BE DAMMED* and on her right by Atsadi Moon who held high a sign that said *CHEROKEE GHOSTS WILL HAUNT DAM RATHER*.

"The residents of Tayanita Village will demonstrate with you today, Mrs. Rather," Atohi said. "If the mayor builds his dam, Tayanita Creek will dry up and we'll have no natural source of water." He held the bridle of Franny the mule, who was hitched to a wagon. Eight-year-old Moki Pace sat on the driver's bench holding the reins.

Atohi was the elected leader of the twenty-one young people who had traced their heritage to the Eastern Band of Cherokee Indians, taken Cherokee first names, and committed themselves to spending two years living together in a manner that honored their ancestors. In the summer of 2015 a core of fifteen had each contributed ten thousand dollars of their Withers inheritance to establish Tayanita Village on nine acres owned by the chief's father at the intersection of Old Dirt Road and Possum Road. Together they bought and erected fifteen small green canvas yurts for lodging and a very large yurt for a Council House, constructed a brick-sided kitchen and a brick-sided bathhouse with showers and composting toilets, planted a vegetable garden, installed free-standing solar panels to provide electricity for their smart phones, computers, and lamps, and painted the old barn. They kept a couple of nanny goats named Grass and Weed, a rooster named Brewster, and some forty chickens—Buff Orpingtons and Broilers—in addition to Franny, numerous cats, and John Hicks's dog Bear, a hundred-pound Newfoundland mix.

In his early thirties, Atohi was the only Villager with a family. His wife Ayita and his son Moki lived in Cherokee, North Carolina, where Moki was in third grade at Cherokee Central School, but they were home for spring break. Every Wednesday night at eleven o'clock Atohi convened the Villagers in the Council House for a lesson in Cherokee culture. A middle-school social studies teacher, Atohi was an expert in Cherokee traditions.

"And if we can't get water from the creek, Tayanita Village will have to buy its water from the city," Chief Pace continued.

"Over our dead bodies will that happen," shouted John Hicks, who emerged with Bear from the Council House carrying a large sign with the word *DAMNATION*. John Hicks, who had discovered his kinship with Elijah Hicks, second editor of the *Cherokee Phoenix*, worked as the IT guy for the Witherston Police. He was usually called by his full name, John Hicks.

"In the nineteenth century whites killed our ancestors and destroyed Saloli Village to build Witherston. Now the whites want to destroy Saloli Valley, where our ancestors are buried," John Hicks said. "Haven't they already done enough to wipe out our people?"

"Wipe out Wather!" Moki yelled.

"Stop the mayor!"

"Keep nature natural!"

"That's telling 'em, Christopher."

"Fellow Villagers, protect the remains of a thousand years of Cherokee civilization," John Hicks said. "Block the damn mayor's dam!"

"Damn the mayor!"

"Damn the dam!"

"It's time to bring out our bows, Villagers!"

"And arrows!"

"And tomahawks!"

"It's time to move!" Rhonda called out.

Rhonda picked up Coco Chanel and got into her Volt with Gretchen in the right front seat and Neel and Gandhi crowded together behind them. Chief Pace climbed into the wagon beside Moki. Ayita, John Hicks, and Bear got into the back. Jon and Gregory maneuvered a cart pulled by Sassyass into third position. Renoir rode between them, sitting upright like a human.

They were followed by a motorcade of one tractor, six cars, most of them loaded with Tayanita Villagers, and one van painted purple with *ZAMORA WINES* lettered in pink. Jorge, Jaime, Beau, and Eric, with Jorge driving, brought up the rear. Eric held Mighty in the front seat, and Jaime and Beau held Sequoyah in the back seat.

A patrol car trailed them.

"Where is Molly Schlaughter?" Gretchen asked Rhonda. "She's our weapon against Mayor Rather."

"Maybe we'll find her at the farm."

෧෩෧

"Thanks for returning my pipe, Jaime," Eric said from the back seat. He put the pipe case into his vest pocket.

Jaime had told him about their morning with Neel and Cherokee Woman.

"I hope we see your pipe again," Jorge said. Jorge was driving.

"Where's your mom?" Jaime asked Eric. "She's supposed to give a speech today."

"What do I know? Last night my stepfather said she went to visit a friend. Maybe in Rome. She misses Rome. He said she'd be back here soon."

"What are you all singing today?"

"'Lonesome Valley,' 'Tom Dooley,' 'Bad Moon Rising,' 'On Top of Old Smoky.' I'd proposed 'Purple People Eater,' but Tony likes folk music."

"Who was Tom Dooley?" Beau asked.

"Tom Dooley was actually Tom Dula, a former Confederate Soldier who fatally stabbed his lover Laura Foster in 1866, right nearby in North Carolina. He'd gotten her pregnant. He was hanged for murdering her."

"I can't imagine killing your own girlfriend," Beau said, "especially when she's carrying your baby."

"Who was purple?" Jorge asked. "The people or the people eater?"

Jaime started strumming his guitar and singing. "It was a one-eyed, one-horned, flying purple people eater, one-eyed, one-horned, flying purple people eater, a one-eyed, one-horned, flying purple people eater. Sure looks strange to me."

"I've been thinking," Eric said. "Do you all believe that enforcing the law is enforcing justice?"

"Most of the time," said Jaime.

"Not always," said Beau. "The law upheld segregation for a hundred years. That was not justice."

"I mean more locally. Your mother and my stepfather enforce laws that have been passed," Eric said to the twins. "And your mother too, Beau, as a judge. So what if they knew that someone had committed a crime that did not cause injustice, that actually brought about justice? Would they have to enforce the law anyway?"

"Like if a poor woman shoplifts a carton of milk from a store to feed her baby?" Jaime asked.

"Well, okay. So would your mother or my stepfather have to arrest that shoplifter?"

"Mom wouldn't. She has a heart."

"I read about a homeless woman who got put in jail

for shoplifting a stick of deodorant," Jorge said. "She just didn't want to stink when she looked for a job. And it was from a big store with a hundred sticks of deodorant on its shelves. How fair is that?"

"How fair is it for a rich country to let some people be homeless," Eric said. "But there are laws that evict you from your home if you can't pay the rent. And police officers enforce those laws."

"We need to run for Congress and make better laws," Jorge said.

"You run, bro."

"I'm thinking about it, Jaime. Really. After college."

"My mother and I could have been evicted from our apartment in Atlanta when my father left us," Eric said. "My mother wasn't making enough money to pay the rent, buy us food, and pay off her truck. Even with me working at the convenience store. That's why she married Sam. A lot of good that did."

"How come you all came here?"

"My mother got a job in the mayor's office."

"That must have upset you."

"Well, we needed to do it. Anyway, I'm just saying that sometimes you have to break the law to get justice."

Jaime parked next to Gregory's donkey cart. "Hi, Sassyass! We're here!"

"I see our mother," Jorge said.

Eric looked around. "I don't see mine."

CHAPTER 5

Sunday Afternoon, March 12, 2017

From her seat on the stone wall Mev saw the flock of white chickens scatter when Rhonda emerged from her Volt and unleashed Coco Chanel. Lidia and Emmett had adopted eight chickens when Dan and Rhonda had liberated four thousand Broilers from Dan's eighteen-wheeler during the December 2015 snow storm. Now the flock numbered twenty-seven egg-layers and a rooster named Oh Lordy. They ranged freely in the cow pasture and across the front lawn, except when chased into their coop by Rufus, a two-year-old Border Collie.

Rhonda ascended the steps of Emmett and Lydia's porch. She spoke to the gathering crowd through her battery-powered mic. "Why don't we want a dam?" she yelled.

"Because we don't want a flood!" The crowd yelled back.

Rhonda repeated, "Again. Why don't we want a dam?"

"Because we don't want a flood!"

"That's good, folks. We don't want Saloli Valley to be flooded if the dam is built. And we don't want Witherston to be flooded if the dam breaks."

"No dam, no flood," Lottie shouted. She had just gotten out of her brand-new lavender all-electric Smart Car. She waved her purple cane.

"Go Aunt Lottie," Jorge called out. "No dam, no flood! No damn flood!"

Jon raised his hand. "Can Mayor Rather swim?"

"He can float!"

Mev saw Grant Griggs park his silver Mercedes-Benz coupe beside the Arroyo twins' Jetta. He got out of his car and joined protesters.

"No damn flood," Atsadi Moon shouted. "May I speak?"

"Of course," Rhonda said. "Right after Gretchen Green and Chief Pace."

Gretchen, with Gandhi at her side, spoke for five minutes of the long-term suffering of farmers that the dam would cause just for the short-term gratification of boaters. She concluded by saying, "The mayor wants to sacrifice Saloli Valley people we know, some of whom may have unwisely voted for him instead of me, for city people we don't know who will bring gas-powered boats up here on weekends and pollute our natural environment with fumes and noise. Mayor Rather will exchange our happiness for prosperity."

"You got it, Ms. Green," Atohi Pace said. "Prosperity does not equal happiness."

Atohi, with Moki at his side, then spoke for five minutes of the immorality of taking water for the lake from people living downstream from the dam. He concluded by saying, "For thousands and thousands of years here nature provided her bounty for all. Now a few individuals with temporary power will decide who will have access to nature's bounty and who will not. I ask you all to call your representatives to the Town Council and tell them what you think."

"Councilman Atsadi Moon, would you like to speak now?" Rhonda handed him the mic.

"Hello, friends of nature," Atsadi said. "To all you who voted for me, thank you! I will do my best to protect our mountains, streams, and valleys from human destruction."

"Go Atsadi!"

"Now I have a momentous announcement to make," Atsadi continued. "Jaime and Jorge Arroyo have discovered a Cherokee grave not far from here. I can't disclose the actual location, but I can disclose the contents. A human skeleton, a gold nugget, and a Cherokee ceramic pot. Dr. Neel Kingfisher has verified that the bones belong to a young woman and the fetus she was carrying. He has notified the Georgia Historic Preservation Office. Since the bones are hard and dry, a geneticist may get DNA from them that will prove the woman was Native American."

"What does that mean for us, Atsadi?"

"If the woman was Native American, we can argue that Mayor Rather would be flooding sacred burial sites."

"How soon will we find out whether she was Native American?"

"In a couple of days, maybe. There's a company in Atlanta called Who R U that will do it in twenty-four hours. Is that right, Dr. Kingfisher?"

"The state archaeologist will come out tomorrow and take the bones to the lab for a DNA analysis. We may get a report by Tuesday," Neel told the crowd. "By the way, if you want a DNA ancestry test to see whether you might have Native American ancestry yourself, you can. Who R U will trace your genetic heritage for a hundred dollars. All you have to do is send them your spit."

Gretchen raised her hand. "What if everybody in Witherston gets a DNA ancestry test, including Mayor

Rather? Neel will pay for it, won't you, Neel?"

"What? Oh, yes. Of course, my love."

"We'll see how we are related to each other. And if Mayor Rather learns he has Native American genes himself, maybe he'll withdraw his dam proposal."

"Mayor Rather does not have Native American genes, Gretchen," Grant said.

"Well, Grant. He doesn't think he does. I didn't think I did either. But I do. Five percent of my genes are from a Native American population. That's the news from my spit. I wonder what the news from your spit will be."

"You're not getting any news from my spit," Grant said. "I'm not getting a DNA test."

"Don't worry, Mr. Griggs," John Hicks said. "An ancestry test is not a paternity test."

"It's the opposite," Gretchen said. "By the way, two percent of my genes are from Neanderthals."

"I would have guessed more," Grant said.

"Maybe you have Native American ancestry, Grant," Gretchen said.

"Maybe Mr. Griggs is my long lost grandfather," Atsadi said.

"Great grandfather," John Hicks said.

"You all shut up," Grant said. "Okay, I'll send them my spit."

"I'll send mine," Lottie said.

"I'll send mine," Eric said.

"I'll send mine," Jorge said.

"I'll send mine too," Jaime said.

"But yours will be the same as mine, Jaime, since we're identical."

"Let's mix up our spit. Anyway, it doesn't matter."

"Let's send Feather Jo's spit."

"Chickens don't have spit."

"*Hijos! Por favor*," Paco said.

"I'll get the test," Rhonda said. "And I'll make Rich get it."

"KNN will get it, all of us!" Christopher Zurich said.

"I'll order a case of vials, and we can have a spitting party," Gretchen said. "Tomorrow night at Green Acres. Six o'clock. Let me know by email if you're coming. Don't eat ahead of time. After the spitting Neel and I will provide Kombucha tea and seaweed snacks."

"Oh, wow," Jaime said.

"And for those of you who don't share dear Gretchen's culinary preferences, I'll provide wine and cheese," Lottie said. "And cokes."

The crowd bellowed their assent.

"What a great project for Witherston," Gretchen said. "Witherston will show the world there's no such thing as racial purity. People can hardly be prejudiced against racial groups whose genes they share."

"What if we find out that we're all very, very, very closely related to each other, like second cousins," Christopher said. "I'll have to go to Idaho to find a wife."

"Remember the song 'I'm My Own Grandpa?'" Jorge said.

"I may not be very closely related to you all," Beau said. "But I'll get the test anyway."

"And after the Kombucha tea we'll do yoga."

"Not me, Gretchen. I don't do yoga. I'm not a seaweed-eating, Kombucha-drinking, carrot-chomping yogi like you."

"So you will spit and split, Mr. Griggs?" Jorge said.

"Inhale deeply, Grant," Gretchen said. "And then exhale slowly, slowly, slowly."

"Why are you here, Mr. Griggs?" John Hicks asked.

The crowd turned to look at Grant.

"To see what you Indians are up to."

"We're talking about our ancestors, who may be buried in Saloli Valley, which your wife wants to flood."

"The grave may be almost two hundred years old, they figure," Atsadi said. "Dr. Kingfisher recognized the design of the ceramic pot as from the early nineteenth century. The state archaeologist will carbon-date the bones."

"If he doesn't hurry the grave site will disappear under Mayor Rather's lake," John Hicks said.

"That's why I'm making this announcement, John Hicks," Atsadi said. "The grave is of historic importance to the preservation of our people's history. Mayor Rather's lake will obliterate the remains of the great Cherokee civilization. I say, how can our Town Council possibly vote for a dam? Certainly not in good conscience."

"May I speak?" John Hicks asked.

"Go ahead, John Hicks," Atsadi said.

John Hicks ran up the steps and took the mic.

"Ladies and gentlemen, dogs and bird," he said. "Which is more powerful? The forces of nature or the equipment of humans? When humans block the natural flow of water through a valley, we make nature our enemy. So nature fights back. Nature breaks dams. Just think of the 1977 dam break in Toccoa that apparently Mayor Rather and Mr. Griggs know something about."

"May I speak, Mr. Hicks?" Grant held up his hand.

"When I finish, Mr. Griggs," John Hicks replied. "Folks, do you think that Mayor Rather and his architects are smart enough to anticipate all the changes they will bring about to our land if they try to control the forces of nature? Are they smart enough to control the rains that could make the lake overflow the dam? Are they smart enough to keep the rest of our ecosystem stable after flooding the valley and drying up the creeks downstream? Folks, I ask you, is Mayor Rather that smart?"

"No!" Rhonda shouted.

"No!" the crowd roared.

"May I speak now, Mr. Hicks?"

"I yield the porch to the honorable attorney Mr. Grant Griggs," John Hicks said, handing Grant the mic and bounding down the steps.

"Thank you," Grant said. "Ladies and gentlemen, first let me respond to Mr. John Hicks. I know little more about the Toccoa disaster than you all do. I have no idea what this Donna Dam person is referring to. Mr. Hicks, whose intelligence I respect, is also wrong about the relationship of humans to nature in the twenty-first century. We humans are not battling the forces of nature. We are harnessing the forces of nature for our own good. We have harnessed flowing water to generate electricity. We have harnessed electricity to light our buildings. We have harnessed fossil fuels to run our cars. In the twenty-first century we have harnessed the power of the wind and the sun to heat our homes. We humans number seven and a half billion. We can no longer live lightly off the land like your Cherokee ancestors did, Mr. Hicks."

"Maybe if your European ancestors had lived lightly off the land, Mr. Griggs, we humans would not number seven and a half billion," John responded.

"Whom would you eliminate, Mr. Hicks? The poor people who can't afford food? Would you let them starve so that others could live lightly off the land?"

"Why do we Witherstonians need a lake?" Gretchen called out.

"We Witherstonians don't need a lake, Gretchen," Grant responded. "We would enjoy a lake. We don't need water sports. But we would get pleasure from water sports. We indulge our desire for pleasure because we're human. We humans are pleasure-seeking animals."

"Your definition of pleasure is not mine, Grant," Gretchen said.

"Mine neither," Lottie said.

"Time to eat!" Emmett called out.

To Tony Lima's arrangement of "Tom Dooley" and other Appalachian folk songs the crowd feasted on Gretchen's roasted vegetables, Emmett's hamburgers, and the Zamoras' wine. Mev stayed on the stone wall listening to the music and watching Sassyass and Franny nuzzle each other and Rufus, Renoir, Gandhi, and Bear romp in the pasture. When on duty she neither drank nor ate. She'd volunteered to attend Rhonda's demonstration because Deputy Staples wanted to go fishing.

The band concluded its concert with Annie and Eric singing "Bad Moon Rising" accompanied by guitar, violin, and harmonica. Rhonda, holding Coco Chanel, joined them and belted out the last stanza herself.

> "Don't come around tonight.
> Well, it's bound to take your life.
> There's a bad moon on the rise."

"Hello, Catherine," Mev said as the young *Webby Witherston* editor approached her. "I bet you're looking for news."

"I am, Detective Arroyo. *Witherston on the Web* needs all the news we can find."

"Or make," Mev said with a smile. Mev was a close friend of Wyatt and Margaret Perry, and she'd seen their daughter grow up. "We're all waiting to see the consequences of your publishing Donna Dam's letters."

"Or make," Catherine repeated. "Right. Publishing Donna Dam's letters is probably influencing events. I have qualms about whether I should have done it."

"Information always influences events, Catherine. And there's no disentangling influences. Don't worry about it."

Catherine told Mev what she'd learned about the weather in Toccoa on November fifth, 1977. "So I think that the mayor is lying," she said.

"How about investigating what happened in Toccoa that Saturday, Catherine? You have access to the *Toccoa Record* archives, don't you?"

"I do, Detective Arroyo. And I will."

છબ્ઝ

On her way home Mev took Jake's call.

"Mev, we've got bad news I fear. The Petes found a battered red Kia pickup hidden in the woods a hundred yards south of the burned shack. Pete Senior just called me. He will get the Vehicle Identification Number and contact the Department of Motor Vehicle Registration tomorrow."

"I'll call you later, Jake. Let's keep this information to ourselves for now."

"I'll tell the Petes."

WITHERSTON ON THE WEB
Sunday, March 12, 2017

BREAKING NEWS
3:00 p.m.

Bones and Pot Discovered in Saloli Valley

Yesterday afternoon Jaime and Jorge Arroyo made a momentous discovery. They found a skeleton buried with a ceramic pot and a gold nugget.

Dr. Neel Kingfisher, who accompanied the Arroyo twins and Beau Lodge to the grave this morning, said he suspected the bones belonged to a Cherokee woman and her fetus. Because of the Cherokee pottery design, he guessed that the grave dated back to the early 19th century. Dr. Kingfisher, who is of Cherokee descent, is familiar with 19th-century Cherokee pottery.

Dr. Kingfisher said that DNA in the bones could prove the woman was Native American. He asked that the exact location of the grave not be revealed until the state archaeologist, Dr. Carter Ellis, excavates the site, possibly tomorrow. Dr. Kingfisher does not want grave robbers to find it. The gold nugget and the pot are worth a lot of money.

Today at Rhonda Rather's demonstration against Mayor Rather's dam project, Councilman Atsadi Moon said that the discovery should make the mayor withdraw his proposal for a lake. He said that a lake would obliterate the Cherokee people's past because it would flood Cherokee graves.

On Friday at 1:00 p.m. Mayor Rather will present his dam plan to the Town Council for a vote. Witherstonians will see then whether Mayor Rather and other individuals on the Town Council care about Cherokee history.

Amadahy Henderson, Reporter

CHAPTER 6

Sunday Evening, March 12, 2017

*H*ola, querida!* Where have you been?" Paco
greeted Mev with a hug and two kisses, one on
each cheek, as he had done since they'd first
met in Madrid two decades ago. At the time he spoke no
English, and Mev, who was in her junior year abroad
studying Spanish, spoke to him in elementary Spanish.
While learning to communicate in each other's language
they'd fallen in love.

"I've been briefing Catherine on recent events. And
she's been briefing me."

"You're home in time to go to Aunt Lottie's with us.
I made a *tortilla*," by which Paco meant a Spanish potato
and onion omelet.

Jaime and Jorge came down the stairs with hair still
wet from the shower.

"Hi, Mom."

"Hi, Mom."

"You all go on over to Aunt Lottie's," Mev said. "I'll
clean up and be there in a half hour."

"Come here, Mighty!" Jaime called. "Wanna go to
Aunt Lottie's?"

He opened the door, and Mighty raced across the

driveway to join Sequoyah, Renoir, and Gandhi in Lottie's woods.

By the time Mev arrived, Lottie's other guests—Jim, Lauren, and Beau, Jon and Gregory, Gretchen and Neel, as well as her own family—were seated at Lottie's long table eating Paco's *tortilla*, Gretchen's Shrimp Casablanca, Gregory's collard greens, Jon's bread, and Lauren's sautéed mushrooms, with Lottie's abundant Spanish red wine. Doolittle, perched on Jaime's left wrist, held up a half-eaten shrimp with his left foot.

"Hello," Doolittle said.

"Hello, Doolittle. Hello, everybody. I apologize for coming late."

"We've been celebrating the boys' archaeological discovery, Mev," Neel said.

"We're gonna go down in history, Mom," Jorge said.

"Which case occupied your time today, dear?" Lottie asked her. "The fire, the dead body, or Donna Dam?"

Mev accepted a glass of wine. "All of the above."

Lottie filled a plate for her.

"We've been talking about our DNA party tomorrow night," Gretchen said. "I'm getting thirty vials to collect our spit. We'll find out where our ancestors lived."

"I wouldn't miss it, Gretchen," Mev said.

"We'll have a big bash. Rich and Rhonda are coming, and Grant and Ruth," Neel said. "Also Chief Pace, Atsadi and Amadahy, and possibly some of their friends from Tayanita Village."

"Gregory and I are coming," Jon said. "We'll get proof that Gregory is Cherokee."

"I already know I'm Cherokee, Jon. Bozeman is a Cherokee name," Gregory said. "And my family is from Oklahoma."

"Doolittle wanna dinner," Doolittle said.

"Aunt Lottie," Jaime said, giving the parrot another

shrimp and moving him to the perch atop his cage. "Eric really likes birds. May we bring him here to meet Doolittle sometime?"

"Of course."

"Eric knows lots of bird calls," Jaime said.

"We can't tell the difference between an owl's hoot and Eric's hoot," Beau said.

At that moment they heard a familiar call, *Who-cooks-for-you, who-cooks-for-you-all.*

"That's a barred owl," Jaime said. "It's in the woods down by the creek."

"Or that's Eric," Beau said.

"May Jaime and Beau and I be excused, Aunt Lottie?" Jorge asked. "We'd like to investigate."

Then they heard a gunshot. And a second one.

The three boys raced out the back door followed by Mighty, Sequoyah, Renoir, and Gandhi. And everybody else.

"Someone's shooting our chickens!" Jaime yelled. "Help!"

"They've killed Henny Penny," Jorge yelled. "And Feather Jean."

Then they heard a third shot.

Beau fell to the ground.

"Beau! Beau's been hit!" Jaime yelled. "Help!"

"He's been shot in the head!"

"Mom! Dad! Come here!"

The dogs raced into the woods.

Beau lay on the ground, the left side of his head bleeding. He opened his eyes.

"I'm okay," he said, holding his hand over his ear. "But I think my ear's been shot off."

Lauren and Jim fell to the ground beside their son.

"Beau, Beau, my dear Beau," Lauren sobbed.

"I'm okay, Mom," Beau said. "I'll live."

Jim examined Beau's head. "You're right, Beau. The bullet went through the top of your ear."

"Let's get some alcohol, Lottie," Neel said.

"I'm calling the police," Mev said. She called nine-one-one. "This is Detective Arroyo. There is a shooter in the woods at three-oh-one North Witherston Highway, home of Charlotte Byrd. Please send police."

Moments later they heard a siren.

"I think Beau will be okay," Jim said. "The bullet just grazed his ear. But we need to clean him up."

"We need alcohol, a couple of towels, and a blanket," Neel said. "Jorge, could you please bring us the blanket in my jeep."

"I'm on it."

Lottie brought out two clean hand towels and a bottle of vodka. "This is the only alcohol I have other than wine," she said. "Will it do?"

"It will do," Jim said. "Thanks, Lottie." He cleaned his son's wound.

Neel covered Beau with the plaid blanket.

"Thanks, Dr. Byrd. Thanks, Neel," Beau said. "Pop, will I lose my ear?"

"No, son. But you'll have a little nick there. A mark of distinction."

The dogs returned from the woods.

Pete Junior pulled into Lottie's driveway in his patrol car, followed by Jake in the Chevy Tahoe. The two men rounded the house with guns drawn.

"The shots came from the woods. Over there, behind our house." Mev pointed in the direction of the creek.

"I'll bet the shooter's gone now," Jorge said. "The shooter was shooting our chickens and accidentally shot Beau. That's what I think."

"And the shooter ran away because he thought he'd killed Beau," Jaime said.

"That's hit and run," Jorge said.

"I'll check out the woods," Pete Junior said, and sprinted into the dark with his gun in his right hand and his flashlight in his left.

Mev pulled Jake aside. "We need to be looking for some connections here, Jake," Mev said. "Too many unusual events have transpired in too few days to be coincidental."

"Right. The fire with the fatality. The cave with the bones. The letters from Donna Dam. The protest against the mayor's lake proposal."

"And tonight's shooting. Let's see. The boys saw the explosion. The boys found the Cherokee grave. Rich Rather and Grant Griggs did something the night the dam broke in Toccoa in 1977. Rich, Grant, and Grant's wife Ruth support the building of a dam here in 2017. Donna Dam does not."

"We should focus on the crimes, Mev. The shooting tonight. And the fire fatality. And if the fishing shack was set on fire intentionally the fatality is probably a murder."

"And if Beau had died—God forbid—the shooting tonight would have been at least manslaughter, if not murder."

"Why would anyone shoot the boys' chickens?"

"To scare the boys? To punish them for something? Paco and I will talk to Jaime and Jorge tonight."

"I have to call Amadahy back. She called me on my way here. She listens to the police scanner and doesn't miss a thing."

"Tell her what we know. Beau got wounded in the ear. We don't know who shot him, or whether it was intentional or unintentional."

"It's not hunting season, Mev."

"Someone thinks it is for chickens."

ɞʣɞ

Jaime and Jorge told their parents the whole Blue Boulder story, including their smoking marijuana, hiding Eric's pipe in the cave, finding the bones, seeing the man in the canoe, and receiving the anonymous threat to their lives.

Jaime explained that the threat to their parents' lives was the reason they had confided only in Neel.

Jorge showed them the text message from XXX.

"Beau got one too," Jorge said.

"We were mostly afraid for you, Mom," Jaime said. "If we had told you and you had looked for Canoe Man, Canoe Man would have killed you, and we'd be responsible."

"*Hijos*," Paco interrupted. "If you had told us we would all have decided together what to do. You are no longer children. You are sixteen years old. We are a team."

"Your father's right, boys. We'll figure this out together."

"You know what I think?" Jorge said. "I think that Canoe Man killed somebody in the fishing shack, set off an explosion, and escaped in a canoe so that nobody would see his car nearby."

"Or his truck," Mev murmured.

"He must have brought the victim to the shack in the canoe, or else that person's car would have been outside," Jaime said.

"Maybe Victim didn't know he'd be a victim. Maybe Canoe Man and Victim were planning something together."

"Maybe Victim was a she, and Canoe Man and Victim went to the shack to make love."

"And then he blew her up? I don't think so," Paco

said. "Where did he suddenly get the dynamite? And the gasoline."

"The man in the canoe must have planned ahead," Mev said. "He must have carried up the dynamite on a previous trip."

"Or he brought Victim to the shack earlier."

"Why wouldn't the victim drive there and park on the road?" Mev asked.

"Because his or her car would be seen, and maybe recognized. He or she must have been doing something illegal."

"And then Canoe Man shot Feather Jean and Henny Penny to scare us."

"And would have shot the others when we ran out. So instead he shot Beau."

"I think we're getting somewhere. Boys, would you give me permission to discuss the situation with Beau?"

"Sure, Mom."

"Sure. We'd have told him that we talked to you anyway."

"May I talk to Beau's parents? They have a right to know what put their son in danger."

"Sure, Mom. Thanks for asking our permission," Jaime said. "I'll tell Beau he can show you his message from XXX."

"And you can tell Chief McCoy," Jorge said.

"I'll tell Chief McCoy tomorrow."

"*Hijos*," Paco said. "In the future don't keep big secrets from us. Okay? We need to be able to help each other."

"Okay, Dad. Do you want me to tell you if Jaime makes love to Annie?"

"Jorge, Shut up!" Jaime said. "I'll keep that a secret from you."

"*Hermano*, we don't have secrets, remember? I tell you stuff."

∾∾

Mighty was already asleep at the foot of Jaime's bed when the twins turned the light out.

"I feel better now that Mom and Dad will help us with the case."

"Me, too. You know what? We forgot to tell them that Canoe Man said 'Shit,'" Jaime said.

"He must not have been happy to see us."

"Canoe Man spoke the word out loud, Jorge. Loud enough for us to hear it. We may recognize his voice if we hear him say the word again."

"Maybe that's what he's worried about. That's why he shot our chickens. He's trying to scare us."

"Do you think the shooter was aiming at Beau?"

"Because Beau's black?"

"No. Because Beau knows something."

"That Beau doesn't know he knows."

"We all know stuff we don't know we know, bro."

"Do you think you and I know the same stuff we don't know we know?"

"Probably. At least we do now. But when we separate, we'll have different stuff we won't know we know," Jaime said.

The boys grew quiet.

"*Buenas noches, hermano*," Jorge said.

"Don't go to sleep yet, Jorge. We've still got to figure out something."

"What?"

"Why did the shooter aim at Beau?"

"How did the shooter know that Beau would be with us at Aunt Lottie's?"

"How did he know we'd go outside when we heard an owl?"

"Maybe it was the shooter who hooted."

"Eric knows we eat at Aunt Lottie's on Sunday nights.

"But the shooter couldn't have been Eric," Jorge said. "Eric wouldn't shoot Beau."

"We should tell Beau that Canoe Man may come back."

"Text him."

Jaime Arroyo
iMessage
Sunday, March 12, 11:01 p.m.

Are you awake

Yes

R u ok

Am ok but with bandage on my head

*Canoe man may think you recognized his
Voice. You may be in danger*

Really

*We told parents about canoe man
They will tell your parents*

*Ok
I will talk to them*

Dont tell anybody else. Not anybody

Not Eric

Ok
Eric doesnt know

Can you go with neel to see cherokee woman's bones at ten tomorrow?

Yes

We will pick you up before ten
We r glad u r ok

Good night

"Done."

"Let's figure this out tomorrow, Jaime."

After a minute Jaime said, "So you really thought that barred owl's call was Eric?"

"I thought he might have been trying to reach us."

"He would have texted Beau."

"Do you think Eric was the owl we heard last night right before Canoe Man went by?"

"I asked him this afternoon. He said it was an owl."

"Do you believe him?"

"I don't know."

"Did you tell him about Canoe Man?"

"No."

"Don't forget not to set your alarm, Jaime."

"And I won't forget not to get up early, Jorge."

"And I won't forget not to go to school."

"*Buenas noches, hermano.*"

"*Buenas noches.*"

Jaime's phone rang. "Who's that?" He looked at his phone. "Who could that be?" He answered. "Hello...Hi,

Eric. You're up late…Okay. We'll pick you up at the gas
station at five forty-five or so…No problem. Good
night."

"What was that about?"

"Eric wants to go with us to the DNA spitting party."

"Does Eric know about Beau being shot?"

"I don't think so."

"He'll find out tomorrow night."

"*Buenas noches, hermano.*"

"*Buenas noches.*"

⌒⌒⌒

*Today I looked into the grave of a Cherokee
woman. I intruded into her sacred space.*

*She was pregnant when she died. Was she
married? Perhaps she was, perhaps she wasn't.
No big deal for a Cherokee woman in a tradi-
tionally matriarchal society, where Cherokee
women and men alike had sexual freedom. At
least they did until the descendants of Europe-
ans "civilized" them, forced them into patriar-
chy and Christianity, and told them their "earthly nature" was sinful.*

*But this young woman was shown respect
by her fellow Cherokees. She was buried in a
traditional fashion in a rock grave with a gold
nugget and a Cherokee pot. I hope she was
loved.*

*The young woman lived through a turning
point in Cherokee history. In the early nineteenth century, the Cherokees were converting
their centuries-old egalitarian ways of govern-
ance into a representative democracy to please
their white conquerors. In 1827 they adopted a*

*constitution that resembled the American Con-
stitution and that gave political power to men
only. The Cherokee women lost the authority
they had had for centuries in tribal decision-
making.*

*All that remains of the people my Cherokee
ancestors were before colonization is a percentage of our genes.*

*We will never know this Cherokee woman's
name. We will never know what she looked like,
how she spoke, how she walked, whom she
loved, what she thought about. The land has
swallowed her life.*

*But this week, two centuries after her death,
we will know her genes. What will they tell us
about who she was?*

Neel closed his journal. Then he opened it again and
wrote another paragraph.

*Descendants of the European colonialists
fight nature here, there, and everywhere—in our
bodies, in our land.*

"Gretchen," he said. "Get your jacket. Let's sit on
the porch and look at the full moon."

"And have a glass of wine."

"I love you, white woman."

"I love you, red man."

WITHERSTON ON THE WEB
Monday, March 13, 2017

NEWS

Beau Lodge Is Shot in Ear

8:00 a.m. Chief Jake McCoy and Deputy Pete Koslowsky Junior were called to the home of Dr. Charlotte Byrd at 301 North Witherston Highway last night at 8:35 p.m. to investigate a shooting. According to Chief McCoy, Beau Lodge and Jaime and Jorge Arroyo, all age 16, had gone outside after Dr. Byrd's dinner party to search for a barred owl who had hooted in the woods near the creek. They heard two shots and then the screams of their chickens. A third bullet struck Beau in his ear. Dr. Jim Lodge, Beau's father, said that he would bandage Beau's ear and that hospitalization would be unnecessary.

Feather Jean and Henny Penny died.

Chief McCoy said that he had no clue to the identity of the shooter and that he actually didn't know whether the shooting was intentional or unintentional. Readers may ask how someone could unintentionally shoot Beau's ear in the light of the full moon.

Chief McCoy will continue to investigate the case. He is looking for the bullets.

Amadahy Henderson, Reporter

Arson Is Suspected in Explosion

8:00 a.m. Chief Jake McCoy, with Detective Mev Arroyo and Mayor Rich Rather, held a news conference at noon yesterday in front of the Municipal Building. The three officials answered questions about Saturday evening's explosion of a wooden shack on the east bank of Saloli Stream. Witherston Police suspect arson.

The hot fire caused one human person to become deceased. The bones of this unknown person have been taken to a DNA lab in Atlanta for analysis.

What will the lab find? The person's sex? The person's race? The person's health? Maybe all of that.

Amadahy Henderson, Reporter

LETTERS TO THE EDITOR

To the Editor:

Who is Eleanor Roosevelt?

Sally Sorensen
Keep Nature Natural

To the Editor:

In southern Appalachia the forces of nature

have shaped our mountains, valleys, rivers, and streams since the Earth cooled four billion years ago. And our mountains, valleys, rivers, and streams have shaped human existence since the first humans arrived here 10,000 years ago. Five hundred generations of humans lived with the forces of nature. Now humans want to shape our mountains, valleys, rivers, and streams. We want to control the forces of nature. At least Mayor Rather does, and all the other humans who use the equipment of civilization to rearrange the landscape for their own convenience.

Does Mayor Rather think that he can change a part of the ecosystem without changing the whole ecosystem?

Gregory Bozeman, Witherston

To the Editor:

If Mr. Wilker would like to know what I was doing on Saturday, November 5, 1977, I can tell him. I was campaigning with my mother and my friend Sharron for passage of the Equal Rights Amendment in Columbus, Georgia. That's what we did on Saturdays in 1977.

Gretchen Green, Witherston

EDITORIAL

It rained all day in Toccoa on November 5, 1977, before the dam broke at 1:30 a.m. on No-

vember 6. Why is that important? Because Mayor Rather has stated that he and attorney Grant Griggs, who were fraternity brothers at the time, had spent the day bass fishing on Barnes Lake. The rain must have filled their boat. Did Mayor Rather tell the truth, that he and Mr. Griggs sat in their boat fishing for bass in heavy rain? Did Mayor Rather misremember? Or did he lie?

On the evening of November 5, Marco's Pizza and Pool Hall on the bank of Barnes Lake had hosted a long-planned tournament. "Some players came from as far away as Athens to play pool and drink beer," the local newspaper reported. "The restaurant stayed open all night after the dam broke, because local customers could not return to the flooded town in the dark."

Were UGA students Rich Rather and Grant Griggs at that pool party? Was Donna Dam?

Journalists seek to publish the truth. We are investigating. So are the Witherston Police.

Catherine Perry-Soto, Editor

WEATHER

Cloudy this morning, with a high of 50 degrees. But here comes the rain again. Rain will come down in sheets this evening. Sheets of rain. Rainy sheets. Sheety rain. Sheety sheety rain.

Low tonight of 40.
I can't stop the rain.

Tony Lima, Weather Warbler

NORTH GEORGIA IN HISTORY:
THE WITHERS
By Charlotte Byrd

After losing his father in 1838 and his mother in 1848, Harold Francis ("Harry") Withers enrolled in classes at the University of Georgia. But he failed to graduate. In 1851 he was expelled for disrupting the May commencement exercises when he rode a horse wearing academic regalia into the Chapel. The horse was wearing the academic regalia, not Harry. President Alonzo Church, who was a retired Presbyterian minister and a harsh disciplinarian, gave "public intoxication" as the reason for Harry's removal from the campus. Apparently, President Church found Harry's bottle of bourbon more offensive than the horse's cap and gown.

The circumstances of Harry's expulsion from UGA offer the only evidence I have encountered in my research that any member of the Withers family had a sense of humor.

In the Panic of 1857, Harry cashed in some of his gold and invested in the newly formed Antler Rifles manufacturing company. That same year he married Patience Gray and took her back to Saloli Creek, where they built a log mansion on the site of the old family cabin and raised their son Withers Francis Withers, who became known as "Witty" for no obvious reason.

Harry Withers did well during the War Between the States. Because his wealth and the Confederacy's conscription laws of 1861 al-

lowed him to do so, when the war broke out Harry hired 36-year-old John Sando, of Cherokee descent, to take his place on the battlefield. Private Sando was killed in Chickamauga in 1863. Antler Rifles prospered with the wartime demand for rifles, and by 1865 Harry's investment had quadrupled.

Harry died in 1882 at the age of 52. In his will he left Witty Withers $9 million in Antler Rifles stock and an untold fortune in gold.

Cartoon by Jorge Arroyo

Mayor Rather sat on a wall, Mayor Rather had a great fall, and all the king's horses and all the king's men couldn't put Mayor together again.

CHAPTER 7

Monday Morning, March 13, 2017

W here's the pot?" Jaime exclaimed. "The pot's gone! And the gold nugget."

"Someone's been here, Dr. Ellis!" Jorge called out. "We see bones, but that's all. And the bones have been messed up."

Jaime and Jorge were lying on their stomachs peering into the hole where they'd left the skeletons of the woman and child just twenty-four hours before. Jorge was holding the flashlight.

Carter Ellis looked at Beau. "Who knew the location of this burial site?"

"Amadahy Henderson and her boyfriend Atsadi Moon. They followed us here yesterday," Beau said. "Amadahy is a reporter for *Webby Witherston*."

"That's *Witherston on the Web*, our local online newspaper," Neel interjected. "But I'm confident that Amadahy and Atsadi would not have robbed a Cherokee grave. They are both part Cherokee. They would have respected it."

"Our parents knew," Jaime said as he and Jorge backed out of the cave and rejoined Dr. Ellis and Neel on the granite outcropping. "But they wouldn't have told anybody."

"And Canoe Man knew," Jorge said. "Canoe Man must have figured out from Amadahy's article that we'd found Cherokee Woman right here. Remember, Jaime, you were holding a trowel when he turned his flashlight on us?"

"Who is Canoe Man?" Carter asked.

"We don't know who Canoe Man is," Jorge said. "Canoe Man may be a murderer." He looked at Jaime. "Should we tell the story?"

"Dr. Ellis, if you will promise not to tell anybody, we'll give you the details," Jaime said. He looked at Neel for confirmation.

"You can trust Dr. Ellis, boys. And of course you may trust me to keep your secrets."

"I promise to keep your information confidential," Carter said. "I speak mostly with the dead anyway. And they're not talkative."

Jorge, Jaime, and Beau told Carter and Neel the story of their Saturday afternoon.

"We had a spiritual experience," Jaime said. "We smoked marijuana and imagined the thoughts of boys our age who lay on these rocks twelve thousand years ago."

"Our friend Eric mimicked the call of a red-shouldered hawk. *Kee-rah, kee-rah, kee-rah,*" Jorge said. "And the call of a barred owl. *Who-cooks-for-you, who-cooks-for-you-all.*"

"We wondered if boys twelve thousand years ago heard those same birds," Jaime said.

"After a while we heard someone on the ridge," Beau said, "and we decided to bury Eric's pipe to keep Eric out of trouble."

"Eric split when we found out Deputy Hefner was on the ridge," Jaime said. "He was afraid of being arrested."

"Jaime still had Eric's trowel in his hand when we heard the explosion up Saloli Stream and saw the fireball. We got up on Blue Boulder to see the fire. Then we heard someone paddling a canoe down the creek right by us," Jorge said.

"When he got close enough for us to see him he aimed his flashlight at us. I held the trowel over my eyes," Jaime said.

"The light was blinding," Jorge said. "So we couldn't see the man."

"How do you know the person in the canoe was a man?" Neel asked.

"We heard him say 'Shit,'" Beau said.

"Why I'll be damned. His mother didn't teach him any manners," Carter said.

"Stay on task, Carter," Neel said.

"Please don't tell anyone what we heard, Dr. Ellis. Canoe Man threatened to kill one of us if we talked," Jaime said.

"You know who else knew about this grave, Beau? Eric knew," Jorge said.

"But Eric is a good guy," Beau said. "He's not a grave robber."

"Let me excavate the site and take the bones to the lab," Carter said. "How do I love bones? Let me count the ways."

"Jaime, Jorge, Beau, when you look at bones, always remember they belonged to somebody, a person who had ideas, feelings, memories, joys, sorrows—just as you have, but different from yours, always different from yours," Neel said. "The person's whole world died when his or her heart stopped beating. The Cherokee woman whose bones you found grew up in a community of friends and relatives whom she loved and who loved her.

Imagine the fullness of her life when you look at her bones."

Beau closed his eyes. "I'm imagining."

"She was born in this valley, she played in this stream, she fished, hunted foxes, listened to birds, tended a garden, cooked, slept and dreamt," Neel continued. "She became a woman and conceived a child. She felt the child move in her womb, and then she died. We'll never know what she thought about when she stood on Blue Boulder and looked out at the water."

"When I imagine her life I feel sad," Beau said.

"Why, Beau? She lived on beautiful land," Jorge said.

"She'd made love," Jaime said.

"I feel sad because I think about her dying. How in just one instant her whole inner life stopped. Poof. Everything she'd thought about, gone. Gone forever. The only thing she left behind was her skeleton, and a pot with a gold nugget that someone has stolen."

"She probably left happy memories of herself in the people who knew her. That's a form of immortality, Beau," Neel said. "Maybe the people who knew her told nice stories about her to their children, who told those stories to their children, and to their children's children. That's how the spirit lives on."

"But the only way we—I mean us here—will get to know Cherokee Woman is by looking at her bones."

"Will the bones show how she died?" Jaime asked.

"Possibly," Carter said. "The bones may show she took a bullet or an arrow. If we get some DNA, the bones may show she had a fatal disease."

"That's what I want to find out," Jaime said, "because she died young, not much older than we are, I'll bet."

"Archaeologists like Dr. Ellis keep the past from

vanishing into oblivion," Neel said. "Archaeologists help us imagine the way of life of communities long gone."

"We poke around in the dirt and salvage remnants of what once was," Carter said, "to remind us of what is lost."

"Everything is lost," Beau said.

"Not everything, Beau," Neel said.

"*Who* people are is lost," Beau said.

"Who people are?"

"I get what you're saying, Beau," Jaime said. "The *who* disappears when a person dies, though maybe not the *what*."

"Think of all the *who*s that have disappeared in two hundred thousand years," Jorge said. "Where have all the *who*s gone? Long time passing."

"Bro, do you have to make a joke of everything?"

"I do."

"I like to think that a person's *who* lives on in the memories of the living, in the words we speak, in the ideas we share with each other, in the hopes we have for our future, in what we create," Neel said. "Our own *who* contains the spiritual traces of many *who*s who have lived before us."

"That's like reincarnation, Neel," Jaime said.

"Of a sort," Neel responded.

"As an archaeologist I look at *what* people left behind, and I never find it enough," Carter said. "The Cherokees were a literate people, and we have their written records and accounts of their experiences. But for ninety-nine percent of human societies over the last two hundred thousand years we've got only material remains. Bones, tools, shards of pottery. I'm trying to put together a jigsaw puzzle which has lost ninety-nine percent of its pieces."

"Let's get to work," Neel said. "Dr. Ellis has to finish his excavation before the rain comes."

Carter opened his tool kit. "Yes, time to get started," he said. "I will teach you boys how to excavate a site, or as I like to say, how to hunt underground."

"And I'm going to report the robbery to the police," Neel said.

BREAKING NEWS
2:00 p.m.

Cherokee Pot and Gold Nugget
Stolen from Cherokee Burial Site

Chief Jake McCoy and Detective Mev Arroyo are investigating the robbery of a two-hundred-year-old Cherokee pot and a gold nugget from the burial site that Jaime and Jorge Arroyo and Beau Lodge discovered in Saloli Valley on Saturday. Chief McCoy said that the robbery took place between noon on Sunday and nine o'clock this morning.

According to Dr. Neel Kingfisher, who accompanied the boys to the grave on Sunday morning and again this morning, the thief disturbed the skeletons of a woman and her fetus but did not remove them.

Chief McCoy asks Witherstonians to help find the grave robber. He asks antique dealers in the Southeast to contact Witherston Police if they are offered the pot for sale.

Atsadi Moon, a member of Witherston's Town Council, said, "According to the Native American Graves Protection and Repatriation law, the pot belongs to the Cherokees. Whoever took the pot may deliver it to Tayanita Village confidentially. No questions will be asked. Ta-

yanita Village will give the pot to the Cherokee-Witherston Museum."

This morning state archaeologist Dr. Carter Ellis excavated the site and took the bones to a lab in Atlanta for DNA analysis. DNA analysis will determine whether the deceased person is Native American, as Dr. Kingfisher believes. Dr. Ellis promised a report by Tuesday afternoon.

Amadahy Henderson, Reporter

CHAPTER 8

Monday Afternoon, March 13, 2017

Mev, come look at this DNA report on the victim of Saturday's fire. It just came in."

Mev got up from her desk at the Witherston Police Station and went into Jake's office. Over his shoulder she read the email message.

> *From: M Melton, GBI*
> *To: Chief Jake McCoy, Witherston Police Department*
> *Re: DNA Analysis of Bone Marrow*
>
> *Monday, March 13, 2017, 2:46 p.m.*
>
> *Dear Chief McCoy:*
>
> *A DNA analysis of bone marrow and soft tissue delivered to GBI Division of Forensic Sciences identified the deceased individual as a female 35-40 years old, 52% Native American, 16% French and German, 14% Northern European, 8% Ashkenazi, 4% British and Irish, 3% Iberian, and 3% undetermined. (1.5% of the*

genes are Neanderthal.) Examination of soft tissue showed evidence of dynamite. Examination of the skull showed evidence that a 9 mm bullet had passed from the back to the front of the head, probably causing death. Death preceded destruction of the body by fire.

Sincerely,

Marcus Melton, PhD
Division of Forensic Sciences
Georgia Bureau of Investigation
Decatur GA 30034

"This report tells us a lot about who she was and how she died, Mev."

"The woman must have had one parent who was Native American. Could be Cherokee, Creek, Chickasaw, who knows? I wonder whether anyone is missing from Tayanita Village."

"The Tayanita Villagers are all under thirty. Except for Chief Pace. And they keep track of each other."

"Well, we Witherstonians keep pretty good track of each other too. And nobody has reported anybody missing."

"Not yet."

"The victim was murdered, shot from behind. The dynamite suggests arson. The murderer probably blew up the shack to hide evidence. Since we found only one body we can assume that the murderer escaped the fire, Jake."

"And we've found a truck, which the victim must have driven to the shack."

"Or maybe the victim and the murderer together. They may have known each other."

"Why did the victim, or the murderer, or both, hide the truck?"

"Maybe they didn't want their presence there known, Jake. After all, they were on someone else's property."

"Maybe the murderer hid the truck."

"Maybe the murderer hid in the truck."

"How did the murderer get away?"

"By canoe, Jake, by canoe. Hernando Zamora saw a man get into a canoe—most likely his canoe—immediately after the explosion. The boys saw a man in a canoe paddle past Blue Boulder down Tayanita Creek several minutes later." Mev told Jake what she knew about the man in the canoe and the threatening messages the boys had received.

"Do you think there's any connection between the Donna Dam letters, the murder, the explosion, the texts from XXX, the shot at Beau, and the grave robbery?"

"Yes, Jake, I do. But I don't know what it could be. I don't know whether these events have to do with the mayor's proposal of a lake, which seemed to motivate the letters to the editor, or with money. If I were a betting woman, I'd say that the crimes have to do with money.

"Who knew the location of the Cherokee burial site?"

"Jaime, Jorge, Beau, Neel, and Eric."

"I think we need to bring Eric in for questioning, Mev."

"Can we wait a day, Jake? I want to talk to Jorge and Jaime first. Just give me twenty-four hours, okay?"

CHAPTER 9

Monday Evening, March 13, 2017

Lottie, Mev, and Paco drove up Bear Hollow Road to Neel and Gretchen's white frame farmhouse and parked by the garden fence. Lottie shooed away the chickens with her cane so that Gretchen's other guests could park there too. Jorge, Jaime, and Eric, trailed by Jim, Lauren and Beau, pulled up a minute later. Beau exited his mother's Prius carefully, for his head was wrapped in a huge white bandage.

"Whoa, Beau! What happened to you?" Eric exclaimed.

"I got shot," Beau said. "No big deal."

"Yes, big deal," Lauren said. "Beau got shot in the ear last night behind Lottie's house."

"Here's what happened, Eric," Jorge said. He recounted the story, mentioning the chickens but not mentioning his suspicion of Canoe Man.

Neither Lauren nor Jim mentioned the man in the canoe either.

"I'm so sorry, Beau," Eric said. "Crikes, I don't know what I'd have done if you'd been killed."

Jon and Gregory, in Gregory's red pickup, and Rhonda and Rich, in Rich's black Chrysler, arrived. They parked beside each other and hurried to join their friends on the veranda. Lightning cracked the sky, and rain poured down.

As Lottie rang the doorbell she heard Gretchen exclaim, "Neel, they're here already! Shoot! I haven't vacuumed."

Lottie turned to the others and said, "Pretend you didn't hear that."

Gretchen opened the door with a big smile on her face, gave Lottie a hug, and exclaimed, "I've been waiting all day for you all."

"That's because Gretchen wants her Kombucha cocktail," Neel said, coming up behind her. "Welcome to Green Acres, everybody."

Gandhi, Swift, and Ama emerged to greet them.

"I brought wine," Lottie said, as Paco carried the case into Gretchen's kitchen.

"Wow, your dining room table looks like my chemistry lab bench," Jaime said.

On the table were thirty blue paper cups, each holding a glass vial, a pen, and a peel-off label.

Grant and Ruth Griggs, Catherine Perry-Soto and Dan Soto, Atohi Pace, John Hicks, Atsadi Moon, and Amadahy Henderson all appeared within the next ten minutes. Finally Christopher Zurich, Mona Pattison, Annie Jerden, Hernando Zamora, and Sally Sorensen showed up in Colonel Sorensen's new Ford Escape.

"KNN is present," Christopher shouted as he walked in. "We're here!" He was carrying a homemade sign that said: *SAVE CHEROKEE GRAVES—SAY NO TO DAM RATHER.*

"Hello, Christopher," Rich said, greeting him. "Are you of voting age?"

"No, sir."

"Happy to hear that," Rich said.

"Whoa, Beau," Christopher exclaimed. "What happened to you?"

"I took a bullet from a chicken hunter," Beau said.

"What?"

"Everybody who RSVP'd is present now," Gretchen said, looking at her clipboard. She had been checking off the names of her guests.

Neel ushered the group into their spacious living room. Floor-to-ceiling shelves held Neel's books of literature, art, philosophy, and medicine and Gretchen's books of organic gardening and vegetarian cuisine. A corner curio cabinet held his collection of Cherokee bone knives. Gretchen's black cat Barack dozed on an old leather sofa. Two oak rocking chairs faced the huge hearth.

"Will everybody please take a paper cup, use the pen to write your name and email address on the label, and stick the label on the vial," Gretchen said. "Now for the next five minutes please fill your vial to the halfway mark with your saliva. I'm taking some loaves of bread out of the oven to help you salivate."

"Jaime and I are sharing a vial," Jorge said. "So we'll be done before anybody else."

"No fair!" Christopher complained. "They'll eat all the bread before we're through spitting."

Gretchen and Neel's guests got to work generating saliva and depositing it into their vials. But after a minute of concentrated effort Jorge got the giggles and spewed saliva all over Jaime. The giggles were contagious. Before long everybody was spewing as much saliva outside their vials as inside. Their task took closer to ten minutes than five.

"Now cap your vial, label it, and give it to Neel," Gretchen said. "Neel and I will take the vials to Atlanta tomorrow morning. Now who would like a glass of Kombucha?"

"I wouldn't," Rich said.

"Who would like a glass of wine?" Lottie asked.

"I would," Rich said, "unless you have bourbon."

"We're serving a red blend from Zamora Wines and a chardonnay from Frogtown Cellars," Lottie said.

"Rhonda dear, will you please remind me why we're here," Rich said.

"Because you are Witherston's mayor, Rich dear. And the people who voted for you will expect you to join this search for our community's ancestral roots."

"That's right, Mr. Mayor," Atsadi said. "Even the folks who voted for Gretchen Green, such as all twenty-one of us Tayanita Villagers, no offense intended, will expect you to disclose your heritage."

"Offense taken," Rich said.

"Thank you, Tayanita Villagers," Gretchen interjected. "I will run again."

"May I weigh in on this, Mr. Mayor, even though I too voted for Gretchen?" Lottie asked.

"Did anybody in this room vote for me?"

"I did, Rich," Grant said.

"So did I," Ruth said.

"You all don't count," Rich said.

"I would vote for you for state senator if you withdrew your dam project," John Hicks said. "Seriously."

"I would campaign for you," Gretchen said.

"If you campaigned for me, Gretchen, I would drink Kombucha and eat seaweed."

"Anyway, I find this DNA ancestry project very exciting," Lottie said. "We historians tend to focus on political differences between groups, cultural differences, religious differences. But if we could compare the genomes of all seven billion people in the world we would notice a whole other set of relationships. We would see genetic connections."

"We are fam-i-ly," Jaime intoned.

"The history of humanity is inscribed in our DNA," Lottie said. "Don't you all find that beautiful?"

"I do, Lottie. And I like the idea that our genetic identity depends on our ancestors' love-making, not war-making," Gretchen said. "Here's the lesson, folks. If you want to influence the future, make love, not war."

Jaime looked at Annie. "Good idea," he said.

"And make love with someone of different ancestry," Beau said, "like my mother and father did."

"And we got you, Beau!" Lauren said. "Lucky us!"

"In a hundred years, most Americans will look like you, Beau," Jaime said.

"Then I'll have an easier time getting a date," Beau said.

"Then you'll be one hundred and sixteen years old," Jorge said.

"You can ask me for a date, Beau," Sally Sorensen said. "I'll go out with you. Now, while we're sixteen."

"You will?"

"Sure. Just ask."

"Do you want to go out to lunch tomorrow? To Gretchen Green's Green Grocery?"

"Great idea," Gretchen said. "I'll fix you all a fabulous vegetarian lunch."

"Thank you, Beau. I will meet you there at noon. How did you know I was a vegetarian, Mizz Green?"

"May I ask why I am spitting in a vial with all you folks who voted against me? Is this some kind of sixties bonding ritual?"

"You're here to show the world that you, Mr. Mayor, like the residents of Witherston whom you represent, are happy being a mongrel, just like everybody else," Gretchen said.

"I'm not a mongrel."

"I'm a mongrel," Eric said. "My mother is half Cherokee."

"She is?" Mev asked. She looked at Jake.

"We're all mongrels," Neel said. "There's no such thing as racial purity. Everybody on Earth had parents with different DNA."

"Here a mutt, there a mutt, everywhere a mutt mutt," Christopher sang. "Old MacDonald had a farm."

"E-I-E-I-O," Jaime sang.

"Here's why we invited you, Mr. Mayor. If you turn out to have Cherokee ancestry, then you won't want to flood Saloli Valley, which is our ancestral cemetery," Atsadi said. "Our ancestors' spirits are here."

"My ancestors' spirits are in heaven. And I don't have Cherokee genes," Rich said.

"I'll wager you do," Neel said. "In your last campaign, you said your family has lived in Georgia since 1797. That's probably ten generations in Cherokee country. And each of those copulating individuals was the product of hundreds of generations of copulating individuals, each of whom brought to their union a unique genetic history. You're a mongrel like everyone else."

"Wow, Neel. That's cool," Jaime said, pulling up the calculator on his iPhone. "Let's see. If I calculate right, Mayor Rather, you have one thousand twenty-four great, great, great, great, great, great, great, great grandparents."

"And half of them are women, Mr. Mayor," Jorge said.

"Do you think that not a single one of them had any Cherokee genes, Rich?" Rhonda asked. "I bet I have Cherokee genes."

"I'm sure you have," Rich said.

"I have Cherokee genes," Gregory said. "I'm hoping I'm related to the woman in the grave Jorge and Jaime found."

"Me, too," Atsadi said. "I'm hoping she's my great, great, great, great, great, great, great grandmother."

"Me, too," Amadahy said.

"Me, too," Jon said.

"You, too, white man?" Gregory said to Jon.

"I once had black hair. Actually, I once had hair," Jon said, "before I met you."

"We may all be kin," Neel said.

"If we find that we're all kin, maybe we won't kill each other," Gretchen said. "If we do we'll be committing kinicide."

"I'll put away my tomahawk," Neel said.

"Me too," John Hicks said.

"One last task for everybody," Neel said. "On your way out please sign this document authorizing me to make your DNA results public. I'd like them to be transmitted to me on a single document."

"And I'd like to publish the results," Catherine said. "Is that okay with everybody?"

"You're already hard on me, Mizz Webby Witherston," Mayor Rather said.

"I'll sign."

"I'll sign."

"I'll sign."

"Okay, I'll sign," Rich said.

"So will Ruth and I," Grant said.

Everybody signed.

* භදහ*

The rain was still heavy when the party ended. As Mev stood on the veranda waiting for Lottie and Paco to emerge from the house, Eric approached her.

"Detective Arroyo, may I talk to you confidentially?" he asked.

"Certainly, Eric. Let's sit down over here." She pulled two chairs together.

"I would like to report someone missing. My mother. She left our house Saturday morning after I'd gone to work and didn't come home Saturday night or Sunday night."

"Oh, Eric. I'm so sorry. Where do you think she went?"

"I don't know. My stepfather said she went to visit friends in Rome. But she'd planned to speak at Mrs. Rather's rally yesterday. That's why I think something's wrong."

"I'll call Sam." Mev had her fellow officer on speed-dial. "Sam, Eric's here with me at Gretchen Green and Neel Kingfisher's farm. He says his mother is missing...Does she often leave without telling you where she's going?...Well, since you haven't heard from her in forty-eight hours, do you want to file a Missing Persons Report?...Okay. I'll meet you in your home in a few minutes."

Mev turned to Eric. "Do you want to ride with me?"

"Yes."

Mev and Eric caught up with the rest of the guests.

"Lottie and I'll hitch a ride home with the boys, Mevita," Paco said.

"And I'll hitch a ride home with my folks," Beau said.

"I'll see you all later." Mev kissed Paco.

Eric showed Mev the way to an older double-wide mobile home in the Old Pines trailer park. A Witherston Police patrol car was parked in front. A Harley-Davidson

Street 500 motorcycle and an old green Datsun pickup were parked in a detached garage.

Sam opened the door. "Hi, Eric. Come in, Mev," he said. "Would you like a Bud? Or a Diet Coke?"

"No, thanks, Sam. I'm here on business. How are you doing?"

"I'm worried. Molly hasn't called."

"Can you give me a photograph of Molly? And tell me what she was wearing when she left?"

"I can give you a photo of her. It's in my room," Eric said. He disappeared into the back.

"She was wearing blue jeans, a black turtleneck, a brown corduroy jacket, and sneakers," Sam said.

"Where did she say she was going?"

"She said she was going to Rome to see a friend. She still keeps in touch with her friends there."

"Has she contacted you since she left?"

"No, but that's not unusual."

"Was she angry at you?"

"No. Absolutely not. She kissed me goodbye, as she always does."

"What kind of car was she driving?"

"Her Kia pickup, ten years old or so. Red. Not in good shape."

"Here's a picture of her with me," Eric said, coming into the living room. "We look a bit alike, don't you think, Mrs. Arroyo?"

"I do, Eric. You both have black hair, long black hair. Your coloring is the same, and so are your dark eyes. Your mother is a beauty. I have to ask you an indelicate question. Could she have gone to meet your father?"

"That's where I think she went," Sam said.

"No, I don't think so," Eric said. "We haven't heard from my father since he left us."

"May I look around?" Mev asked Sam. "May I look into your bedroom?"

"I'd prefer not, Mev," Sam said. "The bedroom is a mess. I'd be embarrassed, and so would she. Would you mind waiting till tomorrow? I'll make the bed and clean up in the morning."

"Maybe she'll come back tonight, Sam. Please let me know immediately if she does."

ぐんぐん

"Hi, Mr. Mayor. This is Mev." Mev called Rich Rather on her Bluetooth as she was driving away. It was nearly nine o'clock.

"Hello, Mev. To what do I owe the honor of your phone call so soon after the party? Was I a problem?"

"No, Rich, but we do have a problem. I'm filing a Missing Persons Report on Molly Schlaughter. Eric told me she'd left their house on Saturday morning and has not returned. Officer Staples confirmed."

"Well, suffering cats! I thought she'd be in my wife's parade."

"She didn't show up, Mr. Mayor."

"I'll be darned."

"Do you have any idea where she might have gone?"

"No idea. No idea at all."

"Thanks, Mr. Mayor. We'll keep you informed."

Mev disconnected and called Jake.

"Jake, will you come with me to Officer Staples's house, now? Molly Schlaughter is missing."

"Since when?"

"Since Saturday morning. Eric talked to me after the spitting party tonight. I'm betting Molly was the person who died in the fire."

"And that she drove to the fishing shack in her truck?"

"She owned an older red Kia truck, I found out from Sam."

"Why did she hide it in the woods, I wonder," Jake said. "Where did she live?"

"Eric took me to their house tonight. In Old Pines Mobile Home Park."

"That's out Ninovan Road near Tayanita Creek."

"Molly is half Cherokee according to her son. Jake, can we search Sam's house tonight? We don't need a warrant if Sam consents."

"I'll pick you up in thirty minutes. If Sam objects, we'll get a warrant."

☙☙☙

"Hello, Sam," Jake said when Sam opened the front door. "Detective Arroyo and I are concerned about Molly Schlaughter's disappearance. Would you mind if we searched your house now for clues to Molly's disappearance?"

"Be my guest, Chief. I want to find Molly as much as you do. I just cleaned up our bedroom."

"Did you know where her truck could be?"

"No. With her, I suppose."

"Is Eric here?" Mev asked.

"No. He left a few minutes ago. I don't know where he went."

"Have a seat while we look around, Sam," Jake said.

Thirty minutes later, Mev called out from the bedroom.

"I found this box in the closet, Jake. It's labeled 'Toccoa.'" Mev carried it to the dining room table.

"Come here, Sam," Jake said. "Let's look at this together."

"Are you familiar with this box?" Mev asked Sam.

"Where was it?"

"Top shelf of your bedroom closet."

"I never looked up there," Sam said.

Mev extracted three large manila envelopes from the box. The first was labeled *FLOOD*. The second was labeled *OBITUARY*. The third was labeled *MAMA'S LETTER*. Mev opened the first envelope. Dozens of yellowed clippings from the *Toccoa Record*, the *Athens Banner-Herald*, and the *Atlanta Constitution* fell onto the table, most of them from November 1977. They were accounts of the collapse of the Kelly Barnes Dam and grainy pictures of overturned trailers and flooded homes. Among them was a glossy yearbook photo of a teenager with black eyes and long black hair, on the back of which was printed in pencil "Donna Jumper, Stephens County High School."

Sam picked up the photo.

"What do you know about this, Sam?" Mev asked.

"Only that Molly's maiden name was Jumper."

"When did you meet Molly?"

"I met her a year ago February, right after she'd gotten divorced from Buck Schlaughter. I spent a couple of weeks in Rome training to be a cop. I had been employed as a security guard, and I thought I could make more money in law enforcement.

"Did she talk about her mother?"

"No."

"Who is the obituary for?" Jake asked Mev.

Mev opened the second envelope.

"It's for Donna June Jumper. It was published in the *Toccoa Record* on March 10, 2016."

"What does it say?"

Mev read it aloud.

"'Donna June Jumper, 55, of Toccoa, died on Tuesday, March 8, 2016. Born in Toccoa on December 28, 1960, Donna was the daughter of Mona Rider Jumper and Len Jumper, both deceased. She graduated from Stephens County High School in 1979 and shortly thereafter moved to Rome, Georgia. In 1998, she returned to her hometown, worked at Henderson Falls Park, and became active in the First Baptist Church of Toccoa. Survivors include her daughter Molly Ann Schlaughter and her grandson Eric Schlaughter, both of Rome. A graveside service will be held at 2 p.m. on Saturday, March 12, at the Toccoa Baptist Church Cemetery. Pastor Carson Brothers will officiate.'"

"Now let's see the letter," Jake said.

The manila envelope marked MAMA'S LETTER held a smaller white envelope on the front of which was written *To Be Opened Upon My Death*. It had been opened. Mev took out a four-page hand-written letter on yellow legal paper and read it aloud.

"'My dear Molly Ann:

"'I know I won't live long with lung cancer. Nobody does. I write you this letter to tell you the story of your conception, a story so sad and so humiliating I could never bring myself to tell it to you while I was alive.

"'In my attic you will find a cardboard box labeled *Toccoa*. It contains all the newspaper accounts I could find of the flood that destroyed my childhood home on Sunday, November 6, 1977. They are for you and Eric, so that you all will know what happened when the dam broke.

"'On Saturday night, November 5, 1977, my best friend Abbie Hawk and I went to a pizza restaurant on the shore of Barnes Lake. We liked to go there on Saturdays to dance with the boys on the football team. About ten o'clock Abbie and I met two handsome older guys from the University of Georgia who invited us to ride around the lake with them in a van, a white van with no windows in the back. I was flattered so I accepted their invitation. Abbie did not.

"'I hate to tell you this part, because what happened is all my fault. The rain was pouring down hard, as it had for days, and the road was very muddy. So we parked the van near the dam, and the three of us crawled into the back. We sat on blankets and talked. Then one of the guys brought out a bottle of Jim Beam, and we drank it all. It was the first time I'd tasted alcohol. I got very drunk, what you'd call 'falling-down drunk.' I am ashamed to say it, but I started kissing both guys and then made love to one of them, or maybe to both. I don't know. I had never had sex before. I was sixteen years old, a junior in high school.

"'We were still in the back of the van when we heard the dam break. It was one-thirty Sunday morning. All I remember is that one of the guys said "We've got to get out of here." The next thing I knew they'd taken me back to the pizza place, where I drank Coca-Cola, sobered up, and spent the rest of that awful night talking about the dam with Abbie and the football players. The restaurant stayed open, and the manager fed us pizza until morning.

"'As soon as the sun rose, Abbie drove me home—or at least to the street address where the trailer I called home had been. The flood had smashed it against a tree.

"'The next day I think it was I met First Lady Rosalynn Carter, who came to Toccoa from Washington to offer comfort to us.

"'My mother and I didn't have much to start with, but we lost all that we had. We stayed with Abbie's family until we found an apartment. Abbie shared her clothes with me.

"'In December, I learned I was pregnant. I wanted an abortion. My mother was horrified. She called me a slut, but she was very religious and did not let me have an abortion. So I dropped out of high school and stayed home that spring semester. Of all my friends only Abbie came over. Abbie was Cherokee like me, and we'd always stuck together. My other friends disappeared. Abbie said that their parents wouldn't let them associate with me—like my pregnancy could be contagious.

"'You were born on August first. I went back to school in the fall, took extra courses, and managed to graduate on time. My mother helped me raise you till you were almost three. Then she died of breast cancer. I took you and moved to Rome, where I got the job at the supermarket.

"'Although I left Toccoa in 1981, telling Abbie I'd never return, I am happy to be back here in my hometown. I am finally at peace with my life.

"'I do have much to regret. I bore you out of

wedlock. You never had a father. I couldn't buy
you pretty clothes. You had to work at the age of
thirteen. I couldn't send you to college. But I
thank the Lord Jesus I did not have an abortion,
because I got you, dearest daughter, and I have
loved you from the moment you were born. And
I was blessed to have had the time on Earth to
see your Eric grow up.

"'Molly Ann, I know you're going through
difficulties. You've had a hard life. Stay strong.
I wish I could be there for you.

"'Do you want to know who those two college guys were? I can tell you now that I'm
gone. They were Rich Rather, who is the mayor
of Witherston, and Grant Griggs, who is a lawyer in Witherston. I never saw them again. One
of them is your father.

"'Talk to Abbie if you like. She has kept the
secret with me.

"'Your devoted mother
"'Mama Donna
"'February 5, 2016.'"

Mev and Jake looked at Sam. Sam looked at the
floor, head in hands.

"Did you know of this letter, Sam?" Mev asked.

"No, no," Sam replied. "Molly didn't mention it to
me."

"Did Molly ever say who she thought her father
was?" Jake asked.

"No."

"So Molly kept secrets from you?"

"I guess she did."

"Have you ever met Abbie Hawk?"

"No."

"We will take this box with us tonight, Sam. I assume you have no objections," Jake said.

"No objections."

"May we also take Molly's hair brush? We will need her DNA."

"Sure, Chief. Do you think she's dead?"

"Let's talk tomorrow morning in the office," Jake said. "Will nine o'clock suit everybody?"

☙❧

"Well, Mev, I think we've just identified Donna Dam," Jake said as he started his engine. "Donna Dam must be Molly Ann Jumper Schlaughter, who is using *Webby Witherston* to get back at the men who ruined her mother's life."

"Who drove her truck to the fishing shack for who knows what reason and died in the fire."

"*Probably* died. We need confirmation."

"Most likely died."

"We need to know whether Rich and/or Grant figured out that Donna Dam was Molly."

"And that Molly was the daughter of Donna Jumper."

"Who probably hasn't entered their thoughts for forty years," Jake said.

"Because they fulfilled their ambitions, Jake. Rich finished college, married wealthy Rhonda, moved to Witherston, built a beautiful home, sold used cars, sent their daughter through college, became mayor, inherited two hundred and fifty thousand dollars from Francis Hearty Withers, and lived happily ever after. Grant finished college, went to law school, married Ruth, moved to Witherston, built a beautiful home, practiced law, sent their daughter through college, inherited two hundred and fifty thousand dollars from Francis Hearty Withers, and lived happily ever after."

"What you're saying is that both Rich and Grant have a lot to lose if their secrets are exposed by Donna Dam."

"Or by a paternity test."

"A paternity test could prove expensive for one of them. Do you suppose money is Molly's ultimate motive?"

"That would be my guess, Jake. Molly grew up poor, cared for by a single mother. When she learned that either Rich or Grant was her father she must have resented their wealth. Her first husband was in and out of jail. He left her with no money. Sam earns thirty-one thousand a year. She would earn less than that. She could certainly use a settlement to send Eric to college."

"And she would have known about old Withers's bequest to the residents of Witherston."

"Most certainly. The news of his bequest went all over Georgia. So she applied for the job in the mayor's office and moved to Witherston to find out more about Rich and Grant."

"In the mayor's office she could learn just about anything folks in Witherston were doing."

"In the mayor's office she might have learned something about Red Wilker, as well as Rich and Grant."

"We have two motives here that implicate Molly, money and justice. She would like to stop the dam project, because she knows that dams break, and she would like to get the child support her biological father owes her."

"She's a black-mailer. And black-mailers get killed, Jake. She was also black-mailing Red Wilker for something. We need to consider him as a possible murderer."

"Let's talk to him tomorrow after we interview Rich and Grant."

"We do need a paternity test. Fortunately, we've collected Rich's and Grant's DNA, which Neel is taking to Who R U tomorrow morning. Do we need a search warrant to use their DNA for a paternity test, to see whether the woman who died in the fire is the daughter of one of them?"

"Not if they give consent," Jake said. "Let's interview those two gentlemen after we talk with Sam tomorrow morning. How about coming by my office when you get to work? I'll email them to come in at ten and eleven. We'll talk with them separately."

"And I will get in touch with Eric. Poor boy."

"You'd better tell Beau too."

"I'll see you when the birds chirp," Mev said as they drove up to her house.

Jake's cell phone rang. "Hello, Catherine," he said. He listened for a moment.

"Don't mention the letter," Mev whispered.

"Yes, Catherine. Detective Arroyo and I have been talking with Deputy Staples. This evening Eric reported his mother missing. We have reason to believe Mrs. Schlaughter died in the fire. We also believe she was the so-called Donna Dam."

"Good night, Jake," Mev said as she shut the car door behind her.

Jake continued to talk with Catherine.

❧❧

Mev couldn't reach Eric on his cell phone, so she left word with Sam for Eric to call her.

"Thanks for calling, Eric," Mev said when he called her twenty minutes later. "Would you be able to come

over to our house tonight?...Thanks. We'll see you shortly."

Mev called Lauren and told her that Eric's mother
was probably Donna Dam, who was probably dead."

"Oh, Mev. Poor Eric. We're coming over."

She then reported the latest developments in the case
to her family.

"I may not tell Eric everything, boys," Mev said. "So
could you let me be the lead investigator on our team tonight?"

"Sure, Mom."

"Sure, Mom. But please keep us on your team."

At ten forty-five Eric walked through the Arroyos'
front door, removing his helmet and black leather jacket.
He appeared startled to see Mev, Paco, Jaime, Jorge, Lauren, Jim, and Beau sitting around the dining room table.

"What's up?" he asked.

"Sit here," Mev said, pulling out a chair for him.
"Would you like some hot chocolate?"

"No, thanks, Detective Arroyo."

Mev told him that the victim of the fire was a female
in her late thirties or early forties, that she was half Cherokee, and that she was probably his mother.

"Of course there's still a possibility that the body is
not your mother. We'll have to confirm her identity with
a DNA comparison. We'll deliver her hair sample to the
GBI tomorrow."

Eric looked distressed.

"I thought the body might have been my mother," he
said. "Too coincidental. A fire fatality and my mother
missing at the same time."

"Do you know why your mother might have gone to
the fishing shack?"

"No."

"Have you ever been there?"

Eric hesitated. "Yes, once or twice with Hernando Zamora. The shack is on his property. It's pretty run down."

"May I ask why you and Hernando went there?"

"To smoke marijuana. Are you going to arrest me?"

"No, Eric. Don't worry about that. But I have to ask you another question. Did you know your grandmother, your mother's mother?"

"Mama Donna? Yes, I did. Why?"

"Did she ever talk about your mother's father?"

"No. No, she didn't," Eric said. "But Mama Donna did say that she was Cherokee and my mother's father was not."

"Did your mother say who her father might be?"

"No, Detective Arroyo," Eric said. "I think I'd better go back home now. I have to work tomorrow."

"Eric, do you want to spend the night at my house?" Beau asked.

"Thanks, Beau. But I'd better go on home."

"Will you be alright?"

"Yes. I'll be alright. Not happy, but alright." Eric got his helmet and his jacket and started toward the door. "Detective Arroyo, could you please keep me informed on your investigation?"

"All the way, Eric."

℮⁊℮⁊

"Move over, Mighty," Jaime said as he got under the covers. Mighty moved over just enough to allow Jaime to stretch out along the edge of his bed.

Jorge turned off the light and crawled into his bed.

"I wonder if Eric knows that his mother's father was either Mayor Rather or Mr. Griggs," Jaime said.

"If he knows, he didn't let on."

"I wonder if he knows that his mother was Donna Dam."

"Eric and his mother might have been working together."

"I can't believe Eric would be involved in sending those letters to *Webby Witherston*."

"Would we work with Mom if she were doing something against the law?"

"We might, because we love her."

"Who do you think killed Eric's mother, Jaime?"

"Canoe Man, obviously."

"But who is Canoe Man?"

"Probably someone who was afraid of her."

"If she was Donna Dam, then Mayor Rather and Mr. Griggs would have been afraid of her."

"But they didn't know she was Donna Dam."

"Good point."

"Maybe she was blackmailing them, you know, privately. Like for money."

"And when one of them found out that Donna Dam was Mrs. Schlaughter—"

"He killed her," Jaime said. "In the fishing shack."

"And escaped in a canoe."

"What would Eric's mother be doing in the fishing shack?"

"Maybe Eric told her about smoking marijuana there, and she went to look at the place."

"Maybe Eric took her there."

"And left her? Geez, Jaime, do you think Eric killed her? His own mother?"

"No. No, I don't. Eric loved his mother. Anyway, he couldn't have killed her. He was with us Saturday afternoon."

"But he could have seen Canoe Man. Remember, we heard a barred owl hoot right before Canoe Man went by.

That could have been Eric warning us."

"Maybe he recognized Canoe Man."

"Let's tell him about Canoe Man. That can't do any harm."

"But Mom is leading the investigation."

"And we're helping her."

"I'm getting sleepy, bro."

"*Buenas noches, hermano.*"

"*Buenas noches.*"

☙ℰ❧

It was almost midnight when Neel sat down with his journal to collect his thoughts.

> *Who would have stolen the gold nugget and the Cherokee pot? Only someone who has no empathy for anyone unlike himself, only someone who cannot imagine being someone else.*
>
> *But in the history of humanity a hundred billion people have had little empathy for those they viewed as unlike themselves. That's the source of war—between families, between tribes, cities, and nations, between races. Gretchen would say, between humans and other animals, whom we humans mistreat with no compunction. I think of what I learned from my father and mother: "Before we can truly understand another person, we must walk a mile in their moccasins. Before we can walk in another person's moccasins, we must first take off our own."*
>
> *Whoever robbed Cherokee Woman's grave does not recognize his kinship with humans of cultures different from his own. He is someone who cannot walk a mile in another's moccasins.*

WITHERSTON ON THE WEB
Tuesday, March 14, 2017

NEWS
8:00 a.m.

Fire Victim May Be Molly Schlaughter

Molly Schlaughter, Mayor Rather's secretary, may have been the person who perished in Saturday evening's fishing shack fire. And she may have been Donna Dam.

According to a forensic DNA report from the Georgia Bureau of Investigation, the bones found in the fire's ashes were those of a 35-40-year-old female who was half Native American and half white.

Chief Jake McCoy and Detective Mev Arroyo were puzzled about the victim's identity until they received other information later in the day.

At a gathering at Gretchen Green and Neel Kingfisher's house Monday evening, Eric Schlaughter revealed that his mother, Molly Schlaughter, was half Cherokee and half white. He told Detective Arroyo that his mother had left their house on Saturday morning and had not returned. Detective Arroyo and Chief McCoy visited Molly Schlaughter's home, which she shared with her son and her current husband Deputy Sam Staples. They found evidence there that Molly Schlaughter was the daughter *of Donna June Jumper, who witnessed the collapse of the Kelly Barnes Dam on Sunday, November 6, 1977, at 1:30 a.m. Donna June Jumper considered herself to be a full-blooded Cherokee.*

Molly Schlaughter was born Molly Ann Jumper in Toccoa on August 1, 1978. She grew up in Rome, Georgia, where she married Nat Schlaughter. She kept his name when they divorced in 2015.

Detective Arroyo and Chief McCoy suspect that Mrs. Schlaughter authored the two letters to Witherston on the Web questioning the whereabouts of Mayor Rich Rather and Attorney Grant Griggs on the night the dam broke and asking them to take a paternity test. She signed those letters "Donna Dam."

The forensic DNA report also stated that traces of dynamite were found in the victim's soft tissue, supporting Chief McCoy's suspicion that the fire was deliberately ignited.

Amadahy Henderson, Reporter, and Catherine Perry-Soto, Editor

---

LETTERS TO THE EDITOR

To the Editor:

Here is a list of endangered species that have been found in Saloli Stream:
Holiday Darter (fish)
Flame Chub (fish)

Popeye Shiner (fish)
Piedmont Blue Burrower (crayfish)
*The Endangered Species Act of 1973 pro-
hibits actions which kill or injure endangered
wildlife "by significantly impairing essential be-
havioral patterns, including breeding, feeding,
or sheltering."*

*If Mayor Rather builds a dam and turns
Saloli Stream into a lake, he will break this law.*

Jaime Arroyo
Member of KNN
Witherston

To the Editor:

*I bet that the coyote who ate Buffy Saint-
Cherokí ate Pastor Clement's goat Esmerelda.*

Christopher Zurich
Witherston

NORTH GEORGIA IN HISTORY:
THE WITHERS
By Charlotte Byrd

*Withers Francis ("Witty") Withers, born in
1858, became a rabid proponent of racial purity
during Reconstruction. In the 1880s he published a series of 8-page pamphlets under the
rubric Essays for the Preservation of the White*

Race. In the one titled "God's Plan" Witty wrote, "In God's eternal and immutable rank order of living things, only the white race is fully human. Therefore miscegenation is an abomination equivalent to bestiality."

In 1881 Witty married the Savannah socialite Obedience Olmstead whom he had met at her debutante ball the previous Christmas. Although living in Dahlonega at the time, Witty had been invited to the prestigious event for his reputed wealth. He fathered a son in 1889, Hearty Harold Withers whom he called "HaHa," and a daughter in 1900, Penance Louise Withers.

HaHa pleased his parents. He graduated from the University of Georgia with a degree in history, married his second cousin Maud Olive McGillicuddy of Savannah, and in 1915 became father to Francis Hearty Withers, his only son. He registered for the draft in 1917 but was not called to service.

Penance Louise displeased her parents. In 1915 she joined the Georgia Young People's Suffrage Association and rode on a float in their Atlanta parade. In 1925, when her father marched on Washington with the Ku Klux Klan, she wrote a letter to the Atlanta Constitution protesting the state's anti-miscegenation law, which had been on the books since 1750. On Valentine's Day of 1930 she married her Cherokee lover Mohe Kingfisher in a private ceremony at the Lumpkin County Courthouse. Neither Witty nor Obedience attended the wedding. Witty disinherited her.

Witty Withers manifested what wisdom he possessed when he cashed out his stock in Antler

Rifles in 1928, 10 years after the end of World War I and 12 months before the Crash of 1929. He was financially liquid when stock prices plummeted and could be purchased for pennies. At his death in 1931 he left his entire fortune to HaHa.

After their marriage Penance Louise and Mohe moved to Tahlequah, Oklahoma, where his family welcomed them. They died together in a bus accident in 1931, shortly after their son Neel Kingfisher was born.

Orphaned at the age of 3 months, Neel Kingfisher was adopted by Cherokee relatives and raised as a Cherokee. He married Ayita Nance and fathered Neel Kingfisher, Jr., who became a physician.

Dr. Neel Kingfisher, Jr., and his wife lost their ten-year-old son to cancer. They divorced, and in 2013 he came to Witherston as director of Withers Retirement Village.

WEATHER

Partly cloudy skies all day. High of 55. Low of 45.

But starting at 11:30 p.m. we're going to have another rainy night in Georgia. Actually, a big storm. I feel like it's raining all over the world.

Tony Lima, Soothsayer

LOST AND FOUND

At 9:30 a.m. on Monday, March 13, Moki Pace of Tayanita Village reported finding a 14-foot-long dugout canoe in shrubbery along the bank of Tayanita Creek. If this canoe is yours, please email chiefatohipace@gmail.com.

CHAPTER 10

Tuesday Morning, March 14, 2017

W ould you all like a cup of coffee?" Jake asked. "Or a pastry?"

"I'm fine, thank you," Mev said.

"I'll take both," Sam said. He helped himself to black coffee and a vanilla frosted doughnut.

They took seats around Jake's pine conference table. Tracker dozed under Jake's chair.

"Am I a suspect in my wife's death?" Sam asked.

"No, Sam, of course not," Mev said. "We three cops are just putting our heads together to solve a mystery."

"Relax, Sam," Jake said. "Let's try to figure this out. We won't have full confirmation of the fire victim's identity until the GBI compares her DNA with the DNA in Molly's hairbrush. But let's assume that Molly was the individual who died in the explosion. Do you know why she might have gone to the Zamoras' shed on Saturday?"

"No."

"Have you ever been there?"

"I've seen the shed from Saloli Stream. I go fishing up the valley."

"I have to ask you, Sam," Jake said. "Did you suspect that Molly was Donna Dam?"

"No. You know, Molly and I are happily married, but we live our separate lives. She doesn't confide in me much."

Mev and Jake were listening to Sam's story about how he and Molly had met when Rich walked into Jake's office unannounced.

"I'm early, chief. I know I'm early. I wasn't supposed to come till ten. But I have to tell you something. I'll tell all three of you. You will find out soon enough." Rich was panting from the climb up the stairs.

"Have a seat, Rich." Jake gave the mayor his chair and leaned against the desk.

Rich peered under the chair at the sleeping bloodhound and sat down cautiously.

"Would you like a cup of coffee?" Mev asked. "A doughnut?"

"I'll take a doughnut."

"Thanks for coming, Rich."

"I've been blackmailed," Rich said. "Blackmailed. By my own secretary, I think. By Molly Schlaughter."

"You're referring to Donna Dam's letters to the editor," Mev asked.

"No, Mev. I am referring to blackmail. Real blackmail, like for money. For almost ten thousand dollars."

"Take a deep breath, Rich," Jake said. "Now tell us about it."

Rich described the email he'd received Friday morning from Donna Dam threatening to expose something he'd done on the night the dam broke if he didn't pay her nine thousand nine hundred dollars. He said he'd decided to pay her even though he'd done nothing wrong, that he'd gotten the cash from his safe at Rather Pre-Owned Vehicles in Dahlonega, and that he had delivered it to the wooden shed at four-thirty Saturday afternoon.

"I got there early," Rich said. "I get everywhere early. Old habit."

"Do you still have the email?" Jake asked.

"I deleted it."

"Did you see anyone near the shed?" Sam asked. "Or hear anyone?"

"No. I just went inside. I was instructed to leave the money on the table, and I did. I left it in a manila envelope. Then I drove away as fast as I could. This morning when I read on *Webby Witherston* that the fatality was probably Molly, and that Molly was probably Donna Dam, I was afraid you all would think I killed her and burned her up."

"Why would we think you killed her, Mayor Rather?" Mev asked.

"Because Donna Dam who was Molly Schlaughter who was my secretary wrote those nasty letters about Grant and me being in Toccoa the night the dam broke."

Jake turned to Sam. "You don't have to stay, Sam. Go on home. The news that your wife was a blackmailer must be hard to bear, so soon after you've learned of her death."

"Or her probable death," Mev said.

"I'd rather stay," Sam said. "I don't want to go home to an empty house."

"Take the day off," Jake said. "The two of us can handle the interviews."

Sam left.

"Mr. Mayor, what were you and Grant Griggs doing in Toccoa on the night the Kelly Barnes Dam broke?" Mev asked.

"I can't remember much. We went fishing, even though, as you know, it rained that day. I think we may have played pool at a pizza joint that night. But we're talking about forty years ago. Can you all remember what you did forty years ago?"

"I don't. I was four years old," Mev said.

"I remember that Sunday morning," Jake said. "I was fourteen. Our minister told us about the flood in church."

"Well, I was twenty. A colt. And feeling my oats."

"Why did you pay Donna Dam?" Jake asked.

"I have a political career to worry about, Chief. I can't let whatever I did forty years ago hurt the good reputation I have built here since then. I'll pay whatever I have to pay to keep it. Wouldn't you?"

"I'm not a politician," Jake said.

"Well, I am. Anyway, Donna Dam, or Molly Schlaughter, was not an honest blackmailer. She sent the second letter to *Webby Witherston* before I had a chance to give her the money. At least her letters will stop now."

"Let me ask you about Molly Schlaughter," Mev said. "Do you know how old she is?"

"Yes, I do. Of course I do. I hired her. She's thirty-nine, turning forty in August. First of August, I think it is. Why?"

"Could she be your daughter, Mr. Mayor?"

"My what?"

"Your daughter. Could you have slept with her mother the night the dam broke?"

"What?"

"Could you be her father? Think. What did you do the night the dam broke?"

"Maybe I was with a girl. I don't remember. That was forty years ago. I slept with lots of girls then. I wasn't this fat. Who is Molly's mother?"

Mev and Jake exchanged glances. Jake nodded.

"Molly's mother was a high school student named Donna Jumper," Mev said. "Have you ever heard that name?"

"Donna Jumper? Donna Jumper. Well, I absolutely never heard the name Jumper. I would have remembered it. Maybe I met a Donna that night," Rich said. He paused and then continued. "Maybe I slept with a girl that night, and maybe her name was Donna."

"Do you remember where that might have been?"

"Hey, I'm the mayor, the duly elected, respectable mayor of Witherston. Do I have to answer your questions about my personal life forty years ago? I say no."

Mayor Rather stood up.

"Would you be willing to take a paternity test, Mr. Mayor?" Jake asked. "Would you be willing to have your DNA used for a paternity test?"

"No! Of course not. Okay, yes, maybe. I've done nothing wrong."

"Thank you, Mr. Mayor. We'll be in touch."

"You all are going to ruin my reputation," Rich said as he opened the office door. "You know Grant was in Toccoa too that night," he added.

"Where was Grant when the dam broke?" Jake asked.

"Grant was with me," Rich said. "I mean, Grant and I were both in Toccoa. We'd gone up there together. I have no idea where he spent the evening."

Thank you, Mayor Rather," Mev said as Rich slammed the door behind him.

"Whew," Mev said.

"Wow, Mev. That's a bombshell. Molly Schlaughter, also known as Donna Dam, used the fishing shack to collect blackmail money."

"And was killed there."

"By whom?"

"By someone she was blackmailing, probably."

"Do you suspect our duly elected, respectable mayor?"

"No. I think our respectable mayor is not competent enough to have blown her up without blowing himself up with her."

Five minutes later, Grant Griggs entered.

"Hello, Chief. Hello, Mev."

"Hello, Grant. Have a seat," Jake said. "Would you like a cup of coffee?"

"No, thanks. I'd just like to get down to business. I'm in a hurry."

"Okay. We'll be quick and direct with you, Mr. Griggs," Mev said. "Have you been blackmailed in the last few days?"

"Me? No! Of course not. Heavens no. What could I be blackmailed for?"

"Let me ask you again. Have you paid any money to stop Donna Dam's letters to *Webby Witherston*?"

"Let me answer you again. No."

"Does the name Donna Jumper mean anything to you?" Mev asked.

"No."

"Did you have a sexual encounter in Toccoa on the night the Kelly Barnes Dam broke?" Jake asked.

"I don't recall! What is this? I thought I was invited for a conversation. This is an interrogation."

"Do you want a lawyer?"

"No. I am a lawyer! Why would I need another lawyer?"

"Just asking," Jake said. "Would you consent to a paternity test?"

"What are you getting at, folks? You need to tell me."

"Okay," Mev said. "You know we have evidence that Donna Dam is Molly Schlaughter."

"I can read."

"We also have reason to believe that Molly

Schlaughter was the daughter of Donna Jumper, who was a sixteen-year-old junior at Stephens County High School when she got pregnant. Molly was born on August 1, 1978, just about nine months after the dam broke."

"So? What implicates me?"

"In her first letter to *Witherston on the Web* Donna Dam—that is, Molly—asked you where you were on the night of November 5, 1977. In her second letter she challenged you and Mayor Rather to take a paternity test. It's likely that Molly is dead now. So we are asking you on her behalf. Would you consent to our using your DNA, which you gave Monday night, for a paternity test?"

"Do I have a choice?"

"Your DNA is already being analyzed, so we are simply asking your permission to compare your DNA with Molly's DNA," Jake said.

"Do you think Molly's my daughter?"

"We'd like to rule you out, Mr. Griggs," Mev said.

"How thoughtful of you," Grant said. "Okay, you can compare my DNA to hers."

"Molly's DNA test showed she was half Cherokee, half white," Jake said. "Donna Jumper considered herself a full-blooded Cherokee. We're looking to see who was responsible for Molly's white genes."

"I don't sleep with Indians."

"I have one last question, Grant," Jake said. "Where were you and Rich when the dam broke?"

"In my van. We heard the rumbling. We drove back to Athens right away."

"I too have one last question, Mr. Griggs," Mev said. "Where were you this past Saturday afternoon from four to seven?"

"God in heaven! You all are interrogating me. Well, I don't have an alibi, unless you count fish as witnesses. I was fishing, up the valley."

"In a canoe?"

"Now why would you ask that? The answer is no. I was fishing off the bank."

"The east bank or the west bank?"

"The east bank."

"You would have gone past the Zamoras' fishing shack on your way up Witherston Highway. Did you notice anything unusual there?"

"Now are you asking me whether I lit the fire? I did not. And I did not kill Molly Schlaughter. I was nowhere near that cabin. I didn't go that far up the valley."

"Did you catch any fish, Grant?" Jake asked.

"No, I did not. The fish weren't biting."

"Thanks, Mr. Griggs. We appreciate your coming in."

෴

Amadahy was waiting for Grant on the steps. She rushed up to him with a microphone.

"Mr. Griggs, do you think you could be Eric Schlaughter's grandfather?"

"What? What are you talking about, Ms. Henderson?"

"Eric's mother, Molly Schlaughter, wanted you to take a paternity test. She must have thought you could be her father."

"I am not her father. I could not be her father." Grant said.

"Why would Ms. Schlaughter think you or Mayor Rather was her father?"

"She wants money. Isn't money the reason for every paternity suit?"

"She is dead now. But if you are Eric's grandfather, you may owe Eric some child support."

"So that's what this is all about?"

"Have you thought about reparations, Mr. Griggs?"

"No, Ms. Henderson, I have not. Now please excuse me."

✌✍

"I bet that Grant paid blackmail. What do you think, Mev?" Jake poured Mev a cup of coffee after Grant had departed.

"I bet he did. Ten thousand dollars would be small change to him."

"Do you think he killed her?"

"He had the opportunity, Jake. Apparently he didn't bump into Rich there. At least not according to Rich. But I can't believe Grant would do it. He's not my favorite person, but he's a respectable member of our community."

"Respectable. Like our duly elected mayor."

"And his wife is on the Town Council."

"Let's think. Who would benefit from Molly's death?"

"Anybody else she's blackmailing. Anybody who wants the dam built. How about Red Wilker?"

"We should talk to him. But how about Sam? We can't overlook Molly's husband, Mev. Most murders are domestic affairs."

"Why would Sam want her dead?"

"Money?"

"Let's find out whether Rich or Grant is Molly's father. You'll have to ask Who R U to send samples of Grant's and Rich's DNA to the GBI."

"I'll do it now," Jake said.

Jake emailed Who R U to authorize the transfer of the DNA samples and then emailed Marcus Melton a request to compare Grant's and Rich's DNA with Molly's.

"Marcus works fast, Mev," Jake said. "We should get our answer by Thursday."

Catherine entered Jake's office.

"Good morning, Chief McCoy. Good morning, Detective Arroyo. Good morning, Tracker."

"Good morning, Catherine. What brings you here?" Jake pulled a chair out for her.

"I've found some records that will interest you all." Catherine set several computer print-outs on the table. They were records from the Lumpkin County Tax Assessor's Office.

"Sit down, Catherine," Mev said, glancing at the top document. "These will certainly interest us."

"Grant Griggs and Red. Wilker have bought more than forty acres of land in Saloli Valley. Just within the past year."

"Land where the lake could be?"

"Yes. When I was looking at the Lumpkin County parcel map of the Zamora property, I discovered that Red Wilker owned the property next to the Zamoras on Cattleguard Lane. That surprised me. Mr. Wilker had bought it in September of 2016 from some people in Big Canoe who had kept it as an investment. It never went on the market. Phyllis Graph handled the sale. Look at this Parcel Information Table."

"Witherston will have to buy up this land if the mayor builds his dam," Jake said.

"You've got a big story, Catherine," Mev said.

"There's more. Out of curiosity I looked at the sixteen acres in Saloli Valley next to the orchard where Neel and Gretchen live. Mr. Griggs bought that piece of property on Bear Hollow Road from Mrs. Parker in August of 2016, when she went to an old folks place in Athens. It never went on the market. Griggs got it for fifty-five thousand dollars. It included Mrs. Parker's house, which was falling apart."

"Did you notice any other recent purchases in Saloli Valley, Catherine?"

"One. Mr. Wilker bought eleven acres on the west bank of Saloli Stream from an Atlanta investor named Trent Uptide who used it for hunting. It's just north of Withers Fork on West Bank Road. Purchase date is October of 2016. It never went on the market either. Phyllis Graph was the silent realtor."

"Molly could have heard about the sales from Rich," Jake said. "Being in the mayor's office, she could have overheard the mayor talking."

"I called Blanca Zamora and learned that Mrs. Graph had offered to buy their vineyard. But they're not selling," Catherine said.

"When did Mayor Rather first mention he wanted a lake here?" Mev asked.

"Last summer, at Witherston's Fourth of July barbecue," Catherine said. "I reported in *Webby Witherston* that Mayor Rather had declared that he would make Witherston the most beautiful town in the country by developing a lake here. I thought it was a campaign promise."

"And he got reelected," Jake said.

"I was there, but I don't remember his speech," Mev said.

"Nobody does," Catherine said. "Do you all know anybody who pays attention to what Mayor Rather says?"

"I don't," Mev said.

"I don't," Jake said.

"Grant and Red pay attention to Mayor Rather's declarations," Mev said. "He's the mayor. If Mighty were the mayor they would pay attention to his bark."

"I called Mr. Griggs and Mr. Wilker," Catherine

said. "Mr. Wilker said he bought the Armour and Uptide properties for hunting and fishing. Mr. Griggs said he bought Mrs. Parker's property as a favor to her. He was her lawyer. Personally, I think he stole it from her. You know she couldn't think straight anymore."

"Let's go over to Wilker's Gun Shop, Jake. I'll drive," Mev said.

"Okay. Tracker, stay here."

Tracker opened one eye and went back to sleep.

"I'll go write my Pulitzer-Prize article," Catherine said.

PARCEL INFORMATION TABLE	
Selected Parcel	176B2 A021 (Click for Complete Card)
Class Code (NOTE: Not Zoning Info)	R4
Taxing District	Lumpkin County - General
Acres	16.1
OWNERSHIP INFORMATION	
Name	GRANT HEMMINGS GRIGGS
Mailing Address	47 PINE STREET WITHERSTON, GA 30533
Situs/Physical Address	3500 BEAR HOLLOW ROAD WITHERSTON, GA 30533
VALUES	
Land Value	$55,000.00
Improvement Value	$0.00
Accessory Value	$0.00
Total Value	$55,000.00

LAST 2 SALES		
Date	Price	Purchaser
08-2016	$55,000	GRANT HEMMINGS GRIGGS WITHERSTON, GA
06-1962	$42,500	ROBERT ALVIN PARKER DAHLONEGA, GA

Website last updated March 10, 2017
GIS Maps last updated March 10, 2017

PARCEL INFORMATION TABLE	
Selected Parcel	185B3 A011 (Click for Complete Card)
Class Code (NOTE: Not Zoning Info)	R4
Taxing District	Lumpkin County - General
Acres	15.7
OWNERSHIP INFORMATION	
Name	REDFORD ARNOLD WILKER
Mailing Address	3950 BLACK FOX ROAD WITHERSTON, GA 30533
Situs/Physical Address	2600 CATTLEGUARD LANE WITHERSTON, GA 30533
VALUES	
Land Value	$53,500.00
Improvement Value	$0.00
Accessory Value	$0.00
Total Value	$53,500.00

LAST 2 SALES

Date	Price	Purchaser
09-2016	$53,500	REDFORD ARNOLD WILKER WITHERSTON, GA
01-1981	$34,000	ARMY AND CAROL ARMOUR BIG CANOE, GA

Website last updated March 10, 2017
GIS Maps last updated March 10, 2017

PARCEL INFORMATION TABLE	
Selected Parcel	123G3 C123 (Click for Complete Card)
Class Code (NOTE: Not Zoning Info)	R4
Taxing District	Lumpkin County - General
Acres	11.2
OWNERSHIP INFORMATION	
Name	REDFORD A. WILKER
Mailing Address	3950 BLACK FOX ROAD WITHERSTON, GA 30533
Situs/Physical Address	3600 WEST BANK ROAD WITHERSTON, GA 30533
VALUES	
Land Value	$31,000.00
Improvement Value	$0.00
Accessory Value	$0.00
Total Value	$31,000.00

LAST 2 SALES

Date	Price	Purchaser
10-2016	$31,000	REDFORD A. WILKER WITHERSTON, GA
02-1999	$29,400	TRENT F. UPTIDE DAHLONEGA, GA

Website last updated March 10, 2017
GIS Maps last updated March 10, 2017

espe

"Handsome bear, Red," Jake said as he and Mev entered Wilker's Gun Shop.

"Good morning, Chief. Hello, Mev. That's Bearwithus. I plugged him last Halloween when he was rooting through my garbage. Remember? It was legal. Now what can I do today for the Witherston Police? Do you all need guns?"

"Not guns, Red. We need information. Is there a place where we can talk?"

"We can go into the back. Grace can stay up front."

Mev looked at the bumper sticker taped to the door that Red opened for them: *YOU'RE IN RANGE. BE NICE TO ME.* They entered a dimly lit room full of dead animals, all stuffed. A bobcat on a seven-foot-high tree stump, a raccoon clinging to the bark, a possum on the branch of a dead pine, and an alligator on the floor against the wall. In the corner, a flagstone fishpond, four feet in diameter, with a dozen live goldfish and aquatic plants. A stuffed otter lying on the adjacent boulder. A stuffed rattlesnake curled up beside the boulder with a tiny sign that said *RATTLESNAKE ROUNDUP, WHIGHAM, GEORGIA.* On the wall, a mounted black bear head, a mounted boar head, a mounted deer head with ten-point antlers, and a mounted bass that once weighed twenty pounds. On the copper plaque, Mev read *KISS MY BASS.*

"This is a zombie zoo," Mev whispered to Jake, as they followed Red past a stuffed beaver.

"I heard that," Red said. He opened another door and ushered them into a room with a small metal table and four card table chairs, a Coca-Cola machine, and a cabinet labeled *FIRECRACKERS, SKY ROCKETS, ROMAN CANDLES, SPARKLERS.*

"Coca-Cola anyone?"

"No, thanks, Red," Jake said. "I see you sell fireworks as well as guns."

"I can sell you anything that goes bang," Red said. "I made a couple hundred dollars right before the fourth."

"Do you carry dynamite?"

"I can get it for you in a day. You fixing to blow something up, Chief?"

"No, Red. And we're not here to buy anything."

"They sat down.

"Let us be quick, Mr. Wilker," Mev said. "Have you been blackmailed?"

"What? What are you talking about?"

"Let me put it another way. Did Donna Dam, whom we know to be Molly Schlaughter, blackmail you? Did she send you an email demanding a sum of money?"

"What would I be blackmailed for?"

"Perhaps for buying up land with advance knowledge of the mayor's plans for a lake," Mev said.

"So the reporter talked to you all."

"She did. But right now we're investigating a murder," Jake said.

"We just want to check you off our list of possible suspects, Red," Mev said.

"Thank you kindly. Can we just be friendly about all this?"

"Sure. We're investigating a murder in a friendly way," Jake said.

"Well, I didn't kill her."

"Did you receive an email from Donna Dam requesting money?"

"Not that I know of. I don't check my email regularly."

"Where were you last Saturday afternoon between four and seven?"

"I closed shop and went fishing. By myself. On Saloli Stream. No alibi."

"Where was Grace?"

"In Dahlonega, shopping, all afternoon."

"Thanks, Red," Jake said. "We'll get back to you."

"Goodbye, Mr. Wilker," Mev said, as she and Jake walked by the dead animals to the front of the store.

"Goodbye, Grace," Jake said.

They got into Mev's Camry.

"Well, Mev, do you think Red paid blackmail?"

"Yes, Jake. I think both Red and Grant brought money to the cabin."

"That would make a heap of cash on the table. Nine thousand nine hundred from Rich, probably a similar amount from Grant, and something from Red. Whoever arrived last could have picked up the others' donations, shot Molly, set the fire, and left."

"If one had seen the other, then the two of them know who did it. And they're both covering up."

"Maybe Red and Grant arrived at the same time and committed the murder and arson together."

"And one of them happened to have dynamite in his car? I don't see that, Jake. Red and Grant have lived in Witherston for a long time. They have a lot of friends. I can imagine they'd pay blackmail to preserve their reputations, but I can't imagine they'd kill anybody."

"And Hernando says he didn't keep dynamite in the shack. I believe him."

"Jake, perhaps there were two blackmailers, Molly and the man in the canoe, who probably set the fire."

"We need to find the man in the canoe."

"The boys call him 'Canoe Man,' Jake. They think he tried to kill Beau. I'm starting to think he was Molly's accomplice, as well as her murderer. Here's a theory. After Rich, Grant, and Red had left the cash in the shack,

Sam killed her, pocketed the money, set fire to the cabin, and escaped in Hernando's canoe down Tayanita Creek."

"Do you think Sam is the murderer, Mev?"

"I hate to come to that conclusion, but I don't see who else it could be. Molly may have confided in Sam, shown him her mother's letter, and hatched the blackmail scheme with him. Maybe he thought up the blackmail scheme himself. They may have driven to the cabin together in Molly's truck, with the dynamite and the gasoline. They could have planned ahead of time to explode the cabin."

"How would they have known about the cabin, and about the canoe there?"

"Eric went there occasionally to smoke marijuana with Hernando. Eric could have told them about the shack."

"Mev, could Eric have been in on the blackmail?"

"Good gracious! That hadn't crossed my mind. Eric seems like a good kid. A good kid with bad parents. I doubt that he was involved."

"Eric's had a tough life. Now his mother is dead, his biological father is on the lam, and his stepfather may be a murderer headed to prison."

"We've got to bring Sam in for questioning again, immediately, Jake. This afternoon, if possible. And let's talk to Eric too."

"Let's think about this in my office while we eat our sandwiches."

℮∕℈℮∕℈

Jake's desk phone rang. Jake picked it up.

"Chief McCoy speaking…Hello, Hernando…Thanks so much for telling me…Yes, this is very helpful."

Jake turned to Mev. "Hernando's canoe showed up at

Tayanita Village. Hernando just picked it up. He says he found a red nylon jacket stuffed under the seat. It had the emblem for Rather Pre-Owned Vehicles stitched on the back. Says there's a pink gun in the pocket. It smells of gun powder."

"Oh, no," Mev said.

"Looks like our mayor needs to be arrested," Jake said.

"Oh, no."

CHAPTER 11

Tuesday Afternoon, March 14, 2017

At five to twelve Beau arrived at Gretchen's Grocery. Sally was already there, seated at Gretchen's back table, where Gretchen had laid out a red checked cotton tablecloth, blue handmade ceramic plates, and a very realistic ceramic owl that held a thick candle. Sally had on a short blue-jeans skirt, a red KNN sweatshirt, and knee-high black leather boots. She wore her long blonde hair in one long braid.

"You look nice, Sally," Beau said.

"You do too, Beau, even with that white bandage wrapped around your head."

Beau was wearing khaki pants and a navy turtle-neck sweater. He'd dressed up for his date.

Beau shook Sally's hand, sat down, looked at the owl, and hooted, *"Who-cooks-for-you, who-cooks-for-you-all."*

"Wow, you sound just like a barred owl, Beau. I'm impressed."

"Me too," Beau said, smiling. "Eric taught me that call."

Gretchen brought out a potato-leek soup, collard greens, and home-made whole wheat rolls.

"Thanks for going out with me, Sally. How did your parents react when you told them we were having lunch together?"

"Mom was happy. I didn't mention it to Dad."

"Would he have objected?"

"I don't know. Probably not. He says he's not racist, but he also says people should marry only their own kind."

"Oh. I understand."

"I don't. I say he's racist. He defines 'kind' as color. I define 'kind' as species. I say people should marry only their own species."

"*Homo sapiens* married Neanderthals forty thousand years ago."

"I wonder what their weddings were like."

"If my mother had thought like your father I wouldn't be here."

"And that would be terrible."

"Would your father want you to go out with Eric? Eric is one-fourth Cherokee."

"He wouldn't know if nobody told him, and if Eric cut off his pony tail."

"I wish everybody were of mixed race. Then you all would think I'm normal."

"You're normal, Beau! You're better than normal. You're super."

Gretchen brought out a freshly baked apple pie and cut them each a slice.

"I have to tell you something I just figured out, Sally, but you have to keep it confidential. For now."

"I promise."

"Sally, someone is trying to kill me."

Beau told her about the previous Saturday's events on Blue Boulder, the whole story. He left nothing out.

"Jorge, Jaime, and I think Canoe Man set the fire.

And if he did, he was probably the one who killed Eric's mother. That's why he said 'shit' when he saw us."

"Not a big deal, Beau. Everybody says 'shit,' even my mother."

"If Canoe Man were innocent he would have yelled 'Hey.'"

"Why would he want to kill you, and not Jorge or Jaime?"

"I heard his voice, Sally. He knows that. And he knows me. So he tried to kill me."

"Did you recognize his voice?"

"It sounded familiar on Saturday, but I couldn't place it. Yesterday when I saw Eric at the DNA party I realized whose voice it was."

"Whose?"

"Eric's stepfather, Deputy Sam Staples. I know him. I've been to Eric's house. He knows me."

"Eric's stepfather? That's freaky scary, Beau."

"Right. Freaky scary."

"Do you think Eric is involved?'

"I don't think so. At least I don't want to think so. Eric's my friend. And I'm Eric's friend. He doesn't have any other real friends, except maybe Hernando, and of course Jorge and Jaime."

"Eric couldn't have set the fire. He was with you all."

"Eric left us before the explosion. After the explosion but right before Canoe Man paddled by Blue Boulder we heard a barred owl hoot up on the ridge. Jorge and I thought it was Eric, not an owl. I thought Eric might have been warning us of something. Earlier that day he'd said that if he hooted he'd be sending us a signal of danger."

"Did you ask him?"

"Jaime asked him. Eric said it was an owl. Then

Sunday night my family was at Lottie's house for dinner. After dinner we heard a barred owl hoot in the woods. Then two shots. Jaime and Jorge and I ran outside, and I got hit. I'm wondering if Eric was warning us. Maybe he was there, and maybe he knew his father was going to shoot me."

"You have to tell Mrs. Arroyo."

"I know. But I'm afraid she'll arrest Eric, and I don't want to get Eric in trouble unless he was involved, like if he was an accessory after the fact. First, I need to make sure Eric didn't know about the blackmail."

"Do you think you're in danger, Beau?"

"For sure."

"Could you talk to Eric?"

"I'll try, but he's not answering his cell phone these days."

☙❦❧

Mev and Jake walked into Mayor Rather's office at one-fifteen. Jake shut the door.

"Hello, officers," Rich said. "To what do I owe the honor of your unexpected visit?" He pulled out chairs for them at his small conference table.

"We're here on sad business, Mr. Mayor," Mev said.

"We're arresting you on suspicion of murder," Jake said.

"Whose murder?"

"Molly Schlaughter."

"What? What are you talking about? I didn't kill her. Not me. I didn't kill her."

"Your jacket was found in a canoe that was taken from the fishing shack right before the fire."

"I told you I went to the shack to leave my blackmail money. But Molly wasn't there. Nobody was there. I didn't kill anybody. I wouldn't kill anybody. Why would I kill anybody?"

"Do you own a red jacket with a Rather Pre-Owned Vehicles emblem on the back?"

"Yes. I wear it all the time. It helps business."

"Where is it now?"

"Right here." Rich went to the coat rack where three or four jackets were hung on top of each other. "Well, I thought it was here. This is where I keep it."

"When did you wear it last, Rich?" Mev asked.

"I don't remember. Oh, yes, I do. I wore it Saturday afternoon."

"To the fishing shack?"

"Yes. Maybe I left it there."

"Do you own a gun? A nine millimeter handgun?"

"Yes. I bought it on Saturday. From Red. It was pink. Embarrassing."

"May I see it?"

"Sure," Rich said. Then he hesitated. "Uh, oh. It's in my jacket pocket."

"One matching that description was found there," Jake said.

"Shit! But I didn't use it. I swear! I didn't use it. I never took it out of my pocket. I just bought it for self-defense."

"I am sorry, Rich, but I have to take you in." Jake brought out a pair of handcuffs.

"Don't cuff me, Jake. Please. I'll go with you willingly. Well, not willingly. Shit. This is ridiculous. Ridiculous. I'm innocent. Mev, could you please call Rhonda?"

"You have the right to remain silent."

"I know, I know. You don't have to tell me."

Jake continued. "Anything you say or do may be used against you in a court of law. You have the right to consult an attorney before speaking to the police and to have an attorney present during questioning now or in the future."

"Okay, okay!"

"If you cannot afford an attorney, one will be appointed for you."

"Don't insult me. I can afford one. Mev, please call Grant."

"I'll call Grant, Rich. And I'll call Rhonda," Mev said.

"I'm being framed," Rich said. "Framed. But I can't figure out who doesn't like me, except for Donna Dam."

"Who may be your daughter," Jake said.

As they got up from the table, they heard a knock on the door.

"What's going on?" Amadahy asked.

അഐഅ

WWW.ONLINEWITHERSTON.COM

WITHERSTON ON THE WEB
Tuesday, March 14, 2017

BREAKING NEWS
2:30 p.m.

Mayor Rather Is Arrested for Murder

Mayor Rich Rather was taken into custody at 1:15 p.m. today on suspicion of the murder of Molly Schlaughter.

Here are the facts:

On Saturday, March 11, between 6:30 and 7:00 p.m., the fishing shack on the property of

*Ernesto and Blanca Zamora exploded. Minutes
later Beau Lodge and Jaime and Jorge Arroyo,
who witnessed the fireball from Blue Boulder,
saw a man in a canoe paddle down Tayanita
Creek. In the dark they couldn't identify the
man. A dugout canoe was later found hidden in
rhododendron bushes on the bank of Tayanita
Creek near Tayanita Village. It was reclaimed
by its owner, Hernando Zamora, age 17, who
had kept it in the fishing shack and assumed it
had burned in the fire. Hernando discovered a
jacket labeled "Rather Pre-Owned Vehicles"
shoved under the seat. The jacket, size XXL, belonged to the mayor. A pink 9 mm handgun was
in its pocket. The remains of Molly Schlaughter
were found in the ashes of the fire. She was posi-
tively identified by her DNA. Her death was at-
tributed to a 9 mm bullet through her skull.*

*According to Chief Jake McCoy, Mayor Ra-
ther had purchased a 9 mm handgun from
Wilker's Gun Shop that Saturday morning. Today Mayor Rather could not produce the gun.*

*The mayor said he went to the fishing shack
on Saturday afternoon at 4:30 to pay $9,900
blackmail to a person who called herself Donna
Dam, who had threatened to expose his activities in Toccoa on the night the dam broke, November 5-6, 1977.*

*Donna Dam has been identified as Molly
Schlaughter. Molly Schlaughter was the daughter of the late Donna June Jumper of Toccoa.
Molly Schlaughter was born on August 1, 1978,
almost nine months after the dam broke.*

*Chief McCoy said, "I am disappointed to
say that strong circumstantial evidence incrimi-*

*nates our two-term mayor in the murder of his
secretary, who had publicly challenged him to
take a paternity test in letters to the editor she
had signed Donna Dam."*

*Grant Griggs, who was also challenged by
Donna Dam to take a paternity test, said,
"There's no evidence that Mr. Rather was at the
shack at the time the murder occurred." Mr.
Griggs is Mayor Rather's attorney and lifelong
friend.*

Amadahy Henderson, Reporter

છ૭છ૭

"You are one dumb stump, Rich. Why in God's crea-
tion did you buy a gun?"

Rhonda was visiting her husband in the same jail cell
she had occupied with Dan Soto when she was arrested
for releasing chickens from his chicken truck.

"I was delivering money to a blackmailer, Rhonda. I
thought she might do me harm. I didn't know then that
Donna Dam was Molly."

"Why didn't you tell me about this?"

"You'd have pitched a hissy fit and stopped me."

"And you wouldn't be resting your fat ass here on
this bench."

"Could you scold me later, Rhonda? You need to
help me now."

"Okay. I'll scold you when you get out of jail."

"Thanks."

"Did you walk into the shack holding your gun?"

"Good god, no! It was pink. I had it in my jacket
pocket. That's why I wore a jacket."

"Your red nylon jacket?"

"Yeah."

"Okay, Rich. So what did you see when you went into the shack."

"An old pine table, square. Two old wooden chairs. Fishing gear, like poles and nets and buckets. A collection of flies and lures mounted on a wall board. And stacks of Zamora wine crates."

"What was on the table?"

"A couple of empty cans of Diet Coke. And a dirty ashtray."

"Was Molly a smoker?"

"No. Don't think so. But I smelled cigarette smoke in the shack, come to think of it."

"Did you see any firecrackers?"

"No."

"Gasoline cans?"

"No."

"Did you see a canoe? A dugout canoe?"

Rich closed his eyes for a moment. "No. No, I didn't."

"You're sure?"

"I'm sure."

"Where did you leave your jacket?"

"On a chair. I took it off while I recounted my money. I put the money, almost ten thousand dollars, in a manila envelope and left it on the table. Then I got out of there."

"Leaving your jacket with the gun in the pocket?"

"Yes."

"Lord in heaven, Rich! What do you use for brains?"

"Please, Rhonda."

"Did you see any vehicles parked nearby?"

"No. I didn't look back. I drove away as fast as I could."

"You have to tell Jake all this."

"I'll talk to Grant."

"You're gonna talk to Jake, Rich, or I'm not bothering with you anymore. You hear?"

"I hear."

e/se/s

When Rhonda exited the police station she encountered Christopher Zurich on the steps. He was holding a sign that said: *SAVE POPEYE SHINERS—SAY NO TO DAM RATHER.*

"Hello, Mrs. Rather," Christopher said. "Could you please take my picture and send it to the mayor?" He stood up and positioned the sign to show off his white KNN sweatshirt.

"Happy to do so, Christopher," Rhonda said.

She took his picture with her phone. She said nothing about her husband's current whereabouts.

e/se/s

Beau, his ear still bandaged, was watching Jorge and Jaime toss frisbees to Mighty and Sequoyah in the Arroyos' back yard when his cell phone rang.

"Who's Trig Morton?" Beau asked, looking at his caller ID.

"He owns the Yona Gas Station, where Eric works," Jaime said.

"Hello," Beau said. "Oh, it's you, Eric…Sure. That's fine. Come before dinner. Mom and Dad will be here by seven." Beau disconnected.

"What's happening with Eric?"

"He wants to spend the night with me."

"He must be upset about his mother."

"He didn't show it last night."

"Maybe he's had a fight with his stepfather," Beau said.

ოჯო

Neel read Carter Ellis's email aloud as Gretchen poured their wine, an Antonio Machado red from Zamora Wines.

"'From: Carter Ellis, PhD, Office of State Archaeologist
To: Neel Kingfisher, MD,
Re: DNA report

"'Tuesday, March 14, 2017, 6:01 p.m.

"'Hey, Neel.

"'Great to see you yesterday. Thanks for inviting me to the burial site. I enjoyed meeting your intelligent young companions. Please give my greetings to Jorge, Jaime, and Beau.

"'I have good news. The lab recovered enough DNA in the bones to identify ethnic heritage. You'll get an official report by snail mail in the next week or so, but I can give you the gist of it now.

"'You were right. The skeleton belonged to an adult young woman 18-20 years old of Native American descent. The DNA analysis identifies her as 99 percent Native American, 1 percent undetermined.

"'But here's a big surprise for you. The eight-month fetus the woman was carrying was only half Native American. The DNA analysis identifies the fetus as 50 percent Native American, 45 percent British and Irish, 4 percent northern European, 1 percent undetermined. The fetus was female.

"'Now ain't them some bones! One of Saloli Valley's early white settlers made love to that Cherokee lady and got her with child! I hope he brought her flowers.

"'Oops, I almost forgot to tell you. The lady had syphilis.

"'But the lady did not die from the disease. She died from a .45 caliber bullet through her head.

"'I'll buy you a bourbon next time you're in Atlanta, Neel, and we can imagine what went on in Saloli Valley two hundred years ago.

"'Have a good evening.

"'Carter'"

"Neel, the Cherokee woman was raped! And the rapist gave her syphilis!"

"Whoa, Gretchen. Have a sip of wine. Maybe the sex was consensual. Maybe she loved the white man, the way my white grandmother loved my Cherokee grandfather. Love crosses borders, you know."

"And she got syphilis from her white lover?"

"Maybe she gave syphilis to her white lover. Syphilis was a new world disease. The Native Americans sent syphilis back to Europe with Columbus."

"Whose men spread it all over Europe."

"Women helped, Gretchen."

They sat down to their seafood stew, which Gretchen made with shrimp, scallops, and squid, all fresh from the

Georgia coast, plus a bit of paprika, red pepper flakes, saffron, and sherry.

"Neel, did you read Lottie's column on Sunday? She wrote that Hearty Withers had syphilis."

"Jeepers! So I'm connected to the Cherokee woman through my white Withers ancestors, and not my Cherokee ancestors?"

"Maybe both. Your great great great grandfather Withers may have had a tryst with your great great great Cherokee grandmother's sister."

"I doubt it, Gretchen."

"I don't."

Neel looked at Carter's email again. "The fetus's father had British or Irish ancestry," he said.

"Like the Withers," Gretchen said. "Will you forward Carter's message to Lottie? Lottie will want to write about it."

"Will do."

"How about to Catherine?"

"Of course. This is big news. A real cold case."

CHAPTER 12

Tuesday Evening, March 14, 2017

M om, I invited Eric to dinner and to spend the night," Beau said as his mother walked in the door carrying a canvas bag full of groceries.

"How thoughtful, Beau. When will Eric get here?"

"He was supposed to come over when he got off work."

"I'll cook spaghetti and meatballs."

"I'll call Eric."

Beau did. He had to leave voicemail.

"Eric," Beau said. "Please call me when you get this message. It's almost seven-thirty. We thought you'd be here by now."

At eight, Beau, Lauren, and Jim sat down for dinner without Eric. Beau told his parents he'd recognized Deputy Staples's voice.

"I think Deputy Staples was mad when he saw us because he thought we'd seen him. I bet he killed Eric's mother."

"We need to inform Mev," Lauren said. "Tonight. If Deputy Staples killed Eric's mother he could kill again."

"Eric should have called me by now."

"Call Mev," Jim said to Lauren. "Tell her we're coming over."

"Without Sequoyah, this time," Lauren said to Beau.

സ

Lottie was reading Carter Ellis's DNA report to her family when the Lodges arrived.

"Come in," Mev said as she opened the front door for her friends. "We're all here."

"Hello," Doolittle said from his perch on Jaime's arm.

"Hello, Doolittle," Lauren said.

Lauren hugged Mev and greeted Jorge, Jaime, Paco, and Lottie. Jorge lay on the floor rubbing Mighty's belly, and Jaime sat beside him with Doolittle on his wrist. Doolittle was holding a piece of uncooked penne pasta. Lottie and Paco sipped tea at the dining room table.

"You all are in time for dessert," Paco said. "Mint tea and brownies for everybody?"

"Thanks," Beau said. "We accept your offer."

"Thanks," Doolittle said.

"We're here to talk to you about a police officer, Mev. Deputy Sam Staples," Lauren said. "Beau, do you want to tell what you figured out?"

"Mizz Arroyo, Canoe Man is Eric's stepfather, Deputy Staples. I just realized he was the man who said 'shit.' I know Deputy Staples, and he knows me. I've been to Eric's house." Beau told them what he had told Sally that afternoon.

"Jeez, Beau! If Canoe Man is Eric's stepfather, Eric might have seen him from the ridge," Jaime said.

"Eric may know his stepfather set the fire," Jorge said.

"Eric may know his mother wrote the blackmail messages," Mev said.

"Eric may know too much for his own well-being," Lottie said.

"I think Eric's already dead," Beau said. "Eric knew I was expecting him for dinner tonight. He wouldn't have changed plans without letting me know. I called him and got his voice mail."

"I'm going to call Jake," Mev said. "Are you fine with that, Beau?"

"Sure. Tell Chief McCoy I'm afraid that Deputy Staples killed Eric."

Mev called Jake. After she disconnected she turned toward the others. "Jake and Officer Hefner are on their way to Deputy Staples's home. He'll report to us shortly."

"Okay if we stay here till Jake calls back, Mev?"

"Of course, Lauren. Would you like more tea?"

Jake called back at nine-thirty. Mev listened and said, "I'll be there in ten minutes."

"What did he say, Mom?"

"It's bad news. Chief McCoy and Deputy Hefner found blood on the kitchen floor. They don't know whose it is. Sam's patrol car is there, but his truck is gone. Chief McCoy is putting out an all-points bulletin. I'm going over there now."

"May I go with you, Mizz Arroyo?" Beau asked.

Mev looked at Lauren and Jim. They nodded their consent.

"Could you bring Beau home afterward?" Lauren asked. "We're leaving now."

❧❧❧

Deputy Hefner was taking pictures when Mev and

Beau followed Amadahy Henderson through the front door of Deputy Staples's double-wide.

"Hi, Chief. I heard the APB go out," Amadahy said. "What's going on?"

"I'll tell you in a minute, Ms. Henderson," Jake said. "Thanks for coming, Mev. Hello, Beau. You all stay out of the kitchen, please. We've got to get blood samples for the GBI."

The yellow *CRIME SCENE – DO NOT CROSS* tape stretched blocked the passageway from the living room into the kitchen.

Amadahy leaned over the tape and photographed the blood-stained linoleum with her iPad.

"I will check the two bedrooms," Mev said.

"Okay if I look in the garage, Mizz Arroyo?" Beau asked. "I want to see if Eric's motorcycle is here."

"Go ahead," Mev said.

Shortly thereafter Mev heard Beau call her.

"Mizz Arroyo, come here! I found the gold nugget from Cherokee Woman's grave. And the Cherokee pot." Beau was peering into a cardboard box.

"Are you sure, Beau?" Mev entered the garage. Amadahy followed her.

"He did, Detective Arroyo," Amadahy said. "This is the same rock and the same pot I saw at the burial site Sunday morning."

"Don't touch them. Deputy Hefner will dust it for fingerprints," Mev said. "Jake, come here! We have something!"

"Eric left his cell phone on the kitchen counter," Jake said. "That's not a good sign."

"We can have John Hicks look at it," Mev said.

"Eric's motorcycle is gone," Beau said. "Maybe Eric's trying to escape from his stepfather."

"Or vice-versa," Jake said. "One of them is hurt, but we don't know which one."

"And one of them robbed the grave, but we don't know which one," Mev said.

"Holy rock-o-poly! Look at these bumper stickers," Amadahy called out from the other side of the garage. She had opened the top drawer of a rusty metal file cabinet. She held up one: *DIVERSITY IS CODE FOR WHITE GENOCIDE.* And then another: *WE MUST SECURE THE EXISTENCE OF OUR PEOPLE AND A FUTURE FOR WHITE CHILDREN.* And a third: *CARRY ON, NATHAN BEDFORD FORREST.* "Who is Nathan Bedford Forrest?"

"He was the first Grand Wizard of the Ku Klux Klan," Beau said.

Amadahy opened the second drawer. "Here's a stack of flyers. She pulled one out: *SAVE THE LAND, JOIN THE KLAN.* "A post-it note on it says 'Grand Wizard Robert Jones, July twelfth, 2014.'"

"Why in the world would a white supremacist marry Molly Schlaughter?" Jake asked.

"And right after Molly had opened her mother's letter?" Mev added.

"Maybe he didn't know she was half Cherokee," Beau said.

"She was beautiful," Mev said.

"Let's check Sam's gun racks," Jake suggested.

In a locked glass display case in the garage, they could see nine antique guns on display, seven of them Civil War rifles, one of them a Colt pistol, another a musket.

"Sam spent beaucoup bucks on these weapons," Jake said. "Thousands of dollars."

"What's in here?" Mev asked. She pointed to a cabinet with a solid wood door.

Jake opened his pocket knife and easily picked the lock.

"Here's his real stash of guns, Mev. He's got a nine-millimeter semi-automatic Taurus, a nine-millimeter Bereta, a nine-millimeter Sig Sauer, a couple of other pistols, and four hunting rifles."

After taking inventory Jake sniffed the nine-millimeter weapons. "These have not been fired, at least not since they were cleaned," he said.

"Why would a cop need his own supply of guns," Mev asked, "unless he's got another job on the side?"

"If I were a psychiatrist, I'd say Sam needs guns for his self-esteem."

☾∽☾∽

After dropping off Beau, Mev arrived home a little before eleven. Lottie and Doolittle had left. She heard Jaime playing "Tambourine Man" up in the boys' bedroom. She found Paco cleaning up the kitchen. Paco had set an uncorked bottle of Rioja and two glasses on the table. He poured the wine and handed her a glass. Mev sat down beside him and gave him a kiss.

The wind had started to blow.

Aaah oooh aaah oooh.

"That's a coyote, Paco. Are the chickens penned up?"

"Everybody is where they belong, *querida Mevita*."

"Not everybody," Mev said.

"What's happening, *Mevita*?"

"Let's get the boys down here." Mev called them.

"What's happening, Mom?" Jaime and Jorge followed Mighty down the stairs and sat down at the table. Jorge had his iPad with him.

"Beau found the Cherokee pot and the gold nugget at Eric's house. Either Eric or Sam stole them from the burial site. And either Eric or Sam wounded the other one in their kitchen. Both of them have disappeared. Eric's Harley and Sam's pickup are both gone."

"*Caramba!*" Paco exclaimed. "Do you think Eric will come here?"

"Eric's mother is dead and his stepfather may be a murderer. Eric could be hurt. He has to go somewhere. Maybe he'll go to Beau's house, maybe he'll come here. And he doesn't have his cell phone."

"We've got to help him," Jaime said.

"There's more to this story," Mev said. "Deputy Staples seems to be a white supremacist." She told them about the bumper stickers they'd found.

"Well, Eric is no white supremacist," Jaime said. "His best friend is Beau."

"Eric's not all white himself," Jorge said. "He's a quarter Native American."

"Is Native American a race?" Jaime asked.

"According to the census it is," Paco said.

Jorge opened his iPad. "Look. I've got the U.S. Census categories here." He turned around his iPad for everyone to see.

---

6. What is this person's race? *Mark* X *one or more boxes.*

☐ White
☐ Black, African Am., or Negro
☐ American Indian or Alaska Native — *Print name of enrolled or principal tribe.* ⬐

☐ Asian Indian ☐ Japanese ☐ Native Hawaiian
☐ Chinese ☐ Korean ☐ Guamanian or Chamorro
☐ Filipino ☐ Vietnamese ☐ Samoan
☐ Other Asian — *Print race, for example, Hmong, Laotian, Thai, Pakistani, Cambodian, and so on.* ⬐ ☐ Other Pacific Islander — *Print race, for example, Fijian, Tongan, and so on.* ⬐

☐ Some other race — *Print race.* ⬐

"How white do you have to be to be white?"

"You only have to look white, Jaime. That's all," Jorge said.

"Beau's half white, but he looks black."

"Blackish. So he checks the black category."

"Oh."

"Are we white, Dad? We're half Spanish."

"*Hijos*, Spaniards are European. So if you believe in categorizing people into races—and I don't—we are white.'"

"What if Who R U says we have some African genes?" Jaime asked.

"Then we'll call up the census lady and explain that we're really sorry but we've made an awful mistake for sixteen years and we're really black after all," Jorge said.

"Wow. Who R U may really upset the census lady," Jaime said. "For good."

"*Qué bien!*"

"The census lady will have to invent a whole lot of new categories to put us three hundred and twenty million people into," Jorge said.

"Boys, let me ask you," Mev said. "What has Eric told you about his stepfather?"

"That he collects guns," Jaime said.

"That he likes Confederate stuff."

"We found old guns and new guns in their garage," Mev said. "But none that had been fired recently."

From deep in the woods an owl hooted: *Who-cooks-for-you, who-cooks-for-you-all.*

"That's Eric," Jorge said. "I know it."

"He must be out there," Jaime said, getting up. "Let's go."

Mighty barked.

"*Hijos*," Paco said, "stay here. You could get shot."

"Maybe Eric needs us."

"Sit down," Mev said. "Eric knows he can talk with us."

They waited in silence for a minute.

"Eric wouldn't steal anything," Jaime said. "His stepfather must have done it."

"And when Eric found out, he and his stepfather got in a fight," Jorge said.

"Eric needs us."

"I'll call Jake," Mev said. She pulled out her cell phone.

A clap of thunder rattled the windows. The storm had arrived.

"Wow," Jaime said. "The lightning must have hit really near."

They heard a crash in the woods. It shook the house.

"A tree's come down," Paco said. "By the creek."

"Here's what I figure," Jaime said. "Eric's stepfather is the bad guy, not his mother. Eric's stepfather is the blackmailer. He must have read Donna Jumper's letter and encouraged Eric's mother to write the Donna Dam letters to *Webby Witherston*."

"Maybe he wrote them himself," Jorge said. "Maybe he wrote the blackmail emails too. Maybe he is Donna Dam."

Who-cooks-for-you, who-cooks-for-you-all.

"That's Eric," Jaime said. "He's hooting for us."

"Let's go look."

"Let's take our bows and arrows, in case we bump into a coyote."

"Wait for us," Paco said. "Your mother and I are coming too."

The boys didn't wait. They grabbed their rain jackets, flashlights, and bows and arrows, and ran out the back door with Mighty in the lead. As they headed into the woods they heard another loud clap of thunder.

Jorge kept Mighty in the beam of his flashlight. Barking all the way, Mighty led them down the path toward Founding Father's Creek Trail. He was answered by a howling coyote.

Aaah oooh aaah oooh.

Jaime pulled an arrow from his quiver and drew his bow.

"Don't shoot," somebody called out faintly.

"Who's that?"

"Eric. Help me."

Jorge caught sight of Eric's motorcycle on its side before he caught sight of Eric lying under it.

"What happened, Eric?"

"Are you hurt?"

"I've been shot. By my stepfather."

"Where?"

"On my right side." Eric unzipped his leather jacket. "Here. And I think my ankle's broken."

The wind blew a branch off an old pine.

With the flashlight Jorge and Jaime could see that blood had soaked Eric's jeans just under his belt. Jorge lifted the motorcycle off Eric's left leg.

Eric groaned.

Even in the rain Jorge could see that Eric was sweating.

Paco and Mev reached them.

"I'm calling an ambulance for you, Eric," Mev said.

"I'll go get a blanket," Paco said.

"Where's your stepfather now?" Jorge said to Eric. He had to shout to be heard over the wind.

"I don't know. I found out he killed my mother, so we had a fight. I tried to stab him and only nicked his arm. Then he shot me. I was trying to get to your house, but I couldn't see the path in the dark." Eric closed his eyes.

"Stay with us, Eric! Stay awake!" Jorge said.

Eric did not respond.

"Hang on, Eric!" Jaime said. "Open your eyes. Help's coming."

Mighty started barking furiously.

"I hear someone in the woods," Jorge whispered. "Down by the creek."

Jaime drew his bow again.

"Come out, whoever you are," Jaime shouted.

Lightning struck nearby and lit up the woods. The twins saw no one.

Paco arrived with a plastic sheet, a blanket, and a water bottle for Eric. They covered Eric with the blanket and the sheet but couldn't get him to respond.

Jake and Pete Senior arrived, with Tracker.

Witherston's ambulance arrived.

Eric was still unconscious when the ambulance carried him away to Chestatee Regional Hospital in Dahlonega.

"Chief McCoy, we think someone is in the woods." Jaime pointed toward the creek. "Out there. Maybe on the trail."

Lightning struck again, followed immediately by an ear-bursting clap of thunder. A huge branch fell onto the path.

"This rain will make it hard for Tracker to pick up any scent, but we'll see what he can do. Pete Senior, check out the woods by the creek," Jake said. "Take Tracker with you."

Tracker found nothing. Neither did Mighty or Pete Senior.

"We'll search the area tomorrow, Mev," Jake said. "The rain should stop by morning."

એડ

Cherokee Woman's genes have spoken. A white man had intercourse with a woman of a race he believed inferior to his own. A white man whose religion demanded that he suppress his "earthly nature," whose society prohibited miscegenation, was overcome by sexual desire.

Wouldn't life be easier if we didn't struggle so hard to defeat nature?

Neel put down his pen.

"Time to go to bed, Gretchen."

❧❦❧

"Eric's got no family at all now," Jorge said, moving Mighty from his pillow to the foot of his brother's bed. "We should go see him in the hospital tomorrow."

"We need to tell Beau what's happened," Jaime said.

"I'll text him," Jorge said.

> *Jorge Arroyo*
> *iMessage*
> *Wednesday, March 15, 12:54 a.m.*
>
> *Eric was shot by his stepfather*
> *We found him behind our house*
> *Motorcycle accident*
>
> *Omg*
> *Where is eric now*
>
> *Ambulance took him to Dahlonega hospital*
>
> *Where is stepfather*

Dont know
Do you want to go with us tomorrow to visit
him in hospital

Yes

Come over at ten

Ok

"Done," Jorge said. "Beau's coming with us tomorrow."

"*Buenas noches.*"
"*Buenas noches, hermano.*"

WITHERSTON ON THE WEB
Wednesday, March 15, 2017

NEWS

Sam Staples and Eric Schlaughter
May Be Armed and Dangerous

8:00 a.m. The home of Deputy Sam Staples was the scene of violence yesterday. When investigating the disappearance of Eric Schlaughter, age 17, Chief Jake McCoy discovered blood on the kitchen floor of the mobile home at 550 Ninovan Road that Eric shared with his stepfather Detective Staples, and his mother Molly Schlaughter. Neither Deputy Staples nor Eric was there. Chief McCoy says that the GBI will determine whether the blood belongs to either of the men.

Chief McCoy has put out an all-points bulletin for the two men. He says that Deputy Staples is probably driving his 1997 light green Datsun pickup and that Eric Schlaughter is probably driving his Street 500 Harley-Davidson motorcycle. Chief McCoy said, "I ask all Witherstonians to report to the Police any contact you have with either Sam Staples or Eric Schlaughter. They may be armed and dangerous."

The gold nugget and the Cherokee pot stolen from the grave site were found in Deputy Staples's garage.

Deputy Staples, his wife Molly Schlaughter, and Eric Schlaughter moved to Witherston from Rome, Georgia, last August. According to courthouse records in Rome, Deputy Staples and Mrs. Schlaughter had gotten married on March 19, 2016. Mrs. Schlaughter died in last Saturday's fishing shack fire, presumably.

Amadahy Henderson, Reporter

Mayor Rather is Freed

8:00 a.m. Mayor Rich Rather, arrested yesterday for the murder of Molly Schlaughter, has been released from jail. No charges were filed.

Amadahy Henderson, Reporter

Grant Griggs and Red Wilker
Buy Land to Be Flooded

8:00 a.m. In the fall of 2016 Grant Griggs and Red Wilker purchased land in Saloli Valley where Mayor Rather proposes to develop a lake. In August Mr. Griggs bought the 11-acre property of his client Mrs. Marjorie Parker at 3500 Bear Hollow Road for $55,000. It included her house. In September Mr. Wilker bought the 15.7-acre undeveloped property of Army and Carol Armour at 2600 Cattleguard Lane for $53,500. In October Mr. Wilker bought the 15-acre unde-

veloped property of Trent Uptide at 3600 West Bank Road for $31,000. All three properties are in Saloli Valley above Withers Fork. If the lake is to cover 60 acres, they will be purchased by the municipality of Witherston before the land is flooded.

The realtor was Phyllis Graph.

On July 4, 2016, Mayor Rather declared "I have a dream for Witherston. A lake that will make Witherston the most beautiful town in North America. I will make it happen. Just watch."

Did Mr. Griggs and Mr. Wilker know where the lake would be situated when they made their land purchases?

Catherine Perry-Soto, Editor

EDITORIAL

Witherston has two mysteries to solve. Both involve a sexual encounter between a white man and a Native American woman. Both involve the conception of a mixed-race daughter. Both involve a bullet to the head. The first encounter took place probably in the 1830s, as evidenced by a pre-Trail-of-Tears Cherokee pot unearthed with a skeleton.

The second encounter took place in 1977, as implied by Donna Dam's first letter to the editor regarding an event that occurred on the night of November 5-6, 1977, and her second letter requesting that Mayor Rich Rather and at-

torney Grant Griggs each take a paternity test.

What do the two mysteries have in common?

Let's take the cases in chronological order. Yesterday state archaeologist Dr. Carter Ellis excavated the Saloli Valley grave discovered by Jaime and Jorge Arroyo and took the skeletal remains to his lab for genetic analysis. Today he reported that the bones belonged to a young woman and the eight-month female fetus she was carrying. The young woman was 99% Native American, but, to his surprise, the fetus was only 50% Native American. Apparently the father was predominantly British and Irish, like the Withers who founded Witherston. Dr. Ellis also reported that the Native American woman had contracted syphilis, but had died from a .45 caliber bullet to her head. Murder.

Now let's fast-forward to the present. On Monday Dr. Marcus Melton of the GBI reported that the bones of the individual who died in Saturday's fire belonged to a woman 35-40 years old who was 49% Native American and "16% French and German, 14% Broadly Northern European, 8% Ashkenazi; 4% British and Irish, 3% Iberian, and 3% undetermined." According to Chief McCoy, that woman was probably Molly Schlaughter, aka Donna Dam. Our assumption, based on Eric Schlaughter's statement that his grandmother was Cherokee, is that Molly Schlaughter's mother was full-blooded Native American and her father was white. Molly Schlaughter may have been conceived on the night of November 5-6, 1977, for she was born on August 1, 1978. Like the Native American

woman who died in the 1830s, Molly Schlaugh-
ter was murdered with a bullet to her head.

Dr. Neel Kingfisher commented on Dr. El-
lis's genetic report: "Our bones unite us. Our
pots divide us. We humans are related genetical-
ly and separated culturally." Dr. Kingfisher said
that tomorrow Who R U will deliver a report on
the genetic ancestry of some twenty-five Wither-
stonians, including our mayor.

Witherston Police will solve the second
mystery: Who fathered Mrs. Schlaughter, who
killed her, and why?

Nobody will solve the first, though I suspect
that Dr. Byrd will try.

Catherine Perry-Soto, Editor

POLICE BLOTTER

On Tuesday, March fourteenth, Deputy Pete
Koslowsky Junior arrested a male Witherston
High School student, age 16, for removing bones
from a burial site in Saloli Valley upstream from
Withers Fork. Deputy Koslowsky, who was in-
vestigating the fire at the fishing shack on the
Zamora property when he spotted the student,
said he believed that the grave belonged to a
Cherokee child. This is the second Cherokee
burial site that has been discovered in the last
week. The student claimed that the bones be-
longed to an old nanny goat he had buried for
fun, but Deputy Koslowsky did not accept his
explanation. The student was fined $50 and re-

leased into the custody of his parents.

Dr. Neel Kingfisher has agreed to look at the bones.

LETTERS TO THE EDITOR

To the Editor:

Jaime Arroyo has identified the endangered species whose homes in Saloli Valley my husband's dam threatens.

I would like to point out that my husband's dam also threatens the homes of otters and beavers whose families lived here in peace for 10,000 years before Harry Withers founded our town.

Rhonda Rather
Witherston

To the Editor:

The Endangered Species Act flouts the teachings of the Bible. The Bible decrees that we humans have dominion over fish.

All creatures are not created equal.

Mr. Arroyo, Do you honestly believe that a Popeye Shiner should have dominion over Mayor Rather?

Alvin Autry
Witherston

To the Editor:

Moving water—the creek, the stream, the river—is sacred to the Cherokee people. Should moving water not be special to white people too? Moving water cleans our body, our hearts, our souls. It washes away whatever pollutes us.

Mayor Rather, please do not destroy Saloli Stream.

Your lake would put gasoline into our bodies and noise into our hearts. It would disturb our Cherokee souls, and your soul too.

Mayor Rather, we believe you are a good man. Listen to the sound of water flowing over rocks. Does that not bring greater peace than the roar of outboard motors?

Chief Atohi Pace
Tayanita Village

WEATHER

Sunshine all day. High of 65. Low of 45.
Tour de Lumpkin County this afternoon.
I can see clearly now, the rain is gone.

Tony Lima, Visionary

NORTH GEORGIA IN HISTORY:
THE WITHERS
By Charlotte Byrd

Here we have reached the fourth and fifth generations of the north Georgia Withers: HaHa Withers, that is, Hearty Harold Withers, 1889-1960; and his childless son Francis Hearty Withers, 1915-2015.

HaHa Withers inherited his fortune in the form of cash and gold in 1931, when 73-year-old Witty Withers died of polio in the polio epidemic that summer and 70-year-old Obedience died of heart failure in the fall.

Quick to recognize financial opportunity in the depth of the Depression, HaHa bought 100,000 shares of the Lawrence Company, which had made skin-care products since 1901. On May 23, 1932, the stock was selling for $3.80 a share, an all-time low. For the next twenty-eight years HaHa reinvested dividends, benefitted from stock splits, and bought additional shares of the Lawrence Company until his death in 1960, when he bequeathed to his son Francis Hearty Withers 7 million shares worth a total of $588 million. He also left him gold.

Francis Hearty Withers, always called by his full name, became majority shareholder in the multi-national Lawrence Company. In the 1980s the company redirected its research from the manufacture of beauty lotions to the development of anti-aging products.

In 2002, when Lawrence changed its name to BioSenecta Pharmaceuticals, Francis Hearty Withers joined its board of directors. In a dec-

ade his wealth increased five-fold. Francis Hearty Withers was murdered on May 23, right after his hundredth birthday. In his will he gave $1 billion to the municipality of Witherston and $1 billion to the town's 4,000 residents, divided up equally among us.

Francis Hearty Withers considered the origin of his wealth to be his family. But we know better. His wealth—and now our wealth—originated in the land of the Cherokee Nation.

LOST

Domingo Castillo asks your help in the recovery of Cantinflas. It is the third time this year that the 7-year-old white llama has escaped his pasture in Saloli Valley. Cantinflas may be recognized by his underbite. If you spot Cantinflas, please email Señor Castillo at federicodomingocastillo@gmail.com. Señor Castillo is offering a reward of $100 for information leading to Cantinflas's whereabouts.

CHAPTER 13

Wednesday Morning, March 15, 2017

I'll go with you, boys. I want to interview Eric if he's able to talk. I'm happy to drive."

Jorge, Jaime, and Beau climbed into Mev's Camry. Jaime and Jorge told Beau about finding Eric in the woods.

Halfway down Witherston Highway to Dahlonega Mev got a text from Jake on her Bluetooth. She pressed the PLAY button.

The voice in the box said, "We found Sam's truck parked at the corner of Ninovan and Immookali just a block from your house. Sam was not in it. "

"Mizz Arroyo," Beau said, "Deputy Staples could be on his bike. He has a mountain bike."

"Then he could have been in the woods last night," Jaime said.

"Deputy Staples might have been chasing Eric," Beau said.

Mev pulled into Chestatee Regional's parking lot. So did Amadahy, right behind her.

Eric was out of surgery for his ankle and his bullet wound by the time Mev, the boys, and Amadahy got to his room. But he was too drowsy to say more than a few words. "Where's my stepfather?" he asked.

"The police are looking for him," Mev said.

"I can't go home," Eric said.

"You can stay at my house," Beau said.

"I'd wanted to go bow hunting with you all," Eric said.

Dr. Buddy Harper entered the room just as Eric fell asleep.

"Who is Eric Schlaughter's closest kin, Detective Arroyo?"

"Eric has no kin," Mev replied to the surgeon. "His mother was murdered on Saturday, probably by his stepfather. His father is nowhere to be found."

"I took a forty-caliber bullet from his side, which you may have, Detective Arroyo. Fortunately, it hit no organs. Apparently, it went through nothing but muscle. But if Eric has internal bleeding I may have to send him to Atlanta for exploratory surgery," Dr. Harper said. "And one other thing. Eric may need blood, and he has an unusual type, A-Negative."

"I can put out a call for a donor," Amadahy said. She pulled her tablet from her pocket.

Minutes later Amadahy showed them the announcement.

WWW.ONLINEWITHERSTON.COM

WITHERSTON ON THE WEB
Wednesday, March 15, 2017

BREAKING NEWS
1:44 a.m.

Emergency Call for Blood Donor

If you have blood type A-Negative, Witherston resident Eric Schlaughter, age 17, needs your help. Please call Chestatee Regional Hospital at your earliest convenience. You may be able to save his life.

Eric Schlaughter was taken to Chestatee Regional late last night for a bullet wound and a broken ankle after he was found in the woods behind Detective Mev Arroyo's house. Eric said that he had been shot by his stepfather, Deputy Sam Staples, earlier in the evening. Eric has undergone surgery to set his ankle, but he may have to have exploratory surgery in his abdomen if he has any internal bleeding. For that surgery he would be taken to Atlanta this evening, Dr. Buddy Harper said.

Amadahy Henderson, Reporter

On their way home Mev called Jake to update him on Eric's situation. Then she had Beau talk to Jake.

"Chief McCoy," Beau said, leaning over

Mev's shoulder to make himself heard on Blue-tooth, "I think that Deputy Staples is on his mountain bike...He keeps it in the back of his truck. If it's not there Deputy Staples is probably riding it...Okay, I'll tell her."

Beau turned to Mev. "Chief McCoy said that the DNA of Eric's mother matches the DNA of the person who died in the fire. He just got the report from the GBI."

WITHERSTON ON THE WEB
Wednesday, March 15, 2017

BREAKING NEWS
12:30 p.m.

Deputy Sam Staples Is Wanted for Murder

Chief Jake McCoy has issued an APB for Witherston police officer Sam Staples. Staples is a suspect in the murder of Molly Schlaughter, his wife, whose body was found in the ashes of the fishing shack fire last Saturday night.

Chief McCoy described Staples as "armed and dangerous." Staples has in his possession a Glock 22, issued to him by the Witherston Police Department.

Staples allegedly shot his stepson Eric Schlaughter, age 17, in their home on Tuesday night.

Catherine Perry-Soto, Editor

CHAPTER 14

Y ou may announce in *Webby Witherston* that Friday I will propose a budget amendment to renovate our jail."

Mayor Rather was answering Catherine's questions about his incarceration when he got a call from Rhonda.

"Excuse me, Catherine," he said. "Hello, Rhonda...Yes, thank you for springing me. I'm much obliged...Of course I'm enjoying my freedom. So kind of you to ask, dear...My blood type? A-Negative. Why?...What?...When?...You're taking me to Dahlonega now? Who will lead Slow Pedal?...Okay, okay."

Rich turned to Catherine. "Now I have to give my blood to Eric Schlaughter, whose mother tried to take my money. We have the same blood type. I'll be bled it at Chestatee Regional after Slow Pedal."

"Who will lead Slow Pedal?"

"Rhonda and I will, in her Volt. She wants to make an environmental statement, she says."

"But her Volt has a *NO DAM RATHER* bumper sticker."

"I know. I know. What can I say?"

At three o'clock Mev watched Jaime, Jorge, Beau, and their friends pull up their bikes behind Rhonda's Volt. To her the members of KNN were indistinguishable from each other in their KNN sweatshirts, blue jeans, goggles, and helmets. So were the ten other cyclists, whose faces were hidden by their goggles and helmets. She couldn't tell for sure who was who, though she recognized Paco by his green jacket and Beau by his dark skin. Mev rode in Witherston's patrol car with Pete Junior, who was at the wheel. They would follow the convoy.

"Hello, hello," Mayor Rather called out, standing beside the Volt with his fifty-watt bullhorn. He sported a huge navy sweatshirt that said YOU'D RATHER RATHER FOR MAYOR. "Are you all happy to be here? I am. I am indeed. Are you all ready to pedal slowly down Witherston Highway to Dahlonega? I bet you are."

"Let's go!"

"Let's move!"

"*Vámonos!*" Hernando yelled.

"*Vámonos!*" Christopher repeated. He'd mounted a small hand-lettered SAVE THE FLAME CHUB sign on the back of his bicycle seat.

"Okay," the mayor said. "Stay in single file, so we won't block traffic. The highway is two-lane all the way. Okay?"

"Okay!"

"Great. Great. Now let's get going," Rich said.

Rich waved high a red flag that said: PEDAL SLOWLY 2017 and strapped himself into the passenger seat of the convertible. The top was down. Rhonda honked the horn four times and started the engine.

"Beep, beep, beep, beep, the Volt went beep, beep, beep," Jaime sang.

"And we're off!" Jorge shouted.

Mev and Pete Junior followed the group west on Creek Street and south on Witherston Highway past Yona Street and Black Fox Road. Before the group had reached the town's outskirts a dozen more blue-jeaned, goggled and helmeted cyclists had joined the pack. Mev counted thirty-six riders in all, most of them on mountain bikes like her sons.

Rhonda had initially set a pace of ten miles an hour, but as the bikers picked up speed on the descent she increased her speed to twenty-five miles an hour to stay ahead of the line. Every so often a car passed them.

Fifteen minutes into the trip the terrain dropped away steeply to the right of the roadbed. Mev worried that Jorge, the more reckless of the twins, would take one of the hair-pin turns too close to the embankment and go off the cliff.

She called Rich on her Bluetooth. "Rich, could you please ask Rhonda to slow down? Some of the bikers are riding awfully close to the edge of the road."

"Sure, Mev, but Rhonda will have to slow down slowly. Jorge and Jaime are only a few feet behind us."

On the next curve Mev got a glimpse of Beau, who was third in line. Someone with a black bike helmet was trying to pass him. Was that person sideswiping him? She couldn't tell. Beau was a good rider and maintained his balance. But he'd been pushed close to the cliff. Beau dropped back to fourth position, and then to fifth, and to sixth. What was wrong? Soon Beau was at the end of the line beside their patrol car. Mev rolled down the window.

"Deputy Staples is here," Beau hollered. "Black helmet. He passed me. He's right behind Jaime."

"Oh, no!" Mev hollered back. "Does Jaime know?"

"No."

Mev could see the black-helmeted cyclist now riding alongside the second cyclist.

"Now he's beside Jaime," Beau hollered.

Pete Junior turned on the siren and started to move into the passing lane. But an oncoming car forced him back.

Sam Staples swerved hard to the right in front of Jaime and bumped Jaime's front wheel. He then passed the first cyclist and the Volt, picked up speed, and disappeared down the highway.

Jaime lost his balance, fell off his bike, and hit the pavement. His bike tumbled down the mountainside.

Annie, in third position, braked and jerked to the left, but couldn't avoid Jaime and ran over Jaime's right knee. Jaime yelped and grabbed his knee.

"Oh, Jaime!" she screamed.

Rhonda braked. Jorge's bike hit the Volt's fender, and Jorge flew into the Volt's back seat.

"No," Mev screamed. "No, no, no, no, no!"

Pete Junior braked too. The rest of the cyclists broke formation and stopped. Paco dropped his bike, ripped off his helmet and goggles, and raced to Jaime.

"*Hijo, hijo mío*," he cried. He cradled his son in his arms.

"My knee, my knee. Dad, help me."

"Neel, come here!" Paco called. "We need your help!"

Pete stopped the patrol car, flashed his blue lights, and blocked the lane. Mev got out and ran to Jaime. Jorge leaped out of the Volt.

Rhonda emerged from the Volt's front seat holding Coco Chanel. Rich emerged holding a bag of peanuts.

Jorge grabbed his twin's hand. "You'll be okay, Jaime," he said. "You'll be okay. I'll take care of you."

Neel took off his helmet and goggles and bent over Jaime.

Jaime opened his eyes. "My knee," he groaned. "Something's wrong with my knee."

Neel looked at Jaime's knee.

"You've dislocated your kneecap, Jaime. Now grit your teeth and hang on to my shoulder. This will hurt."

"I'm here, Jaime," Annie said.

Jorge cradled his brother's head. "Close your eyes, Jaime."

Neel held Jaime's knee firmly with his right hand, his thumb on the kneecap, and then yanked the leg straight with his left.

Jaime let out a long breath. "That's better," he said.

"I've put Jaime's kneecap back in its socket," Neel explained to the other cyclists—Beau, Hernando, Sally, Mona, Christopher, Gretchen, Dan, Catherine, and John Hicks. "He'll be fine."

Catherine took pictures with her phone.

"May I have water?" Jaime asked.

Jonathan supplied it. "I hope you like Perrier," he said. "Sorry I don't have lemon slices."

"What happened?" Rhonda asked.

"Deputy Staples tried to kill Jaime," Beau said.

"He tried to kill you first," Sally said.

"How many of you recognized Deputy Staples?" Mev asked.

"I did, for sure," Beau said.

"So did I," Sally said.

"I did too," Jaime mumbled. "I smelled his smoky breath."

"We'll get him," Rich said. "We'll get him. I'll offer a reward."

"How much?" Catherine asked.

"Ten thousand dollars."

"An ambulance is coming," Pete Junior reported.

"Jorge and Paco can ride with Jaime in the ambulance," Mev said. "I hope it will hold a couple of bikes too."

"We'll meet you all at the hospital," Rhonda said. "Rich is giving blood for Eric."

"I am. I am indeed," Rich said.

"We'll see you there," Mev said.

"May I go with you?" Beau asked.

"You can ride with us," Rhonda said.

"I'll go back to Witherston with the others." Neel said.

"I'll lead us back to Witherston," John Hicks said to the cyclists after the three vehicles had departed.

"I'll bring up the rear," Neel said.

"First let me file this story," Catherine said.

WITHERSTON ON THE WEB
Wednesday, March 15, 2017

BREAKING NEWS
5:00 p.m.

Rogue Deputy Pedals Away

Deputy Sam Staples, sought for the murder of Molly Schlaughter, allegedly joined the 35 Slow Pedal bicyclists traveling down Witherston Highway this afternoon. After causing a bike wreck five miles down the road, he broke formation, passed Mayor Rather's pace car driven by Rhonda Rather, and sped away toward Dahlonega. He was not followed.

The accident disrupted the Slow Pedal event. Mrs. Rather braked suddenly, causing three or four bicycle pile-ups behind her.

The bicyclist identified as Staples sideswiped Jaime Arroyo, age 16, on a hairpin turn. Jaime suffered a dislocated kneecap when his girlfriend friend Annie Jerden crashed into him from behind.

Dr. Neel Kingfisher, just behind Annie, put Jaime's kneecap back in place. An ambulance carried Jaime to Chestatee Regional.

Dr. Kingfisher said, "Jaime should have his leg X-rayed, and he'll need to get a brace. But I imagine he'll go home tonight."

"I think we just escorted Witherston's most wanted fugitive out of Witherston," commented

Deputy Pete Koslowsky Junior who, with Detective Mev Arroyo, followed the convoy in the patrol car.

Staples is approximately 5 feet, 6 inches tall, 140 pounds. He shaves his head. He has brown eyes. He is dressed in a black leather jacket and blue jeans. If he is still on his mountain bike, he will also be wearing a black helmet and goggles.

Mayor Rather announced a reward of $10,000 for the capture of Staples.

Catherine Perry-Soto
Editor

CHAPTER 15

Wednesday evening, March 15, 2017

At six-thirty Mev followed Jaime's wheel chair out of the hospital and helped her son to his feet. Jaime had been X-rayed and outfitted with a knee brace and crutches. Mev and Pete Junior would take Jaime and Jorge with them for the trip back to Witherston. They loaded the three bikes onto the rack on top of the patrol car. Rhonda and Rich would take Paco and Beau.

Paco climbed into the back seat of the Volt, which Rhonda had parked directly behind the patrol car. Rhonda got in the front with Coco Chanel, and Rich got in with coffee and a doughnut.

"Mizz Rather, may I run see Eric, just to say hi?" Beau asked, dropping his helmet and goggles in the Volt. He still wore a white bandage over his ear, a small one.

"Please be back in ten minutes, Beau," Rhonda said. "We want to follow the others home."

"Yes, ma'am."

Mev held the door of the patrol car open for Jaime to maneuver himself in. Jorge climbed carefully in after his brother. Then his cell phone rang.

"Hey, Beau…What?…Where?…We'll look."

Jorge reported the conversation to the others. "Eric's not in his room. The nurse said he was going to Atlanta for surgery. She said he was being picked up down here by Eckard Emergency Transport."

"There's an EET vehicle in front of us," Pete Junior said, pointing to a large white Ford Braun just ten feet away. "A patient has just been loaded."

"Here comes Beau," Jaime said.

Beau joined Paco in the Volt's back seat. Rhonda handed him Coco Chanel.

They all watched a young male nurse in blue scrubs close the EET's rear doors and walk around to get in the front passenger seat. But when he reached for the door handle, the EET pulled away.

"Mom, did you see that?" Jorge shouted from the patrol car's back seat.

The nurse rushed to Mev's window. His hospital badge carried the name Zach Smart. "Officer, follow that vehicle. I'm supposed to be in it!" He opened the door to the back seat. "Move over!"

Jorge moved over, and Zach squeezed in.

Pete Junior turned on his siren and flashing lights. The patrol car took off after the EET down Hospital Drive and onto Highway 249 going south.

The EET did not slow down.

"The driver's new," Zach said. "Maybe he didn't know I was supposed to go with him. I'm responsible for a patient named Schlaughter."

"The driver's not stopping. So hang on, folks," Pete Junior said. He brought the patrol car up alongside the EET. Both vehicles were going seventy miles per hour.

"He's doing an OJ, Mom!" Jorge said.

Mev looked at the driver. "Sam Staples! It's Sam! Stop him, Pete."

"He's got Eric," Jorge said. "We've got to stop him!"

Mev rolled down her window. Sam rolled down his, gave her the middle finger wave, and increased his speed. Sam was wearing a white cap and a white jacket with an EET insignia on the left sleeve.

Pete Junior accelerated to keep up. Now they were going seventy-five side by side. But an oncoming car forced Pete Junior to pull back.

Mev took out her gun.

"Don't shoot, Mom! Eric is in there!"

Mev called Sheriff Weston Bearfield for back-up.

Jaime called Beau. "We're following the EET, Beau. Eric is inside. And Deputy Staples is driving!"

The EET hit eighty.

Within minutes a Lumpkin County Sheriff's vehicle, siren screaming, blue lights strobing, entered the highway from a side road in front the EET Braun. The EET was now in second position in a convoy speeding to Atlanta.

"Crimeny! What do you know? The Volt's come up behind us," Pete Junior said, looking in the rear view mirror. "Cheesus bejesus. Rhonda's passing us."

"Oh, my gosh. Now she's trying to pass the EET," Mev said.

"Mayor Rather's standing up. He's holding his bullhorn," Jaime said.

Beau and Paco were busy putting on their helmets. Coco Chanel was standing on Beau's lap with her mouth open and her tongue out. She was clearly enjoying Rhonda's wild ride.

Rhonda moved alongside the EET vehicle.

Then they heard the mayor's voice. Rich Rather was on his bullhorn. "Pull over, you skinny, ugly, hairless runt of a murderer, you!" Rich shouted. "Pull over. I'm the mayor."

In response, Sam honked four times and sped up.

An oncoming truck forced Rhonda back into the right lane.

The sheriff's vehicle was slowing down, forcing Staples to slow down too.

Rich bellowed. "If you can hear us, Eric, get up! I gave blood for you!"

Rhonda once again moved up alongside the EET.

Mev heard Paco yelling in the Volt's back seat: "Grab him, Eric! He killed your mother!"

Suddenly the EET swerved.

Rich shouted. "Go Eric! That's my boy!"

The caravan slowed to sixty, fifty, forty miles per hour.

"Hold on, Eric," Rich hollered through his bullhorn. "Don't let go."

"What's happening, Pete?" Mev asked.

The EET slowed to twenty, pulled onto the shoulder, and stopped.

Rhonda passed the EET and stopped in front of it.

Mev jumped out of the car with gun in hand and approached the driver's side of the EET. She saw what was happening. Eric was strangling his stepfather. Slowly, deliberately.

"I've got him, Eric," she said as she opened the vehicle's door. "I've got him, Mayor Rather."

The mayor was trying to squeeze in behind her to get his hands on Sam.

"Please, Mayor Rather. Let Detective Arroyo do her job," Pete Junior said.

The rotund mayor backed away.

Sam was almost unconscious.

"Let go, Eric. Let go. You don't want to kill him," Mev said.

Eric let go. He was wearing a hospital gown, open in the back. He immediately sat down in the passenger seat.

Pete Junior, with Paco's help, lifted Sam Staples out of the EET vehicle and lowered him to the ground. He cuffed him.

Rich, Rhonda, Beau, Jaime, Jorge, Zach, Paco, Mev, and Eric watched as Pete Junior read Sam the Miranda Warning.

"I am arresting you for the murder of Molly Schlaughter," Pete Junior said. "You have the right to remain silent. Anything you say can and will be used against you in a court of law."

"I know, I know," Sam growled.

"You have the right to an attorney. If you cannot afford an attorney, one will be appointed for you."

"Right," Sam said. "So get me one."

"I'm sure you'll enjoy having Grant Griggs represent you," Rich said.

"Are you okay, Eric?" Mev asked.

"Not great, but okay. Detective Arroyo, I don't want any more surgery."

"But I gave my blood for you," Rich said, coming up behind Mev. "Don't you want my blood?"

"Thanks, sir," Eric said. "Maybe another time."

"Boys," Pete Junior said to Jaime, Jorge, and Zach. "You'll have to find another ride back to Witherston. Sam gets my back seat."

"I'll take you all in the EET," Zack said, "after we take Eric back to Chestatee Regional."

"May I go with you all?" Beau asked.

"Sure," Zach said.

"We'll meet you at your house after you lock up Deputy Staples," Rhonda said to Mev. "You may hold Coco Chanel now," she said to Paco as she opened the car door for him.

"*Muchas gracias*," Paco said.

Mev called Lottie and briefed her. "Looks like we're

having a party tonight, Aunt Lottie. Would you mind getting my house ready?...Thanks. And please tell Gretchen and Neel."

Then she called Jake.

⚘⚘⚘

"Mr. Mayor," Paco said from the Volt convertible's back seat. He had to shout to be heard against the wind. They were approaching Witherston. "Were you serious about the ten thousand dollar reward for capturing Deputy Staples?"

"Sure was, Paco. Sure was."

"I think Eric deserves it. He stopped Deputy Staples."

"Maybe he does," Rich said. "You've got a point. Maybe he does. And maybe I will announce it tomorrow."

Rich called Amadahy on his mobile phone. "Amadahy," he said, "I will have a big announcement to make tomorrow at nine o'clock on the front steps of the Municipal Building...Yes, Deputy Staples is in custody...No, I can't tell you who will get the reward...Yes, here's the story...Yes, you may record it." Rich kept her on the phone for fifteen minutes.

⚘⚘⚘

By the time Mev walked in the door the party was well underway. She heard the Weavers singing "Wasn't That a Time," so she knew Lottie was there.

"Hi, Mom," Jaime said. "We're celebrating." Jaime lay on the sofa with Doolittle on his hand and Mighty at his feet.

Lottie had placed on the dining room table a big platter with apples and carrots, a cutting board with a wheel of Manchego cheese, two baguettes, two bottles of a 2010 Rioja, a case of Coca-Cola, and paper cups, plates, and napkins. Beau, Jorge, and Zach sat on the floor with their backs against the sofa looking at Jorge's iPad. Rhonda held Coco Chanel on her left arm and a cup of Rioja in her right hand while she gave cooking instructions to Paco, who stood at the stove cracking eggs into a skillet. Rich sat at the table eating cheese and drinking wine.

Lottie, dressed in black silk pants and a white silk big shirt with an aqua silk gauze scarf draped loosely around her neck, poured a cup of wine for Mev.

"Let's raise a glass to our favorite detective, dear Mev," Lottie said. "You've solved another crime."

"With the help of everybody in this room," Mev said, raising her glass. "Nobody solves a crime alone."

"Nobody accomplishes anything alone," Lottie said. "Our society always doles out credit to individuals, but it should give credit to the individual *and* all the good people who influenced that individual."

"And all the good people who influenced those good people, and all the good people who influenced those good people," Jorge said, "and all the good people who influenced those good people, and all..."

"Okay, okay, bro!"

"Right, Jorge," Lottie said. "You got it."

"We should also toast Eric Schlaughter," Rhonda said, raising her cup. "He must have tolerated a pile of pain to unbuckle himself from his gurney, stand on his one good foot, grab Sam, and make him stop the EET."

"With his butt showing," Jorge said.

"I guess he heard me calling out to him," Rich said.

"Dear husband! You think Eric said to himself, 'Oh, that's the mayor. I guess I'd better get up and strangle Sam'?"

"No, dear wife. But I did give him encouragement. I did."

"You're a good driver, Mrs. Rather," Beau said.

"Thank you, Beau. I love to drive fast."

"I would like to say something," Rich said. "Let me say something."

Doolittle mimicked the ringing of the phone. "Telephone for bird," the bird proclaimed. "Hi, how are you?" he then said in Lottie's soft voice.

"Fine, thank you. How are you?" Jaime said.

"Fine, thank you. How are you?" Doolittle replied.

"Fine, thank you. How are you?" Jorge said.

"Let me speak," Rich said. "Please."

"Fine, thank you," Doolittle said.

"Go ahead," Mev said.

"Tomorrow I'll announce that Eric gets the ten thousand dollar reward."

"Great," Beau said.

"Woohoo."

"Terrific."

"That will make him so happy."

"He'll be able to go to college."

"I'm going to call him."

"It's too late in the evening, Beau," Mev said.

"Can't we just surprise him?" Rhonda asked.

"Yes, let's surprise him."

"Eric must have hated his stepfather," Paco said. "He seemed to want to kill him."

"Thank goodness he didn't," Mev said.

"Do you think Sam was involved in the blackmail scheme?" Paco asked.

"Maybe he put Molly up to it," Rhonda said.

"Maybe Sam and Molly were in cahoots," Mev said. "They must have driven up to the shack together."

"They parked the truck in the woods, and then they

hid in it when Mayor Rather brought his blackmail money to the shack."

"I smelled cigarette smoke in the shack," Rich said. "Sam must have been there. Sam was a smoker."

"Mom, do you think Sam married Eric's mother to get money from blackmailing Mayor Rather?"

"Eric said his mother had to marry Sam because they were going to get evicted," Beau said.

"Do you all think that Eric knew his mother was Donna Dam and that she was going to blackmail Mayor Rather?" Paco asked.

"I don't," Jaime said.

"Eric is too decent a guy," Beau said.

"But remember what Eric said in the car when we were going to Mr. Gray's farm for the rally? He said that sometimes people needed to break the law to get justice."

"So you think he was defending his mother for writing those letters?" Mev asked.

"I'm sure he didn't know," Beau said. "I'm sure of it. He would have told me if he did. We're friends."

"If I thought Eric knew his mother was Donna Dam, I certainly wouldn't give him the reward money," Rich said.

"Well, dear husband, you don't know that. Eric's just a kid with a runaway father, a blackmailing mother, and a stepfather who killed his mother. He captured his stepfather. He deserves the reward money."

"Rhonda is right, Rich," Mev said.

"And everybody in Witherston will be happy you're giving it to him," Lottie said. "All the voters."

"Okay, Lottie. You've convinced me," Rich said. "I hope you all show up for my news conference tomorrow."

"I'll call the BBC," Rhonda said.

ɞɔɛɔ

Neel wrote in his journal.

> *Genes are nature's form of immortality.*
> *They are what we pass down of ourselves to our*
> *children and our children's children and our*
> *children's children's children and on and on—*
> *until a generation produces no children, and the*
> *family genes reach the end of the line.*
>
> *Those of us without children leave nothing*
> *of ourselves to the future except our molecules*
> *which enter the soil, and perhaps a few*
> *thoughts, which enter the planet's noisy conver-*
> *sation, most often anonymously.*
>
> *I think of words related to "gene": gener-*
> *ate, generation, generic, generosity, genesis,*
> *genitalia. All these words suggest procreation,*
> *reproduction, creation, birth. And then I think of*
> *"genocide," the killing of all that.*
>
> *The murderer of the pregnant Cherokee*
> *woman destroyed her genetic future and that of*
> *her unborn daughter. Perhaps that was the mur-*
> *derer's intention.*

ɞɔɛɔ

At eleven o'clock Chief Atohi Pace stood before the
Tayanita Villagers at the Council House for their weekly
meeting. Moki sat on the ground beside him with a black
kitten in his lap. Torch lamps illuminated the interior of
the yurt.

"Good evening, fellow Cherokees," Atohi said. "Tonight we gather to consider a proposal by John Hicks.
The floor is yours, John Hicks."

John Hicks rose from the bench and turned to address his fellow Villagers. He wore a black sweatshirt that said *HAPPY HALF-BREED*.

"Hello, Cherokee brothers and sisters!"

"Hello, John Hicks!"

"You all know Eric Schlaughter," John Hicks said. "Eric is one quarter Cherokee. I propose that we invite him to join Tayanita Village and make his home with us."

"Great idea," Atsadi said.

"I can tell you all about Eric," Amadahy said. "Catherine asked me to prepare an obit for him when we found out he'd been shot. Just in case."

"Speak, Amadahy."

Amadahy pulled out her tablet and read: "Eric entered high school in Rome in 2014. He already had a good voice, so he joined a band called the Owl Bards as their lead singer. And he joined a bird-watching club called the Red Woodpeckers where he learned the calls of the pileated woodpecker, the crow, the red-shouldered hawk, the bald eagle, and the barred owl. He made the honor roll. In August of 2016, Eric moved to Witherston with his mother Molly Slaughter and his stepfather Deputy Sam Staples. Here he joined KNN and Tony Lima's Mountain Band. His favorite song is 'Purple People Eater.'"

"Eric has no family now," Atsadi added.

"I have nominated Eric because he is one-fourth Cherokee and proud of his heritage," John Hicks said. "And because I like him."

"Is there any more discussion?" Chief Pace asked. He paused and said, "Hearing none, I ask you to raise your right hand if you wish to invite Eric Schlaughter to join Tayanita Village."

The twenty-one Villagers raised their right hands.

"Eric Schlaughter is now a member of Tayanita Village," Chief Pace said. "I will extend the invitation to-morrow. Now let's get in our circle for the prayer."

Chief Pace intoned:

> "May the warm winds of heaven
> blow softly upon your house.
> May the great spirit
> bless all who enter there.
> May your moccasins
> make happy tracks
> in many snows,
> and may the rainbow
> always touch your shoulder."

ℰↃℰↃ

"Jaime, are you awake?"

"I am now."

"What if Eric was in cahoots with his mother? What if Eric knew his mother was blackmailing Mayor Rather?"

"We don't even know if Eric knew his mother was writing those *Webby Witherston* letters, bro."

"How do we find out?'

"We ask him."

"And he's going to tell us the truth? I don't think so, Jaime. If he was involved in blackmail, he'd have a mile of misery ahead of him."

"Can we talk about this in the morning? I'm meditating on my knee now."

"Oh. I'm so sorry about your knee, Jaime. I'm so sorry about your accident. You scared me."

Jorge got up and gave his brother a hug.

"You're a good brother, Jorge."

"Here, I'll take Mighty to my bed," Jorge said.

"Buenas noches, hermano."
"Buenas noches.

WITHERSTON ON THE WEB
Thursday, March 16, 2017

NEWS

Deputy Staples Is Arrested for Murder

8:00 a.m. After a ten-minute chase on Highway 249 south of Dahlonega, Deputy Sam Staples was apprehended and arrested for the murder of his wife Molly Schlaughter.

Here is the story Mayor Rich Rather told of the event"

"About 6:30 I came out of Chestatee Regional Hospital, where I donated blood to save young Eric Schlaughter's life. I immediately saw that something was wrong. A male nurse was loading an EET medical transport vehicle with a patient who didn't seem to want to go. The driver just sat in his seat and didn't get out to help. He had a cap pulled down over his face. I got suspicious right away. I'm telling you, right away.

"When the nurse started to get into the EET vehicle, the driver took off, just about knocking the nurse down. He headed toward Atlanta.

"Deputy Pete Koslowsky Junior and Detective Mev Arroyo were in the patrol car behind the EET. Jaime and Jorge Arroyo were in the back seat. The nurse jumped into the car with them. Then Pete Junior turned on his siren and took off in hot pursuit.

"I leapt into my wife's Volt. Paco Arroyo and Beau Lodge were already in our back seat with my wife's dog. I said to Rhonda, "Follow Pete Junior!" She took off, and in a minute we caught up. That Volt has great pick-up. It's really a fine car for regular people, not just eco-maniacs.

"I could see that Pete Junior was not going to push the EET off the road, so I figured Rhonda and I would have to do it ourselves. I told Rhonda to pass the patrol car. When we pulled up beside the EET, I could see Sam Staples driving. I yelled at him through my bullhorn and got Eric Schlaughter to attack him. Beau had told us that Eric was the patient in the back. Eric heard me, got up, and strangled Sam. Or almost strangled him. I could see Eric hated the guy, really hated him.

"Detective Arroyo and Deputy Koslowsky arrested Sam for murder. Now he is safe in the Witherston jail. I will be in the courthouse when he is tried. I sure will."

Chief Jake McCoy hired Sam Staples as a deputy in August of 2016. Chief McCoy said he had been impressed by Staples's record as a private security guard for several large manufacturing plants in Atlanta. Staples was recommended for the Witherston Police position by BioSenecta Pharmaceuticals.

Chief McCoy and Detective Arroyo searched Staples's home on the evening of March 13 and found evidence that Staples was involved in Ku Klux Klan activities. Staples had a stack of flyers that recruited members for the white-supremacist organization. According to our research, flyers such as those were distributed in Atlanta in July of 2014.

They also found the gold nugget and Cherokee pot that had been stolen from the Cherokee grave site.

The arrest of Sam Staples does not close the case of Molly Schlaughter's murder. Many questions remain.

Did Sam Staples know that Molly Schlaughter was half Cherokee when he married her? Did he collaborate with her in blackmailing Mayor Rather? Was the idea his? Why did he murder her?

These are questions Witherstonians want answered.

Mayor Rather will hold a news conference at 9:00 a.m. today on the steps of the Municipal Building.

Amadahy Henderson, Reporter

Mayor Rather Will Renovate Jail

8:00 a.m. After his unfortunate incarceration Mayor Rather has decided that Witherston's holding cell needs a facelift. At Friday's meeting of the Town Council, after the vote on his dam proposal, Mayor Rather will request the following renovations: construction of a small bathroom accessible to the cell with a comfort-height toilet and sink; a daybed and a stressless chair; a writing table and chair; a lamp; pine flooring;

and a new paint job, at a cost not to exceed $10,000.

"We need to show respect for our prisoners," the mayor said. "Some of them may be innocent."

In December of 2015, Mayor Rather's wife Rhonda was detained in the same cell with Dan Soto for releasing chickens from the eighteen-wheeler Mr. Soto was driving.

Catherine Perry-Soto, Editor

Bones Belong to Old Goat

8:00 a.m. Dr. Neel Kingfisher affirmed that the bones a 16-year-old Witherston High School student dug up on Tuesday, March 14, belonged to an old nanny goat and not a Cherokee child.

The $50 fine the student's parents had paid was returned to them.

Amadahy Henderson, Reporter

LETTERS TO THE EDITOR

To the Editor:

Mr. Autry is behind the times, by about a hundred and fifty years. He assumes that since we humans can capture and kill almost any living thing, we don't need to worry about anybody but us. Well, Mr. Autry must not have heard about ecosystems. In an ecosystem we creatures all depend on each other. If the fish of the sea, the fowl of the air, and every other living thing that moveth upon the earth do not thrive, neither do we humans. We cannot survive alone.

Humans are not smart enough to know the importance of every living thing's work in an ecosystem. We don't know all that a Popeye Shiner does to keep other living things in a stream healthy.

Dan Soto
Witherston

To the Editor:

I believe that a Popeye Shiner should have dominion over Mayor Rather.

Gretchen Green
Witherston

NORTH GEORGIA IN HISTORY:
THE WITHERS
By Charlotte Byrd

Yesterday our community received big forensic news. The bones discovered in a grave site in Saloli Valley by Jaime and Jorge Arroyo and Beau Lodge belonged to a pregnant Native

American woman of the 1830s afflicted with syphilis who died from a .45 caliber bullet to the head. Her fetus, according to archaeologist Carter Ellis, was half "white."

Did the father of the unborn child infect the mother with syphilis? Did he then kill her? Who buried her?

We will never be able to answer these questions with certainty, but by trying we can learn a lot about the past.

I reread the 1838 diary of Patience Withers, Hearty Withers's wife. On the evening of Sunday, May 28, two days before Hearty Withers was killed by a Cherokee man, Patience wrote the following:

After dinner my husband cleaned his rifle for the second time in three days. I asked him what he had shot since he had brought home no meat for dinner. He said he took care of a problem. Little Harry asked him what problem. He said miscegenation. Little Harry asked him what miscegenation was. My husband said miscegenation was the mixture of the blood of our white race with the blood of inferior races like the Indians. He said that we whites had to protect our racial purity and that we could not allow our blood to be weakened by Cherokee blood. He also said his life could be in danger. Before he went to bed he drank almost a whole bottle of whiskey.

I worry about my husband. His sight is poor and his hearing is getting worse. He walks with a jerky motion. His syphilis will kill him soon I fear.

Did Hearty Withers murder the young

woman who was buried with a gold nugget and a Cherokee pot? It's possible. But Hearty Withers did not bury her. Her own people did. They gave her a grave.

Did the Cherokee man kill Hearty Withers in revenge for murdering the Cherokee woman? It's possible.

Did Hearty Withers father the unborn child? It's possible.

Hearty Withers's fear of miscegenation was widely held among white people in Georgia in the nineteenth century. That fear was the basis for the following decision by the Georgia Supreme Court thirty-one years after his death:

"...moral or social equality between the different races...does not in fact exist, and never can. The God of nature made it otherwise, and no human law can produce it, and no human tribunal can enforce it. There are gradations and classes throughout the universe. From the tallest archangel in Heaven, down to the meanest reptile on earth, moral and social inequalities exist, and must continue to exist throughout all eternity."

Hearty Withers believed that white supremacy was God's will. He inherited his belief, and he passed it down to his children and his children's children.

Georgia's miscegenation laws remained in effect until 1967 when the United States Supreme Court ruled that, in the decision written by Chief Justice Earl Warren, "Under our Constitution, the freedom to marry, or not marry, a person of another race resides with the individual and cannot be infringed by the State."

WEATHER

Sunshine all day. High of 72. Moonshine all night. Low of 50.

Get you a copper kettle,
Get you a copper coil
Fill it with new made corn mash
And never more you'll toil
You'll just lay there by the juniper
While the moon is bright
Watch them just a-filling
In the pale moonlight.

Tony Lima, Climate Crooner

FOR SALE

Land

Placed on 03/16/2017

Property Type: Land
Street Address: 3500 Bear Hollow Road16.1 acres of woods in Saloli Valley
$60,000 or best offer
Email: <u>phyllisgraph@graphrealty.com</u>

Placed on 03/16/2017
Property Type: Land
Street Address: 2600 Cattleguard Lane
15.7 acres of woods on Saloli Stream
$59,000 or best offer
Email: phyllisgraph@graphrealty.com

Placed on 03/16/2017
Property Type: Land
Street Address: 3600 West Bank Road
11.2 acres of woods on Saloli Stream
$37,000 or best offer
Email: phyllisgraph@graphrealty.com

CHAPTER 16

Thursday morning, March 16, 2017

Gretchen, have you looked at the classified ads this morning?"

"No, sweetie. I've been baking biscuits for you," Gretchen replied. She set a basket with a half-dozen hot biscuits on the table in front of Neel. "And here's your strawberry jam, which I made last week."

"The property on Saloli Stream adjacent to ours is for sale for sixty thousand."

"Hallelujah! Let's buy it, Neel!"

"It's all woods. I've walked through it."

"We won't touch it. We'll save it for the bears."

"I'll call Phyllis Graph in an hour, at nine o'clock sharp."

❦

"*Oye, Blanca*," Ernesto said, looking at his tablet and drinking his coffee. "We could buy the land the Armours used to own for fifty-nine thousand dollars. It's almost sixteen acres."

"*Qué bien*! Let's buy it, Ernesto. We can grow more grapes and make more wine."

Hernando walked into the kitchen. "*Qué pasa?*"

"Hernando, would you vote for buying the Armour property? We could grow more grapes. Someday Zamora Wines will be yours, so we want you to approve."

"Yes," Hernando exclaimed. "Yes, yes, yes. Great idea."

"I will call the lady this morning," Ernesto said. "I will offer fifty-nine thousand dollars, and we will get it by the time the sun goes down."

ℰℐℰℐ

"*Oye, Mevita,*" Paco said. "There are three pieces of land for sale on Saloli Stream. They are posted on *Webby Witherston.*"

"Show me, Paco," Mev said.

"Right here." Paco turned his tablet so that Mev could read the ads.

Mev, Paco, and the boys were at the breakfast table finishing up their scrambled eggs, grits, bacon, and toast. Mighty was on the floor chewing a Beggin' Strip.

"These are the properties that Red Wilker and Grant Griggs bought," Mev said. "Red and Grant were betting on the lake."

"You know what I think, *Mevita*? I think they know something we don't know. I think they know there won't be a lake."

"Grant may be trying to avoid legal trouble, Paco. Ruth is on the Town Council."

"Maybe Mrs. Griggs has told Mr. Griggs she will vote against the lake," Jaime said. "Maybe she read my letter in *Webby Witherston* about the endangered species in Saloli Stream."

"Maybe the mayor saw my cartoon and got all scared," Jorge said. "Maybe he told Mr. Grant he was changing his mind about the lake."

Mev answered her cell phone. "Hello, Jake...I figured Sam had done that...Okay, I'll see you at nine at the mayor's news conference...And by the way, Grant and Red are unloading their properties on Saloli Stream." Mev disconnected.

"What, Mom? What about Deputy Staples?"

"Eckard Emergency Transport reported that one of its vehicles was hijacked yesterday four blocks from Chestatee Regional. The driver was shot in the chest, right side, stripped of his clothes, and left unconscious and naked under a rhododendron bush. The driver's cell phone and wallet are missing. It was a forty-caliber bullet, like the one found in Eric. Same caliber as his police Glock."

"Naked?" Jaime asked.

"Nekkid," Jorge said. "Deputy Staples must have left him nekkid so the guy wouldn't run after the EET vehicle." Jorge giggled.

"Who found him, Mom?" Jaime asked.

"A sixty-year-old lady walking her dog. The dog found him."

"A Great Dane?" Jaime giggled.

"She was an old lady, Jaime. She probably had a Chihuahua. Old ladies like Chihuahuas."

"What kind of dog, Mom?"

"I didn't ask, Jaime."

"*Por favor, hijos,*" Paco said. "Focus!"

 espe

Mev watched the corpulent mayor shake hands with every single person gathered in front of the Municipal Building. There must have been twenty or twenty-five people there in addition to Aunt Lottie, Paco, and the twins, who'd brought Mighty. The KNN members were standing in the street. Mev spotted Christopher, Sally, Beau and Sequoyah, Mona, Hernando, and Annie. Jaime was on his crutches. Annie had her arm on Jaime's shoulder. Beau still had a small bandage on his ear. Beau and Sally held hands. Christopher carried a hand-lettered sign that said *SAVE HUMPTY DUMPTY. SAY NO TO DAM RATHER.*

Mev also spotted Amadahy Henderson and Atsadi Moon, Chief Pace, Catherine, Gregory and Renoir, Neel, Gretchen, and Gandhi, Blanca Zamora, Ruth Griggs, and a number of other Witherstonians she knew only slightly. Pete Junior stood by Rich's side.

"Rich will never stop running for office," Mev said to Jake.

"He's getting ready to run for state senator," Jake replied. "In 2018. I heard he's already asked Grant to manage his campaign."

"Good morning, ladies and gentlemen! And what a good morning it is! Let's hear it for sunshine all day and moonshine all night!"

The crowd stayed quiet.

"I have invited you here this morning to tell you who gets the ten thousand dollars reward money for catching Deputy Staples. Do you all want to know?"

"That's why we're here, Mayor Rather," Amadahy said. "We want to know. Now."

Mev saw Jorge holding up his iPad. She presumed he was recording the announcement.

"Tell us."

"Let's get on with it."

"Well, you all have read how Deputy Sam Staples was caught. Mizz Amadahy wrote a fine story about it in *Webby Witherston.* So I'm here to announce that the recipient of the ten thousand dollars is…" Rich paused. "…Eric Schlaughter!"

Now the crowd clapped.

"Go, Eric!"

"We love you, Eric!"

Jorge appeared at Mev's side. "I've just emailed the mayor's speech to Eric," he told her.

Atsadi Moon held up his hand.

"Yes, Councilman Moon. You may speak."

"Mr. Mayor, will you withdraw your proposal to dam Saloli Stream? There's lots of folks against it."

"You will get your chance to vote tomorrow afternoon, Councilman. But now let's focus on Eric Schlaughter and the good deed he did for Witherston," Rich said.

Mev saw Gretchen raise her hand.

"Yes, Gretchen."

"What percentage of Witherston's voters would have to oppose your dam to get you to change your mind, Mayor Rather?"

"I'm a leader, Gretchen, not a follower of polls. But to answer your question, I'd say fifty-one percent. Yes, fifty-one percent."

"The results of yesterday's poll will be published at two o'clock today, Mr. Mayor," Catherine said.

"Well, well, well. We'll see what my constituents want me to do with their money," Rich said. "I want to lead my constituents in the direction they want me to go."

"Mom," Jorge said, "Eric just called me from the hospital. He wants us to drive down to Dahlonega and pick him up. He's getting released from the hospital. May we go?"

"Sure. Drive carefully."

"He said he needs some clothes. I'll take him some pants of Dad's, and a shirt and jacket. Okay?"

"That's fine."

"He also said he wouldn't accept the reward."

"Why?"

"He didn't say."

☙❧☙

"Hi, Jake. Hi, John." Mev walked into Jake's office at ten o'clock to find John Hicks there with an iPhone in his hand.

"I've got bad news, Detective Arroyo," John Hicks said. "Looks like Eric Schlaughter sent the emails from Donna Dam and the instant messages from XXX."

"What?"

"Eric's iPhone has an app that disguises the sender of emails and messages. The phone had no password, so I could see everything."

"You're saying that Eric was the blackmailer?"

"I'm saying that Eric's phone sent the messages."

"Oh, no!" Mev looked at Jake. "I can't believe it."

"I have to bring Eric in for questioning," Jake said.

"Jaime and Jorge and Beau have gone to Dahlonega to pick him up. What should I tell them?"

"Tell them to bring Eric here, but don't say why."

"John, what else did you find on Eric's phone?" Mev asked.

"An app for calling birds, and a few recordings of birds. A recording of a coyote. Forty or fifty songs. Forty or fifty photos, mostly of birds. A few of a beautiful black girl, and a selfie with the girl by a waterfall."

"Whom did he call?" Mev asked. "Or email? Or text?"

"Someone named Latasha. They communicated day and night."

"She must be the African American girl, Jake. Sam Staples wouldn't have been happy."

"I read a few of the messages, Detective Arroyo. Eric and Latasha were keeping their relationship secret."

"When did Eric send the last message to Latasha, John?"

"Friday night, eleven twenty."

"Nothing on Saturday?"

"None to her. On Saturday night he sent the texts from XXX. I mean, his phone sent the XXX texts."

"Looks like Eric was in possession of his phone when the Donna Dam emails were sent on Friday, Mev."

"But maybe not when the XXX texts were sent on Saturday."

❧❦❧

Checking Eric out of the hospital took longer than the boys anticipated, but eventually they got him settled into the front seat of the Jetta.

Eric wore an over-sized white sweatshirt with the words *REAL MADRID* emblazoned on it, a pair of Levi's, a moccasin on his right foot and a large black surgical boot on his left. Under the sweatshirt he wore a big band-age wrapped around his body.

"You can live with us till you graduate, Eric," Beau said.

"Maybe. Maybe. Anyway, I really appreciate the invitation."

"Why won't you accept the ten thousand dollars, Eric?" Jorge asked from the back seat as Jaime steered the Jetta onto Witherston Highway. "You can use it for college."

"I don't deserve it."

"Why don't you deserve it?"

"I just don't, okay. I'm sorry. I'd rather not talk about it."

"Mom said we have to drop you off at the police station, Eric," Jaime said.

"I'm not surprised," Eric said.

"Chief McCoy probably wants to ask you questions about Deputy Staples."

"Right," Eric said.

ⱺⱺⱺ

"You don't know who XXX is, Eric?" Mev asked him. She and Jake were interviewing Eric in her office. It was noon.

Jake held up Eric's cell phone. "Is this your phone?" he asked.

"Yes, sir."

Jake showed Eric the instant message thread.

"Did you send these texts from XXX?"

"No, sir. I did not. I have no idea who sent them, and I have no idea who XXX is."

"What about Donna Dam?" Mev asked.

"Donna Dam was my mother."

"Did you send emails from Donna Dam to Mayor Rather, Mr. Griggs, and Mr. Wilker?"

Eric hesitated. "I guess I'll tell you the whole story. I've done something awful."

"Do you want a lawyer?"

"Am I under arrest?"

"No. At least not yet."

"I don't need a lawyer. I'll feel better if I tell you everything."

"Go ahead, Eric."

Eric drew a long breath and started talking. "My mother and I are both guilty of blackmail. Moving to Witherston was her idea. She thought we should scout out the place and get to know Mayor Rather and Mr. Griggs. She believed she'd sense who her father was. She saw the mayor's help-wanted ad in *Webby Witherston*, applied for the job as his secretary, and got it. We moved here in August. But blackmailing Mayor Rather and Mr. Griggs was mostly my idea. My mother and I read my grandmother's letter when we cleaned out her house. That was the weekend after my mother married Sam. Sam read the letter too. Anyway, after thinking about it for a while, I got upset that my mother grew up with no father, no money, and no college, while her real father lived in luxury and respectability. I didn't know who her father was—Mayor Rather or Mr. Griggs—but I decided that whichever one he was he owed my mother and me some money. I told my mother we should blackmail them both, since neither would have wanted their Toccoa sex party to be made public.

"When Mayor Rather started planning the lake, my mother got traumatic. She remembered her mother's stories about the collapse of the Kelly Barnes Dam, how many people were killed, how many lives were ruined. She said she owed all her hardships to the dam break. So we hatched the plan to send a letter to the editor of *Webby Witherston* signed 'Donna Dam' opposing the dam. My mother also wanted to humiliate Mayor Rather and Mr. Grant. She figured we could stop the dam and shame Mayor Rather and Mr. Grant at the same time. I'd gotten an app on my phone that let me send out emails under another name, so we sent both the blackmail emails and the letters to *Webby Witherston* under the name of Donna Dam."

"Why did you all include Red Wilker in the first letter to the editor?" Mev asked.

"My mother had found out that he and Mr. Griggs had bought Saloli Valley land. She guessed they were planning to sell it to Witherston at a profit if the Town Council approved Mayor Rather's lake project. My mother said that everybody was making money off the dam but us."

"Who actually sent the emails?" Jake asked.

"I sent the blackmail emails Friday morning. We asked Mayor Rather and Mr. Griggs each to pay nine thousand nine hundred dollars. We asked Mr. Wilker to pay five thousand dollars. I also sent the first *Webby Witherston* letter, the one that was printed Saturday morning.

"But my mother wanted to send a second one Saturday afternoon if Mayor Rather or Mr. Griggs didn't pay the blackmail, so I left my cell phone with her while I went with Beau and Jorge and Jaime to Blue Boulder. I figured my cell phone had burned up in the fire."

"Why collect the blackmail at the fishing shack?" Jake asked.

"I'd been there a couple of times with Hernando Zamora. It was secluded but accessible."

"How did Sam Staples get involved?"

"My mother met Sam Staples right after she divorced my father. We were running out of money, so she married the guy. I never liked him, and he never liked me. I wanted my mother to keep our blackmail plan a secret from him, but she told him anyway."

"He was a law-enforcement officer. He should have reported the plan to me," Jake said.

"Eric, you were with Jaime and Jorge and Beau Saturday afternoon, but you left them when you found out that a patrol car was on the ridge," Mev said. "Did you see the explosion?"

"Yes. The patrol car had gone, so I stayed up there a few minutes and watched the shed burn."

"Did you see the man in the canoe paddle by Blue Boulder? Did you recognize him?"

"I did. I recognized my stepfather in the canoe. I

hooted to warn Beau and the twins, but I guess they thought I was an owl."

"Why didn't you report it, Eric?" Jake asked.

"I was scared, Chief McCoy. I was scared of my stepfather because he could kill me. And I was scared of you because you could put me in jail. I felt responsible for everything bad that was happening. Because of me, my mother's dead."

"Where were you on Sunday night, when Beau was shot in the ear?"

"I was with my girlfriend Latasha. She drove to Dahlonega and met me at Effie's Tavern. We do that on Sundays. We had to keep our relationship secret because my stepfather is a member of the Klan. Latasha is smart and funny and really beautiful, but my stepfather hates blacks. He calls Beau, Blackie."

"What do you think happened, Eric?" Mev asked.

"I think my stepfather went with my mother to the fishing shack Saturday afternoon to collect the blackmail money, parked my mother's truck in the woods, and hid in it with my mother when Mr. Griggs, Mr. Wilker, and Mayor Rather brought their blackmail money. At some point after that, either my mother or my stepfather sent the second letter from Donna Dam, the one daring Mayor Rather and Mr. Griggs to take a paternity test. And then my stepfather shot my mother, took the money, blew up the shack, and escaped in the canoe. I think my stepfather planned ahead. He knew about the fishing shack from me."

"What about the dynamite?"

"He must have brought dynamite in his truck. You'll have to ask him."

"Why do you think he shot Beau?"

"Actually, I think he probably meant to shoot the chickens, to intimidate Jaime and Jorge."

"Did you steal the gold nugget and the Cherokee pot, Eric?"

"No, Detective Arroyo. I didn't. I would never rob a grave."

"What happened Tuesday night?"

"I was in a rage by the time I got home from work. I walked into the kitchen, found my stepfather counting money, and accused him of murdering my mother. He denied it. He said that he'd gotten twenty-five thousand dollars from someone who owed him money."

"Are you sure he said twenty-five thousand dollars, Eric?"

"Yes, ma'am. That's what he said."

"Jake, that means that probably all three men brought money to the shack Saturday afternoon. But go ahead, Eric."

"Anyway, I didn't believe his story. I socked him. He socked me. I grabbed a knife and stabbed him on his left arm. He pulled a gun and shot me in the side. I got on my Harley and tried to reach your house. I wanted to tell you what had happened, Mizz Arroyo. I went up the path by the creek so my stepfather couldn't follow me in his truck. I must have hit a root behind your house because I crashed. I was unconscious for a while. Then I came to, but I couldn't get out from under my motorcycle. So I hooted like an owl and howled like a coyote. I wanted Jorge and Jaime to hear me and come out. I didn't want my stepfather to hear me. I thought he might be following me."

"He probably was, Eric," Mev said.

"The storm was pretty scary. I thought I was going to die out there before anybody could find me."

"Eric, we are not going to keep you," Jake said. "But we have to find a place for you to stay. You need rest and medical care."

"Eric will stay with the Lodges," Mev said. "Jim can change Eric's bandages and watch for signs of infection. I'll take him over there tonight."

"I'd appreciate that."

"Eric, let's go to my house now for lunch."

Mev helped Eric out of his chair.

Eric winced as he put weight on his booted foot. "Will I be arrested for blackmail, Chief McCoy?"

"Probably not if you testify against Deputy Staples."

"I'll testify. Where is he now?"

"In jail. In our holding cell. It's not comfortable. He'll be there till his trial."

⇜⇝

"*Who R U* has emailed me their report. You're sixty-six percent Native American, Gregory."

"Is that all? I thought I was at least seventy-five percent."

"And both of you have some Ashkenazi Jewish genes."

"I didn't know I did," Gregory said.

Neel was seated with Jon and Gregory at Gretchen's back table. Gretchen was bringing out a platter of cucumber and black olive sandwiches to follow their pea soup.

"Let's see the letter," Jon said.

Neel showed them the letter signed by a Dr. Charles D. Beagle.

"Ohhh myyy gawd," Jon exclaimed. "Our ever-so-distinguished white mayor is twelve percent Native American!"

"We've got to get the news out," Gretchen said. "Maybe the mayor will withdraw his dam proposal if he knows his great grandmother is lying out there in Saloli Valley just about to drown."

"Let's have a DNA ancestry disclosure party. At our place tomorrow night," Jon said. "Are you game, Greg?"

"I'll email the invitations, folks," Gretchen said. "And I'll bring a ton of shrimp for you all to grill."

"I'm game," Greg said.

WITHERSTON ON THE WEB
Thursday, March 16, 2017

BREAKING NEWS
2:00 p.m.

Poll Shows Majority of Witherstonians
oppose Dam Rather

A *Witherston on the Web* telephone poll taken late yesterday shows voters in our community to be slightly opposed to the creation of a Lake Witherston. Here are the numbers:

51 % Opposed
46% In favor
3% Undecided

The Witherston Town Council will meet tomorrow at 1:00 p.m. in the Council Room of the Municipal Building to vote on Mayor Rather's proposal for a lake. Mayor Rather says that visitors are welcome as always.

Catherine Perry-Soto

CHAPTER 17

Thursday afternoon, March 16, 2017

*F*rom: Gretchen Green *gretchen-hallgreen@gmail.com*

To: Rich Rather, Rhonda Rather, Jorge Arroyo, Jaime Arroyo, Mev Arroyo, Paco Arroyo, Charlotte Byrd, Grant Griggs, Ruth Griggs, Amadahy Henderson, John Hicks, Annie Jerden, Beau Lodge, James Lodge MD, Lauren Lodge, Atsadi Moon, Atohi Pace, Mona Pattison, Catherine Perry-Soto, Eric Schlaughter, Sally Sorensen, Dan Soto, Hernando Zamora, Christopher Zurich

INVITATION, Thu 03/16/2017, 2:23 p.m.

You are invited to a picnic tomorrow (Friday) evening at the home of Gregory Bozeman and Jon Finley, 650 Yona Road, to learn your genetic ancestry. Come at 6:00.

Gretchen Green
Sent from my iPad

ↄ✎ↄ

"Well, I'll be dab-nabbed, Rhonda. Gretchen Whole Grain has just invited us to a party at Jon and Gregory's place. She's invited the same gaggle of liberal geese who went to her house Monday night. Look."

Rich showed Rhonda the invitation on his phone.

"How lovely," Rhonda said.

"Now we're going to get all cozy together—me and everybody who voted against me—and tell each other who our ancestors were."

"Sounds like fun to me. Email Gretchen that I'll bring four pecan pies."

"I'll bring bourbon."

ↄ✎ↄ

Mev and Jake were updating Catherine when Jake's computer beeped indicating the arrival of an email. Jake glanced at the screen.

"Excuse me," he said. This is an email I've got to read now."

From: M Melton, GBI
To: Chief Jake McCoy, Witherston PD
Re: DNA Analysis of Bone Marrow
Thursday, March 16, 2017, 3:09 p.m.

Dear Chief McCoy:

A comparison of the DNA samples of Mr. Richard Rather and Mrs. Molly Schlaughter shows a close familial relationship, most likely that of father/daughter.

A comparison of the DNA samples of Mr.

Grant Griggs and Mrs. Molly Schlaughter shows no familial relationship.

Sincerely,

Marcus Melton, PhD
Division of Forensic Sciences
Georgia Bureau of Investigation
Decatur GA 30034

"How very interesting," Jake said. "Our mayor is Molly's father."

"May I see?"

"You might as well, Catherine. It's news."

Catherine looked over Jake's shoulder and read the email aloud.

"How do you suppose Rich will react?" Mev asked.

"Now I have a huge story," Catherine said. "Thank you, Chief!"

"Catherine, you cannot—I repeat, cannot—publish your story before we contact Eric and the mayor."

"I'll call Rich," Jake said.

"And I'll tell Eric. He's at my house with the boys. I'll tell him in person."

❧❧❧

"Why would the chief of police be calling me now? I've been proven innocent," Rich said to Rhonda. He picked up the phone. "Hello, Chief. How are you this fine afternoon?...What can I do for you?...What? What?...For certain? How could that be?...Yes, yes, of course. Of course I'll welcome Eric into our family...Of course...You say this story will be in *Webby Wither-ston*?...Four o'clock?...I'll tell Rhonda. Thank you for informing me." Rich turned to Rhonda. "Eric is my grandson," he said. "Mine. There's DNA proof."

"Terrrrrific!" Rhonda went over and hugged Rich. "Maybe he'll move in with us," she said.

"Catherine's going to call me."

Catherine did, within the minute.

"Hello, Catherine. Yes, I'm delighted. Truly delighted. Yes, you may quote me. Just say that I've always wanted a grandson, and now I've got one. And that maybe we'll go fishing together…Yes, and Rhonda is happy too. She's dancing around the living room she's so happy."

ఌఁఌఁ

"The mayor? The mayor is my grandfather?"

"Yes, Eric," Mev said. "He's a good man."

"For a politician," Lottie said.

"Whoopee," Jorge said. "Eric, you're Humpty Dumpty's grandson!"

"Jorge," Paco said. "Give the mayor a little respect."

"Okay, Dad. Eric, you're Rather Round's grandson."

"*Hijo!*"

"That makes Rhonda your grandmother, or your stepgrandmother," Jaime said. "That's not bad, Eric. Maybe she'll get you a dog. She volunteers for the TLC Humane Society in Dahlonega."

"My mother and I blackmailed the mayor. And Mr. Griggs too, and Mr. Wilker," Eric said.

"Anybody else?" Jorge said.

"Just return the money, apologize, and say you're checking yourself into rehab," Lottie said.

"Let me talk to Jake," Mev said.

ఌఁఌఁ

BREAKING NEWS
5:00 p.m.

Mayor Is Eric Schlaughter's Grandfather

Mayor Rich Rather is the father of the late Molly Schlaughter. A DNA paternity test conducted by the GBI has confirmed Mayor Rather's paternity. Mayor Rather is therefore the grandfather of Eric Schlaughter, age 17, who was released from Chestatee Regional Hospital today after being shot Tuesday night by his stepfather, Witherston police officer Sam Staples.

Upon hearing the news Mayor Rather said he was delighted. "I've always wanted a grandson, and now I've got one. We'll go fishing together."

Eric Schlaughter has confessed to concocting jointly with his mother Molly the scheme to blackmail Mayor Rather, Grant Griggs, and Red Wilker. But Chief McCoy said he would be granted leniency in the judicial system for turning state's evidence against Staples.

Catherine Perry-Soto, Editor

❧❧❧

"What? My grandson is my blackmailer?"

Rhonda had just read Catherine Perry-Soto's article to Rich.

"Was," she said. "I'm sure he regrets what he did."

"How can I be a good grandfather to my blackmailer?"

"If you'd been a good father to your daughter you would not be in this pickle, Rich."

"If I'd been a husband to Molly's mother, you would not be in this pickle either, Rhonda. You wouldn't be here at all."

"Right. Not here."

Rich looked at his cell phone. "Flying pigs, it's Grant calling."

"Hello, Grant," Rich said. "I'm not surprised you called. Not surprised at all...Yes, I am happy about it. 'Delighted' is what I said...Thank you for reminding me...Yes, well, Ruth will find out tomorrow...Thanks for calling, Grant." Rich disconnected. "Grant's enjoying the news," he said. "He had to remind me that my grandson is one-fourth Cherokee."

"Will you withdraw your dam proposal now?"

"Why should I do that?"

"Eric may have ancestors buried in Saloli Valley."

"I can't withdraw it now. I'll look weak."

"You can proclaim that you are the leader of fifty-one percent of Witherston's voters."

"Maybe Eric will work on my campaign for state legislature."

"We've got to call our daughter and tell her she's got a nephew."

℘℘℘

"The call's for you, Eric," Paco said, taking the phone to Eric. "It's Mrs. Rather."

Eric was lying on the Arroyos' sofa with his foot elevated on a pillow. Jaime was sitting on a chair with his braced leg on an ottoman and with Doolittle on his hand. Jaime was teaching Doolittle to take a peanut out of his mouth. Beau was sitting on the floor, rubbing Mighty's belly. Jorge was sitting at the dining room table writing his *Webby Witherston* column. Paco and Mev were sautéing *calamares* in the kitchen. Lottie had gone home.

"Hello, Mrs. Rather," Eric said. "Yes, I just found out…Thank you. I really appreciate your invitation, but I'll be staying with the Lodges my senior year, unless I go to jail for blackmail…Of course. I'll be happy to have dinner with you all next week. Thanks…Goodbye."

Eric handed the phone back to Paco. "Now they like me."

"I just read that coyotes mate for life, and both parents raise the pups," Jorge said. "The female coyotes are pregnant now. They'll give birth in April."

"What's the gestation period?" Jaime asked.

"Sixty-three days, just like dogs."

"If coyotes mate for life and we kill one, we'll make the pups fatherless," Eric said.

"What would we do with the dead coyote?" Beau asked. "We wouldn't eat the meat."

"We'd put his head over our fireplace for people to *oooh* and *aaah* over our good aim," Jorge said.

"How undignified for the poor coyote," Beau said.

"Do you all really enjoy hunting?" Eric asked. "If you don't eat the meat, aren't you just testing your archery skills on a moving target?"

"I'm starting to identify with the coyote," Beau said. "Let's just take pictures."

The phone rang again. Paco looked at caller ID and said, "Hello, Chief Pace…Yes, Eric is right here." He handed the phone again to Eric.

⌒⌒⌒

After dinner Neel sat down at the kitchen table, with Swift at his feet, to write in his journal.

Tomorrow some thirty of us Witherstonians will look into our deep past, our endlessly deep

past. The DNA ancestry report will tell us some-
thing about where our fairly recent ancestors
lived, since human populations diverged over
time and left traces of their differences on our
genome. But it won't tell us who our original
ancestors were because we have no original an-
cestors. No living being on earth has original
ancestors. If we went back a hundred thousand
years and looked at our genome we would find
in it traces of our ancestors for the previous
hundred thousand years, long before our ances-
tors were human.

I understand why the story of Adam and Eve
is so compelling. It is the story of an origin.
People want to know the origins of things. But in
life there are no origins.

೮/ᄋᄃ/ᄋ

"How does your knee feel, Jaime? Still sore?"

"Probably better than Eric's ankle feels. He'll be laid up longer than I will."

"Mighty can sleep with me again tonight."

Lauren and Jim had picked up Beau and Eric after dinner, and Mev and Paco had gone to bed. Jaime lay in bed watching Jorge browse the internet on his iPad.

"Tomorrow we find out our genetic ancestry, Jorge. I wonder what Mighty's genetic ancestry is," Jaime said.

"We should have sent Who R U some of Mighty's spit."

"Can you be serious, bro?"

"I'll try," Jorge said. "Hmm, according to one article dogs and wolves evolved from a common ancestor between eleven thousand and sixteen thousand years ago, before humans developed agriculture."

"So humans were around for thousands of years before they had dogs to keep them company. How sad."

"Here's something," Jorge said. "A DNA ancestry kit for testing dogs! Only $60 on Amazon. It gives you, quote, the percentage of the different breeds found in your dog's genes."

"Let's test Mighty."

"We'll find that Mighty is part terrier, part lab, part toy poodle, part Great Dane, part Chinese hairless crested dog, and part wolf, with some Neanderthal blood."

"You know what? If we could find the genetic ancestry of every animal and every plant on the planet we would have the whole history of our biosphere. We would know everything."

"Not everything, Jaime. We'd know *what* happened in evolution, but we wouldn't know *why* it happened. We wouldn't know how volcanoes or meteors or human activity affected evolution."

"Or prejudices."

"Right."

"Still, we'd know a lot, Jorge. Sequencing everybody's genome—or at least the genomes of a thousand plants and animals—would be like hearing echoes of the big bang."

"Do you know how many humans have ever lived, Jaime?"

"No."

"I can find out. Hmm. Wikipedia says between a hundred billion and a hundred and fifteen billion."

"Suddenly I don't feel very important."

Jaime reached over to turn the light off.

"*Buenas noches, hermano.*"

"*Buenas noches.*"

WITHERSTON ON THE WEB
Friday, March 17, 2017

BREAKING NEWS
8:00 a.m.

Deputy Staples Taken to Dahlonega

Deputy Sam Staples, who was apprehended on Wednesday for the murder of Molly Schlaughter, will be transported this morning to the Lumpkin County Jail in Dahlonega by Deputies Pete Koslowsky Senior and Pete Koslowsky Junior. Staples will await trial there.
   Eric Schlaughter, son of Molly Schlaughter and grandson of Mayor Rich Rather, has declined to accept the mayor's $10,000 reward for Staples's capture.

Amadahy Henderson, Reporter

OBITUARY

Molly Schlaughter

Molly Ann Jumper Schlaughter (1978-2017), daughter of the late Donna June Jumper of Toccoa and Richard Rather of Witherston, died on Saturday, March 12 at the age of 39.
   Molly Schlaughter grew up in Rome, Georgia. According to her son Eric Schlaughter, alt-

hough she had to work fifteen hours a week at McDonald's, she graduated from Rome High School at the top of her class. Her yearbook shows she played the flute in the marching band, sang in the choir, acted in musicals, and served on the student council. Molly married her high school boyfriend, Nat Schlaughter, in June of 1996 and went to work as a secretary in the police department. She gave birth to Eric, her only child, in the year 2000. In 2016 she and Eric, with her second husband Samuel Staples, moved to Witherston, where she became Mayor Rather's secretary.

Eric said he would be forever grateful to his mother for teaching him to sing.

Amadahy Henderson, Reporter

LETTERS TO THE EDITOR

To the Editor:

Today the Town Council will vote up or down the mayor's proposal to turn Saloli Valley into a lake. I hope my fellow members of the Council will remember the line from Joni Mitchell's 1970 song "Big Yellow Taxi."

"They paved paradise and put up a parking lot."

Smitty Green
Witherston

WEATHER

Sunny skies, no clouds, no rain, no storms, no twisters. High of 76. Low of 58.
Just a perfect day.

Tony Lima, going south of the border down Mexico way

EDITOR'S NOTE

Dr. Byrd's column "North Georgia in History" will re-appear on March 27. Dr. Byrd is taking a week off to conduct research at the University of Georgia for her book "The History of Witherston." She is seeking information regarding the activities of Witherstonians during Prohibition.

Catherine Perry-Soto

CHAPTER 18

Friday morning, March 17, 2017

Will the meeting of Keep Nature Natural please come to order."

Beau pounded his gavel on the pine picnic table. A bright purple band aid on his ear had replaced Thursday's larger white bandage.

"Order, order!" Jorge shouted at Mighty, Sequoyah, and Bear, who were wrestling noisily near the creek. "Order in the woods!"

Eric sat on one long bench with his booted foot propped up on his back pack. Jaime, still wearing his knee brace, sat on the other with his leg stretched out. Annie, Sally, Mona, Jorge, Hernando, and Christopher squeezed together on the remaining bench space. John Hicks stood behind Beau.

"We have a visitor today," Beau said. "John Hicks. You all know him. He has an invitation for us. John Hicks, would you like to have the floor?"

"Thanks, Beau," John Hicks said. "Thanks, everybody. I am carrying a message from Chief Pace. Tayanita Village would like for KNN to be our partner. Or you might say, Tayanita Village would be your partner.

Here's how it would work. One of you would be a representative of KNN to Tayanita Village and would sit in on our weekly meetings, and one of us—preferably me—would be a representative of Tayanita Village to KNN and would sit in on your weekly meetings."

"Why would we want to be your partner?" Christopher asked.

"Because together we would have greater power in the Witherston community," John Hicks said. "In the future, when something threatened our natural environment we'd wage our campaign to save our land together. Besides, our missions are the same."

"What's your mission?" Annie asked.

"It is to live with the forces of nature, not against them. We honor our Cherokee ancestors and their predecessors for living here thousands of years without destroying the land that sustained them. Isn't that what KNN stands for—Keep Nature Natural?"

"It is," Annie said.

"We've already done something important together, folks. We've kept Mayor Rather from building his dam."

"We have?" Jaime asked.

"We have," John Hicks said. "I have inside information from Atsadi Moon."

WITHERSTON POLICE DEPARTMENT

INTERNAL MEMO

DATE: 03-17-2017

TO: Chief Jake McCoy
FROM: Detective Mev Arroyo
RE: Arrest of Sam Staples for Murder of Molly Schlaughter

    An abundance of circumstantial evidence implicates Witherston Police Officer Sam Staples in the murder of his wife Molly Schlaughter. Here is the timeline of Staples's activities that I have constructed with the help of Eric Schlaughter:
    Tuesday, March 8, 2016: Donna June Jumper died, leaving a letter to her daughter Molly Jumper Schlaughter to be opened upon her death.
    Saturday, March 19, 2016: Staples married Molly Schlaughter.
    Saturday, March 26, 2016: Staples helped Molly and her son Eric clean out Donna Jumper's house. They found the letter. Staples was present when Molly and Eric opened the letter. They learned that Molly had been conceived on the Saturday night of November 5-6, 1977, the night the Kelly-Barnes Dam broke in Toccoa, and that her father was either Rich Rather or Grant Griggs.
    Friday, July 15, 2016: Molly Schlaughter took a job as Mayor Rather's secretary.
    Friday, July 22, 2016: Staples took a job as

deputy with the Witherston Police Department.

Monday, August 1, 2016: Staples, Molly, and Eric moved to Witherston. Eric enrolled in Witherston High School as a junior.

Saturday, March 4, 2017: Staples learned from Molly that she and Eric had devised a plan to blackmail Mayor Rather and Mr. Griggs.

Friday, March 10, 2017: Using an app on Eric's cell phone that disguised the sender, Molly and Eric sent emails from the fictitious "Donna Dam" to Mayor Rather, Grant Griggs, and Red Wilker threatening to expose their secrets if they did not deliver money to the fishing shack on the property of Ernesto and Blanca Zamora at 5:00 p.m. Saturday. The emails to Mayor Rather and Mr. Griggs, which demanded $9,900, alluded to their activities on the night on November 5-6, 1977, when Molly was conceived. The email to Mr. Wilker, which demanded $5,000, alluded to his undisclosed land purchases in Saloli Valley.

Molly and Eric also sent the first "Donna Dam" letter to Witherston on the Web threatening to expose the activities of Mayor Rather and Mr. Griggs on the night the Kelly-Barnes dam broke if Mayor Rather did not withdraw his dam proposal.

Saturday, March 11, 2017: Eric left his phone with his mother who said she would need it later in the day to send a second letter to Witherston on the Web. Eric worked at the Yona Gas Station in the morning and then hiked to Blue Boulder in the afternoon with Beau Lodge and Jaime and Jorge Arroyo.

Early in the afternoon Staples and Molly

Schlaughter drove to the fishing shack in Molly's old Kia pickup, which they had loaded with dynamite and a gas can, and parked it in the woods out of sight. They went into the shack, took Hernando's canoe off the wall, and carried it out to the stream bank. Then they returned to the pickup, where they hid while Rather, Griggs, and Wilker delivered their blackmail money.

After Rather, Griggs and Wilker had come and gone, Sam Staples and Molly Schlaughter returned to the shack to collect the money and plant the dynamite. They found Mayor Rather's jacket with a 9 mm pink handgun in its pocket. Using Eric's phone, Molly sent Witherston on the Web the second letter, the one demanding that Rather and Griggs take a paternity test. Staples then shot her in the back of the head with the mayor's handgun.

Staples took Eric's cell phone, the mayor's jacket, and the gun to the canoe. Between 6:30 and 6:45 he set fire to the shack with his wife's body inside, and as the shack exploded he got into the canoe and headed downstream.

As he passed Blue Boulder and entered Tayanita Creek, Staples spotted Jorge and Jaime Arroyo and Beau Lodge on Blue Boulder. He aimed his flashlight at the trio, realized who they were, and saw that Jaime held a trowel. He paddled down to Tayanita Village, pulled his canoe up on the bank, stuffed Mayor Rather's jacket and gun under the seat, and turned the canoe over. He walked to his home in Old Pines Mobile Home Park.

Close to midnight, Staples used Eric's phone to send text messages from XXX to Jorge and Jaime and Beau. Staples threatened the boys with harming their parents if they revealed what they had seen that day.

Sunday, March 12, 2017: Staples read Amadahy Henderson's 3:00 p.m. story in Witherston on the Web about the discovery of a Cherokee grave holding human bones, a valuable ceramic pot, and a gold nugget. He realized that the gravesite must be close to Blue Boulder, because that was where he'd seen the boys. While the protest picnic at the Grays' farm was going on, he drove to the ridge above Blue Boulder, climbed down, found the gravesite, and stole the gold nugget and the Cherokee bowl.

Later that night, Staples went to the woods behind the Arroyos' house and shot two of their chickens, presumably to frighten Jaime and Jorge. When Jaime, Jorge, and Beau came out of Dr. Charlotte Byrd's house, which is next door to the Arroyos' house, Staples shot at Beau. He nicked Beau's ear.

Monday, March 13, 2017: Staples received a visit from Chief McCoy and Detective Arroyo, who found the box with Donna Jumper's letter to Molly. Staples lied to Chief McCoy and Detective Arroyo about Molly's whereabouts.

Tuesday, March 14, 2017: Staples was surprised by Eric when he was counting the blackmail money on his kitchen table. He and Eric got into a fistfight. Eric stabbed his left arm. He shot Eric in the side with his Glock 22. Eric left on his Harley Davidson motorcycle and headed across town. Staples followed him in his truck. Staples abandoned the truck at the corner of Ninovan and Immookali and got on his mountain bike, which was in the truck bed. His whereabouts that night are unknown.

Eric attempted to reach Detective Arroyo's house, but he wrecked his motorcycle on the path by Founding Father's Creek in the thunderstorm. Close to midnight he was found by Jorge and Jaime Arroyo and taken to Chestatee Regional Hospital.

Wednesday, March 15, 2017: Staples joined Slow Pedal and left Dahlonega disguised as a bicyclist. On the way to Dahlonega he sideswiped Jaime Arroyo, causing Jaime to crash. Staples then passed the Volt driven by Rhonda Rather and carrying Mayor Rather. He rode into Dahlonega.

Near Chestatee Regional, Staples ran across an Eckard Emergency Transport vehicle, shot the driver in his side, put on the driver's uniform, and took his vehicle. He called Chestatee Regional, identified himself as Dr. Buddy Harper, and said that an EET would take Eric Schlaughter to Atlanta for surgery.

Once Eric was in the EET, Staples left the hospital and headed toward Atlanta on Georgia Highway 249. He was chased by Deputy Pete Junior Koslowski and Detective Arroyo in Witherston's patrol car and Mayor Rather and Rhonda Rather in Rhonda's Volt. He was captured when Eric, from inside the EET, got up and began to strangle him.

Staples was arrested and taken into custody.

Thursday, March 16, 2017: Eric Schlaughter confessed his role in the blackmail plot.

CHAPTER 19

Friday evening, March 17, 2017

Here's to our mayor," Gretchen said, raising her glass of wine. "I promised to campaign for you if you withdrew your proposal. You did, so I will."

The partygoers had gathered in the spacious living room of Jon and Gregory's old farmhouse.

"Thank you, Gretchen Whole Grain. I'm much obliged."

"I'm telling the truth, Mayor Rather. I will campaign for you."

"Well, pour the Kombucha!" Rich said, raising his glass of Wild Turkey. "And pass the seaweed!"

"*Chin, chin,*" Paco said, clinking his glass with hers.

"*Chin, chin!*"

"*Chin, chin!*"

"The Flame Chub will be most grateful," Christopher said.

"So will the Piedmont Blue Burrower," Jorge said.

"And the Popeye Shiner," Dan said.

"And all of our dead Cherokee relatives in Saloli Valley," Atsadi said.

"And all of our live Cherokee friends in Tayanita Village," John Hicks said.

Rich took a bow. "Now will you all vote for me?"

"I'll give it serious consideration," Rhonda said.

"Fill your plates and refill your glasses," Jon said. "It's time to find out who copulated with who long ago."

"Whom," Lottie said.

"Whom," Doolittle said.

"Fasten your seatbelts," John Hicks said.

Neel moved to the fireplace. Eric limped over to one chair in front of it. Jaime limped over to the other. Beau, still wearing a bandage on his ear, sat down on the hearth.

"Anybody else need to come to our infirmary here?" Jorge called out.

"Are you all comfortable with disclosing your genetic heritage?" Neel asked. "If you aren't you should say so."

"Speak now, or forever hold your peace," Jon said.

"My genes are nobody's business but my own," Rich said. "They're like my medical records, which I keep confidential. I came to this party because Rhonda made me."

"I did," Rhonda said.

"*Chin, chin,*" Gretchen said.

"*Chin, chin.*"

"Why won't you let us know how you came into being?" Lottie asked. "You let us see you in person. How is that different from letting us see what made you?"

"We assume you're not the product of an immaculate conception," Gretchen said.

"If it weren't for your ancestors, you wouldn't be here," Jorge said. "You should be grateful to all of them. Just think, if one of your ancestors had died at birth, he or she wouldn't be your ancestor, and you wouldn't be here."

"And their genes would be lost forever," Jaime said.

"And Eric wouldn't be here either. Eric should be grateful to you too, Mayor," Jorge said.

"Eric may pass your genes on," Jaime said.

"Possibly to somebody who is not all white," Eric said.

"What?" Mayor Rather exclaimed.

"My girlfriend is black," Eric said. "Or at least mostly black."

"So what's the big deal?" Lauren asked.

"Seriously, folks. My genetic ancestry is private," Rich said.

"But you're a politician, Mayor Rather," Catherine said. "You have to disclose your finances and just about everything you've done in your long life if you want to win elections."

"I'm only sixty," Rich said. "I have not had a so-called 'long life.'"

"I understand why you might want to keep your cultural heritage secret, especially if you come from horse thieves," Gretchen said. "But why would you want to keep your genetic heritage secret? Only a racist would find shame in his genetic heritage, and you're not a racist, Rich."

"Of course I'm not a racist, Gretchen!"

"Then why don't you want folks to know your genetic heritage?"

"Okay, okay. I'll do it."

"Go, Mr. Mayor," Jon said. "Maybe I'll vote for you."

"Really, Jon?" Gregory asked.

"I said, maybe."

Neel gave everybody a copy of the letter he had received from Dr. Charles D. Beagle of Who R U.

"Hey, Mr. Mayor, you are part Native American," John Hicks exclaimed as he read it. "You are twelve percent Native American. You'll be a natural grandpa to Eric."

"I am thirty-two percent French and German, but I'm still proud to be Eric's grandfather."

"I'm forty-one percent French and German," Eric said. "And twenty-five percent Native American."

"Eric, your mother was sixteen percent French and German," Neel said.

"Well, she *was* my daughter, Neel," Rich said.

Neel pulled out of his pocket the letter from Dr. Melton of the GBI. "Molly Schlaughter was fifty-two percent Native American, sixteen percent French and German, fourteen percent Northern European, eight percent Ashkenazi, four percent British and Irish, three percent Iberian, and three percent undetermined. Apparently one point five percent of her genes were Neanderthal. The Neanderthal percentage probably came from you, Mr. Mayor."

"Your wife Rhonda is nine percent Native American," John Hicks said.

Rhonda smiled.

"And I am five percent Native American," Gretchen said.

"I'm seventeen percent Native American," Dan said.

"That's your Aztec blood, hubby," Catherine said.

"Mr. Griggs, you're part Native American too," John Hicks said. "Six percent."

"I certainly didn't know that. My father, who did our family tree, did not put any Indians on it."

"Surprise, surprise," John Hicks said.

"Dr. Lodge has some Native American blood too," Eric said.

"I figured," Jim said. "My slave ancestors must have known some Cherokees."

"In the Biblical sense," Jorge said.

"Dad has six percent African genes," Jaime said. "Jorge and I have three percent."

"We're cousins!" Beau said.

"A whole lot of us have Jewish blood," Gretchen said. "I'm three percent Ashkenazi Jew. Lottie is twenty-four percent Ashkenazi. And Mev, the twins, Ruth, Annie, Mona, Rich, Gregory, Jon, Lauren and Beau, Catherine, Rhonda, Rich, Eric, Sally, and Christopher all have some Jewish blood.

"Ashkenazi Jews came from Eastern Europe," Jaime said. "Jorge and I got our Jewish genes from our mother."

"Just imagine all the love-making that has gone on for forty thousand years that resulted in us," Gretchen said.

"Love-making that overcame prejudice," Neel said, "that took place regardless of cultural differences."

"Almost everybody has Neanderthal genes," Lottie said, "except for people whose ancestors were all African. Neanderthals occupied Europe and Western Asia and interbred with Homo sapiens who had migrated out of Africa."

"And then Neanderthals went extinct," Jaime said. "They went extinct about forty thousand years ago."

"Think about being a Neanderthal man, having deep thoughts like ours, looking at birds in the sky, fishing for food in the stream, looking for a place to live," Eric said.

"And a girlfriend," Beau said.

"I'm picturing a romantic moment between a Neanderthal dude and a Homo sapiens chick," Jorge said. "His name was Oof, and hers was Aauugaa. They did it in a cave."

"And look what came of their union, *hijo*, after four hundred centuries," Paco said. "You."

"Would anybody mind if I put Dr. Beagle's letter into *Webby Witherston*?" Catherine asked.

"Go ahead, Catherine, go ahead," Rich said. "Go ahead. If we go back forty thousand years we're probably all related to Oof and Aauugaa."

e/ɔe/ɔ

"Come to bed, Neel," Gretchen said.
"Just one minute, honey."
Neel wrote:

> *Imagine a genetic ancestry party in Wither-ston a century from now. Thirty people of all ages and of indeterminate racial origins compare their reports from the Atlanta-based global corporation Who R U. What do you know? There are no big differences.*

Neel closed his journal. "I'm on my way, Gretchen."

e/ɔe/ɔ

"Jaime, are you awake?"
"No."
"Do you think that Deputy Staples would have shot Eric's mother if he hadn't found the gun Mayor Rather left behind?"
"I'm not awake."
"Oh."
"*Buenas noches, hermano.*"
"*Buenas noches.*"

WITHERSTON ON THE WEB
Saturday, March 18, 2017

NEWS
8:00 a.m.

Mayor Rather Withdraws Proposal for a Lake

Mayor Rich Rather has withdrawn his proposal to dam Saloli Stream. At yesterday's meeting of the Town Council, the mayor explained
his decision as a change of heart. He said,
"When I learned that Saloli Valley was the sacred burial ground of Cherokee people who
lived here for centuries before my own ancestors
arrived, I decided not to let the Town Council
flood their graves."
Ruth Griggs said that Mayor Rather did not
have enough votes to create the lake. She did not
reveal where she stood.
The Council approved the mayor's proposal
to renovate the Witherston jail.

Amadahy Henderson, Reporter

Mayor Rather Has Indian Ancestors

8:00 a.m. Yesterday evening twenty-six
Witherstonians learned of their genetic ancestry.
They have agreed to allow Witherston on the
Web to publish the following letter from Charles

D. Beagle, Senior Scientist at Who R U, to Dr. Neel Kingfisher, who commissioned and paid for the report. Who R U is a company in Atlanta that determines genetic ancestry from samples of saliva.

Dear Dr. Kingfisher:

Here is a preliminary report on the ancestry of the following individuals. A more detailed report will be available at www.peach-pitdna215.com on April 30. Log in with user name neelking and password, which you can change, wru30533nkjr.

Arroyo, Jorge: 49% Iberian; 33% British and Irish; 10% Eastern European; 3% African; 2% Broadly Southern European; 1% Ashkenazi; 2% Undetermined (2.6% Neanderthal)
Arroyo, Mev: 56% British and Irish; 30% Eastern European; 4% Iberian; 4% Broadly Southern European; 2% Ashkenazi; 4% Undetermined (2.7% Neanderthal)
Arroyo, Paco: 89% Iberian; 6% African; 2% Broadly Southern European; 2% British and Irish; 1% Undetermined (2.6% Neanderthal)
Bozeman, Gregory: 66% Native American; 23% British and Irish; 5% Ashkenazi; 2% Iberian; 4% Undetermined (1.2% Neanderthal)
Byrd, Charlotte: 34% British and Irish; 25% Broadly Northern European; 24% Ashkenazi; 9% French and German; 5% Scandinavian; 3% Undetermined (2.7% Neanderthal)
Finley, Jonathan: 49% British and Irish; 28% Broadly Northern European; 8% Broadly

Southern European; 7% Ashkenazi; 6% Finnish; 2% Undetermined (2.7% Neanderthal)

Griggs, Grant: 33% British and Irish; 28% Broadly Northern European; 19% Scandinavian; 11% Broadly Southern European, 6% Native American; 3% Undetermined (2.7% Neanderthal)

Griggs, Ruth: 41% British and Irish; 36% Broadly Northern European; 13% Ashkenazi; 7% Italian; 3% Undetermined (2.6% Neanderthal)

Henderson, Amadahy: 49% Native American; 23% British and Irish; 18% Iberian; 6% French and German; 3% Italian; 1% Undetermined (1.1% Neanderthal)

Hicks, John: (55% Native American; 12% British and Irish; 15% French and German; 14% Iberian; 4% Undetermined (1% Neanderthal)

Jerden, Annie: 39% British and Irish; 38% Broadly Northern European; 7% French and German; 8% Ashkenazi; 5% Scandinavian; 3% Undetermined (2.7% Neanderthal)

Lodge, Beau: 43% African; 31% Scandinavian; 10% British and Irish; 7% French and German; 4% Native American; 1% Ashkenazi; 4% Undetermined (2.4% Neanderthal)

Lodge, James: 86% African; 8% Native American; 3% British and Irish; 3% Undetermined (.1% Neanderthal)

Lodge, Lauren: 62% Scandinavian; 18% British and Irish; 13% French and German; 3% Ashkenazi; 4% Undetermined (2.7% Neanderthal)

Moon, Atsadi: 70% Native American; 19%

British and Irish; 7% Iberian; 2% Broadly Southern European; 2% Undetermined (.2% Neanderthal)

Pace, Atohi: 72% Native American; 17% British and Irish; 7% Iberian; 3% Broadly Northern European; 1% Undetermined (1% Neanderthal)

Pattison, Mona: 36% British and Irish; 31% Broadly Northern European; 11% French and German; 9% Ashkenazi; 9% Iberian; 4% Undetermined (2.7% Neanderthal)

Perry-Soto, Catherine: 49% British and Irish; 30% Broadly Northern European; 7% French and German; 8% Ashkenazi; 4% Scandinavian; 2% Undetermined (2.7% Neanderthal)

Rather, Rhonda: 29% British and Irish; 28% Broadly Northern European; 18% French and German; 9% Native American; 7% Ashkenazi; 5% Finnish; 4% Undetermined (2.7% Neanderthal)

Rather, Richard: 32% French and German; 24% Broadly Northern European; 14% Ashkenazi; 12% Native American; 9% British and Irish; 6% Iberian, 3% Undetermined (2.9% Neanderthal)

Schlaughter, Eric: 41% French and German; 25% Native American; 16% British and Irish; 11% Broadly Northern European; 4% Ashkenazi; 3% Undetermined (1% Neanderthal)

Sorensen, Sally: 41% British and Irish; 31% Scandinavian; 12% French and German; 8% Ashkenazi; 5% Finnish; 3% Undetermined (2.7% Neanderthal)

Soto, Daniel: 44% Iberian; 26% Broadly

Southern European; 17% Native American; 17% Native American; 3% Undetermined (1.6% Neanderthal)

Zamora, Hernando: 85% Iberian; 7% African; 6% French and German; 2% Undetermined (3.3% Neanderthal)

Zurich, Christopher: 66% French and German; 21% British and Irish; 6% Ashkenazi; 4% Finnish; 3% Undetermined (3.7% Neanderthal)

Thank you very much for your business, Dr. Kingfisher. We look forward to working with you again in the future.

Sincerely yours,

Charles D. Beagle, PhD., Senior Scientist
Who R U
215 Peachpit Boulevard
Atlanta GA 30625
www.peachpitdna215.com

Catherine Perry-Soto, Editor

LETTERS TO THE EDITOR

To the Editor:

At the opening of our Cherokee pottery show on Saturday, April 22, the Cherokee-Witherston Museum will display the Cherokee ceramic pot that Jaime Arroyo, Jorge Arroyo,

*and Beau Lodge discovered at Blue Boulder. It
appears to have been made in the early 1830s.*

*I invite all Witherstonians to attend this
event after participating in Witherston's Earth
Day celebrations.*

*Carolyn Foster, Director
Cherokee-Witherston Museum*

WHAT'S NATURAL
By Jorge Arroyo

*Are coyotes native to Georgia? No, they are
not. They are exotic, which means that they are
newcomers.*

*Coyotes migrated here from the western
part of the United States. Since they are adapta-
ble and not picky about what they eat or where
they live, they have spread all over Georgia.*

*Coyotes disturbed ecosystems in north
Georgia when they started arriving here a hundred years ago. They multiplied faster than other predators because there weren't enough
bears and cougars to keep the adult coyote population down. The coyotes ate rabbits, mice,
squirrels, beavers, and occasionally deer. However, hawks and weasels developed a taste for
coyote pups. So in time, ecosystems adjusted to
the coyotes.*

*A newcomer can throw the whole ecosystem
out of balance. All the parts of the ecosystem—
plants and animals—have to adjust to the newcomer's behavior. Everybody relates to every-*

About the Author

Dr. Betty Jean Craige is University Professor Emerita of Comparative Literature at the University of Georgia. She has lived in Athens, Georgia, since 1973. Craige is a teacher, scholar, translator, humorist, and writer. After retiring in 2011, she published a column about animal behavior in the local paper titled "Cosmo Talks" and began writing fiction. Her Witherston Murder Mystery series, set in north Georgia, includes *Downstream*, *Fairfield's Auction*, and *Dam Witherston*.

CPSIA information can be obtained
at www.ICGtesting.com
Printed in the USA
BVOW06s1355261217
503650BV00026B/1380/P